TOWN AND COUNTRY

Kevin Barry is the author of the story collections *Dark Lies the Island* and *There Are Little Kingdoms* and the novel *City of Bohane*. He has been awarded the Sunday Times EFG Short Story Prize, the Rooney Prize for Irish Literature, the Authors' Club Best First Novel Award, and the European Union Prize for Literature. His stories have appeared in the *New Yorker*, and many other journals and anthologies.

Also available from Faber

THE FABER BOOK OF BEST NEW IRISH SHORT STORIES 2004-5
THE FABER BOOK OF BEST NEW IRISH SHORT STORIES 2006-7
NEW IRISH SHORT STORIES

TOWN AND COUNTRY

New Irish Short Stories

Edited and with an introduction
by Kevin Barry

faber and faber

First published in 2013
by Faber and Faber Limited
Bloomsbury House
74–77 Great Russell Street
London WC1B 3DA

Typeset by Faber and Faber Limited
Printed in CPI Group (UK) Ltd, Croydon CR0 4YY

A CIP record for this book is available from the British Library

ISBN 978-0-571-29704-7

FSC
www.fsc.org
MIX
Paper from
responsible sources
FSC® C101712

2 4 6 8 10 9 7 5 3 1

This book is dedicated to the
previous editors in its series:
David Marcus and Joseph O'Connor

Contents

An Introduction KEVIN BARRY ix

Images DERMOT HEALY 1

Earworm JULIAN GOUGH 12

Saturday, Boring LISA MCINERNEY 34

Tiger MICHAEL HARDING 50

Godīgums KEITH RIDGWAY 61

The Second-Best Bar in Cadiz
    ANDREW MEEHAN 76

The Ladder SHEILA PURDY 97

Barcelona MARY COSTELLO 105

The Mark of Death GREG BAXTER 122

Summer's Wreath ÉILÍS NÍ DHUIBHNE 133

The Clancy Kid COLIN BARRETT 158

Hospitals Requests PAT MCCABE 177

The Recital EIMEAR RYAN 199

A Winter Harmonic MIKE MCCORMACK 210

Joyride to Jupiter NUALA NÍ CHONCHÚIR 230

City of Glass MOLLY MCCLOSKEY 243

While You Were Working NEASA MCHALE 265

CONTENTS

Brimstone Butterfly DESMOND HOGAN 280
Paper and Ashes WILLIAM WALL 308
How I Beat the Devil PAUL MURRAY 315

About the Authors 343

An Introduction

Kevin Barry

i

There was a time when the short story looked – to use a great and morbidly descriptive Irish phrase – as if it might turn in to face the wall, and the expectation was of a low-key funeral with a smallish turn-out.

But now?

In every coffee trough and every garret, in the jails and in the hospitals, in university workshops and in secure units, and down the backs of pubs, and on the buses and the trains, short stories are being written; at any given moment, it seems, there are ten thousand maniacs battering their laptops with caffeinated fingers, and stories are scrawled onto the backs of beer mats, or pricked out in blood on the pale skin of the page.

Somehow, the story has come alive again and is wriggling and it has about it all the demonic energy (and the undeniable immediacy) of a newborn infant.

Every story within these covers contains that bawl of life.

ii

Ireland is not so much a country as a planet. Perception operates differently here. When our writers face up to the world, I believe they work off a certain hard-to-define oddness as they set about perceiving it and recording it. Maybe there is a particular tone or note that's sounded often – a kind of laughter in the dark. Or, more specifically, against the dark. You are going to hear that note on so many of these pages.

iii

So I sent out the pleading emails and the begging letters and I made the discreet phone calls, and I waited, in modest expectation, at home in County Sligo. For a while, silence. But then, somewhere among the occult mists of autumn, the stories started to take shape and appear out there, and they came skittering along the road, and I hauled them into the house, one by one, and ran a sceptic's eye over them.

And I was awed. Not just by the quality of the finish and the nimble delicacy of the engineering, but by the sheer variety of the methods employed – there are so many modes of attack on the short story as a form now; these writers are up to all sorts.

There are carefully crafted stories here in a classical mode but there are riffs and rants, too, and stories that employ documentary techniques, or delve into the mystics of psychogeography. There is a historical piece;

there is an eerie blast from the near-future. There are stories that read like miraculously compressed novels; there are dramatic monologues; there are stories that use the pans and fades and jump-cuts of film. There is lots of funny and there is plentiful joy but the contours of our great human aches and sorrows are traced here too.

iv

What the short story at its very best can offer is an intensity difficult to match in the other prose forms. A great story can take all the air out of a room. A great story can make you loosen your collar. A great story can delineate the critical moments of a life – those moments of pregnant arrest – with a sense of shiver and glow, and for the reader those moments can linger within, and for years. They are moments with the clarity and amplitude of hallucination, and they are found in the stories of this book.

v

It is a special pleasure to present an anthology that contains many new voices. There is always a distinctive relish about the work of young and emerging writers, a jauntiness and thrust that comes directly from the very fact of *being* a young writer, which is a haunted and exalted state, and for that writer a time of immense excitement but also of great difficulty, when there is that vast store of Voice inside just waiting to be released but finding the moment, and the opportunity, can seem to take for ever. It's a very cool thing to have these new voices make their clamour on the pages here.

vi

It was with a sense of cackling glee, then, that I sent this book to its publisher. These are Irish short stories, and often they come in the shapes that we know and have loved in the form but also they come at a very interesting moment, I believe, when the story is being considered anew and is being pulled in many strange and unexpected new directions. The Irish story is changing and is pulsing with great, mad and rude new energies.

Watch it now as it spirals and spins out—

Images

Dermot Healy

After Jack retired as a lecturer from the IT college we often saw him with camera in hand honing in on the black windows of deserted cottages above the beach. If the doors were open he'd step inside and haunt the ruin. I could not tell what he was after – the architecture, the stonework, the past – or maybe all of them.

He's a strange bird, said Mrs Jay.

He is.

I could understand what he was looking at when the dead whale was washed in. Jack was at his side for over a week, circling and circling. Some other days he'd head off to the forts and stand centre stage, walk the alts to reach the old man-built defences, and many times head out the rocks to catch the flower-like fossils in his curious lens. That made sense. But why haunt the abandoned? What are you after, I'd ask myself, then one morning there was a knock on my door.

My car has broken down, could you be my cabby for two days, Miss Jennifer? he asked.

Certainly Jack.

I got into the Ford, and he sat in beside me, his camera on his lap, and the haversack at his feet. I turned on the engine.

Where are we for? I asked.

How about above the valley?

Fine.

And so we headed up the road below the mountain on the northern side of the lake. On the way he jumped out and helped himself to a few strands of the white flowers of wild garlic. The smell filled the car when he sat back in. We passed lines of lived-in houses, some thatched, all looking the same way onto the waters below. Above them a couple of streams scored an old path down the cliffs. Cherry-blossom trees shook their wings.

And so began the procedure. Every few hundred yards or so he'd make the sharp request as he'd spy another emptiness. We'd stop suddenly and awkwardly. Then he'd step out to take shots of the ivy-covered walls of roofless ruins, the old blue and yellow doors locked by chains and the darkness floating beyond the old window ledges.

At one old ruin fresh daffodils were shooting up among the debris in the garden.

Mortality is rife, he said, as he caught an image of the flowers.

After each photograph was taken he'd study the snap, tip his chin off the back of the hand that held the camera and look closely at the place in question.

Maybe, he'd say. Maybe.

We shot up a side road where he tried the front door of another deserted house – whose tiled roof was still intact in places – but could not open it. He went round the back and was gone for maybe ten minutes.

Come here, he said, emerging from behind.

I followed him and found he had the back door open. He led me in to the middle room. Underneath a window to the side of the front door sat an old grey wooden piano and across the top lay a huge torn mattress and eight blue cushions. I hit the keys. There was no sound.

Can you hear the music? he said.

I can, I said.

Play another tune, he said, and he watched me stroking the silent notes.

He looked fondly at the gutted armchairs, said something to himself, and a look like aggression came over his face as he smiled.

How did they get a piano up here, back then? he said. The past is like a herd of deer.

We stepped out, he pulled the back door closed, and stood a while, wondering.

A girl in a motorised wheelchair went by with a small dog on a lead.

Off again.

We arrived at what might have been a forge, then on to a deserted post office, an old RIC barracks, a deserted farmhouse with a dog barking out of one of the top broken windows at the tulips and mayflowers sprouting below.

3

A big house makes you lonesome, he said. That place reminds me of my grandmother's home, he said, she lived alone with a dog, and when she was in her seventies she committed suicide.

Dear God.

I should keep my mouth shut. The past has a lot to answer for.

Next we headed to a lonely, empty, big cement-block building out on the main road. It had eight glassless crucifixes on the windows looking in on the dark. That looks like an old school, said Jack. Crows waddled across the tarmac. I parked by a gate into a field across the way and this time he did not try to enter the premises but took pictures from all sides on the road, nursing the lens with steady fingers.

I have been here before a few times, he said.

As the cattle watched me I began to imagine him imagining the kids arriving for the Irish class. Maths. Religion. Sonnets. He went to his knees, and strips of wet hair crossed his bald head. At last he sat in and said in a boy's voice, I have just been talking to a Miss Buckley and a Master Coyle. Oh yes! Study my dears, they said.

And be a good boy.

I will.

Off we go.

As we drove round the lake the waves stuttered as mists flew over.

This valley is renowned for rain, he said.

4

All of a sudden there was a rap of hailstones on the windscreen.

Ah Mother Nature can be very articulate, he said.

Then it was up a side road to another deserted cottage on the side of the mountain. He tried the door and it opened. He disappeared inside and was gone for some time. Up above sheep climbed the sheer side of Ben Bulben and hung there like markers. Old paths crossed over. Down below tractors passed with piles of the first cut of grass in their trailers. When he stepped out he was shaking his head and said Look! and he showed me the photographs in the camera, all in black and white. The first shot was taken from inside a room in the house and was aimed facing a window – through the old wooden crucifix that once held glass panes – that looked down on a steep dangerous fall to the valley and the lake below.

Now look at these, he said.

In the next appeared a kitchen table, with a bottle of Jameson whiskey – quarter full – sitting mid centre; then two chairs facing each other, an old metal ashtray and finally an *Irish Independent* newspaper from years back. We walked in and looked at the scene.

What do you make of that?

He lifted the newspaper, gone wet and black at the edges, with the print slipping into the unreadable, and read out the wandering headline concerning Vietnam, and then placed it back exactly where it had been. As we headed outside to the car a farmer driving black and white sheep and newly born lambs appeared on the lane.

Hallo. Not too bad a class of a day, he said.

We've just looked inside the cottage, said Jack.

Oh yeh?

Just taking photographs.

I'm sure the Bradys wouldn't mind.

I'm glad to hear it. Did you ever see that bottle of whiskey?

No, not me. I have never once stood in that house since they've gone. I couldn't. I just heard the story from neighbours. The brothers took off for America, back in the sixties. The hired car came, and off they went leaving everything behind exactly as it was. They was great in fairness to them. Aye and that house has been empty a long time since then.

Jesus Christ.

And there's no relations in the area. One day the boys might come back. So there you go, good luck folks, take care, and he headed on down with the sheepdog racing and circling at the front.

Now, said Jack, history is a password.

Off we took again through another fall of hailstones and this time headed for an organic café for a bite to eat. On the way we passed a graveyard and he stared at the tombstones. Tranquillity can be very noisy, he said, there's always a war in another land. At the car park an old lady sat on her own in the passenger side of a jeep slowly feeding light-green rosary beads through a finger and thumb. Jack got out, waved to her and took off his wellingtons and lifted a pair of white shoes out of his bag, then off came the jacket and on came a yellow jersey.

We had fish soup and scones, and he ate his ice cream like a child, all tongue and suck. Before we left he ordered two salad sandwiches for takeaway.

When we got back to the car the white shoes and jumper came off and he went into his old gear.

Will you drive me back to the piano house? he asked.

Of course. Could you put on your belt?

Oh dear.

We took off back along the same path, past the school and up the side road, and when we reached the grey debris he stepped out with his bag and his camera, pulled a fifty from his pocket and handed it to me.

I have a favour to ask you, he said.

Go ahead.

Will you collect me in the morning?

Sure thing.

Well, good luck!

What do you mean?

You can collect me here.

What?

Yes here.

Here? I thought you meant back at your house.

No here! I'm going to stay for the night. I will have to wait till after midnight before I sleep. You see I never go to bed on the same day I got up. And when I get up tomorrow I'll head for school, and don't you worry,

7

I have all I need, even a sleeping bag, and he headed round the back with a wave.

Jack, are you sure? I shouted.

I am! came the distant call from someone I could not see.

I drove off filled with guilt past yellow piles of whins and forsythia. I stopped the car and thought can I really leave him there, then went on. I collected the pair of kids in Bundoran, an hour late, and on the way home I began to look at ruins I had never looked at before. My eyes wandered across the fallen walls, broken sheets of asbestos, crunched pillars, old lovers, black windows, shattered little iron gates, the tree shooting up alongside the chimney through where the roof once was.

Ma, keep an eye on the road, said David.

Sorry.

I thought of Jack all that night. In sleep I lost my way; then I dreamed I was carrying a friend's baby in my arms. I found him, or he could have been a she, when I entered a small theatre with infants on stage. Inside the front door to the left was a medical room for training in folk. They were all in long grey gowns. It was here I found the babe. I set off down the town, and it was near my destination that I got the first bite on the edge of my palm. The babe held it tight with his teeth for nearly half a minute.

Then a few minutes later came the bites on two of my fingers.

I handed the child over to the mother, and then an

old businessman took my arm. He'd take my elbow again and again as we started walking round the strange town, and as we did so his head began to droop forward dangerously, and suddenly sometimes he'd go face down from the waist forward.

And no passers-by would help.

At last he straightened up and went on. I woke and wondered, and next morning drove off at nine o'clock to the piano house, lost my way, and started going round in circles. At last I found the correct route.

I knocked on the front door.

Hallo! I called. There was no reply.

I knocked on the back.

Jack!

Again no answer. I pushed the back door in and it swung open on a single hinge. The two rooms were empty and there was not a trace of his gear. Not a sign of anyone. A pile of dust sat in a corner by an old sweeping brush. He had been cleaning up. Jack! I screamed. I began to get that ghostly feeling. The piano sat silent again. Panic set in. I listened to him say he was going to stay in the piano house. Now what had happened? I heard him say *And get up for school*. I leaped into the car and drove down to the old ruins, pulled in at the gate and stepped out opposite the huge dark inside the eight windows.

Jack! I called.

An ass in a field behind me roared. All of a sudden out of one of the black windows of the old primary school came the haversack thrown like a schoolbag, then with the camera round his neck Jack appeared at another window and waved, disappeared, then reappeared out through a door in the side of the building.

You're early, he said.

Good morning.

Sorry about that, missus, I was about to head back above to meet you.

Okay Jack.

We climbed into the car.

I'm afraid Miss Buckley and Master Coyle were not present there this morning, he said.

No?

No. Reality is more complex than the imagination. Look!

And he rolled a few photos for me to look at. First came the sole of a boot stuck in mud. Next came the interior – a long room behind the windows that contained lines of cages made of rusted tin bars.

What are those?

Cages for holding pigs. There were no old desks. There was no school. A farmer informed me this morning that it was a blooming creamery and after it closed, the new owner brought in the pigs.

Oh.

I was wrong, he said, forgive me.

No problem.

He took his camera to his eye to read the images.

So where are we for today? I asked him.

That's a good question, he answered.

I turned the key. We sat there for a few moments with the engine running.

Smile, he said.

He turned the camera on me.

Pretend I'm not here, he said.

Okay.

In the flash I disappeared into the dark.

A second later we took off.

Maybe, he said.

Earworm

Julian Gough

I met TigerBalm on Star Wars Day, in one of 4chan's manga forums. May the Fourth be with you. We sparked straight off. But a bunch of newfags kept making Bin Laden jokes I'd already heard twenty times on Twitter – it had been the anniversary of his death a couple of days earlier – so we swapped over to Skype and talked till dawn, my time.

We got our big idea that first night. He had a head cold, and sneezed something horrible onto his keyboard. It was so gross, I switched off video while he cleaned up. I'd had a Blondie song stuck in my brain all day, and while I waited, I sang the chorus, 'Haaaaangin', on the teeeeele, phooooooone, uh . . .' He told me he hated Blondie. I told him I hated sneezes, and that every time he sneezed, I'd sing. He tried not to sneeze.

We were already thinking of working together, to build something. Game? App? Virus? Some kind of hack? But how could you do something truly outstanding? The world was full of better coders than us, with more resources. The sun was coming up, I was about to shut down for the night, when I realised, he's humming my song. Heh. And then he sneezed again.

He sneezed the idea into being, it went off like an explosion in my head: hackers build viruses, but they only affect computers. Nature builds viruses, but you can't spread them over the Internet. But a song is a virus that you can transmit, over the Internet, to human beings. And I was off . . .

★

TigerBalm was in Washington, DC. I was in Rathenow, one hour west of Berlin, and a couple of decades behind it. Soon we were talking every night. He kept me up late, but that was cool. My father didn't like me going out since my brother had been arrested. Unfuckingbelievable, that they arrest the guys protesting *against* the Nazis. This is not Germany's most enlightened town. The neo-Nazi dickheads I went to school with didn't even know what it meant. It annoyed the police, that was enough.

I was trying to get the money to relocate to Berlin, but that's hard in a town with no decent jobs. I'd been trying for three years, but I couldn't seem to save, I spunked everything on equipment. Hard to resist, with the deals I could get from Broiler. Broiler was one of the few guys I'd got on well with in school. Not that he was there often. He took the train to Berlin most days, like a job. Stealing his way down a list. You just told him what you needed, negotiated a price. He could steal *anything*. He was a legend in Rathenow. So my bedroom filled up with computer gear, until I could hardly get in the door.

★

TigerBalm couldn't see it at first, song as virus. He didn't really get the manipulative genius of bad pop. I mean, Rebecca Black, 'Friday', I found that song hypnotic. It was terrible, a real piece of shit. And yet, 'It's Friday, Friday . . .' I loved it. When everybody was crapping on her, and putting all those brutal comments up on You-tube, I was so angry I bought the single on iTunes. I think it was the first time I paid for music. But I had to, it was a vote for . . . Ach, I don't know. Her innocence. Her stupid, totally commercially exploited and ruined, look-at-me, love-me, why-do-you-hate-me, all-Amer-ican innocence.

That song, man. Because it was so crudely done, you could see, incredibly clearly, what they'd tried to do: mechanically build a perfect song out of parts of old hits. Like Frankenstein, trying to assemble a perfect man from the organs of dead criminals. Jolting it to life with electricity. They'd failed, horribly – 'Friday' was an ugly monster – but imagine it done well . . . Even with 'Fri-day', a lot of people pressed play again, straight after hearing it. For the wrong reasons, sure. But I started to wonder if you could write a song that *forced* you to press play again. That left you no option. Like a wire in a lab rat's brain, BAM, pleasure, hit the button, BAM, pleasure, hit the button . . .

Me and TB would argue about this shit. We'd started spending a lot of time together. Two loners who wanted company, it worked out pretty good. We'd have these epic Skype video calls – four hours, six, eight – where we'd maybe talk twice. Mostly just work away on our shit. It was a lot more fun than listening to my father crying in the next room. Sometimes, I'd play something loud through the big Harman Kardon speakers I'd bought off Broiler, just to see how long before TB was humming it, singing it. I'd take notes.

I started to buy old vinyl 45s at the Flohmarkt in the Optikpark on Sundays. Made a rule: they had to have been number one in some country, any country. And I took my father's vinyl out of the cellar. Kind of weird, listening to them again. Reminded me of Mum, and my dad before the accident.

I found I really liked some of their songs now, songs I'd hated back then. Listening to 'The Winner Takes It All', I couldn't believe I'd hated it so much. All our arguments over Abba came back to me, and I closed my eyes. I wished I could go back and say sorry.

The Christmas I'd told my parents their taste in music sucked, because they wouldn't let me play Rammstein on our hi-fi after dinner. Stormed out, slammed the living-room door, thumped up the stairs weeping. My mother had followed me up to my room. The argument had all been in German till then, but when she came into my room I swore at her in English. 'Fuck you,' I said. 'You can't stop the music.'

As soon as I'd said it, my eyes prickled with embarrassment, I felt a hot, sweaty wave of blushing across my face, down my back, it was such a stupid, American, fake thing to say. But, simultaneously, I meant it.

I'd never sworn at her before. Argued, sure, but never sworn.

She lost it, but she didn't know how to lose it.

She grabbed the iPod off my table and then kind of stood there, shaking, stuck. She wanted to smash it, but it had cost too much. She couldn't overcome a lifetime of conditioning and make the big gesture. I laughed at her and said, 'Go ahead. I'll just download them all again.'

She put it down carefully on the bed and walked out.

It broke something. She wasn't really my mother after that. She was wary, sad. She never again told me what to do. Even when I wanted her to.

She died a few months later. We made it up, kind of, before she died, but I never took it back, never said sorry.

The winner takes it all.

The loser standing small.

Some of my tears fell onto my keyboard, and I had to use cotton buds to dry between the keys.

I put on one of my dad's, the Rolling Stones – he didn't like modern music – and a whole summer came back. Fishing on the Havel. Holidays in Blossin, in a hut in the forest. The communal dining room. The kids' disco. Rain on the roof.

You can't always get what you want.

And I realised there were variables I couldn't control. The memories embedded in songs – they're different for everyone. But there are general principles: summer hits encode summer memories – kisses, freedom, sunshine. Obvious, but a breakthrough. Before, I'd been trying to build the perfect song from scratch. But the stuff I built didn't trigger anything. What I needed were samples that were rich in memories. Songs from hot summers, and Christmas number ones . . .

I built the information into the database.

And I started to study catchiness. That was the key. Buggles, 'Video Killed the Radio Star'. Listen, I'd say, they've put the internal rhyme on the same dropped note, listen: 'In my *MIND* and in my car / We can't re*WIND*, we've gone too far . . .' and this, even better, 'Pictures *CAME* and broke your heart / Put the *BLAME* on VCR . . .' And the way 'heart' rhymes with the 'Rrrrrrrrr . . .' in VCR because by dragging out the VCRrrrrrrrrrr, you are satisfied at some level that the final 't' will arrive eventually. So that rhyme continues through the song forever . . . Hey, what if you layered these unresolved rhymes, so that you had a dozen running by the end of the song, would that be catchy or what . . .

I got a little obsessive maybe.

TB hated this subjective shit, though, and tried to

prove me objectively wrong. He built a mathematical model of the three-minute pop song. It took into account everything, and its relationship to everything else – notes, beats, chord changes, key changes, rhymes, metre, but a lot of subtle stuff too, which is important but doesn't get talked about. Echo, the depth of the reverb. Hell, listen to Prince, 'Kiss' – totally dry, no reverb on anything, amazing . . . And TB's model mapped the height of the vocal relative to the bass drum. The pitch of the vocal relative to the snare. The lag between drum and guitar. Because ultimately it's not about the notes, the beats. It's about the relationships.

The Rolling Stones were really interesting. The drums follow the lead guitar, and the lead guitarist doesn't keep strict time. I'd throw TB's data into an old Linux program for visualising data relations and graph it. 'Satisfaction' looked like a drunk coming home from a party. The analogue relationships – the 'mistakes' – gave the recordings their power. MIDI had fucked that up by mapping music onto a grid. Every element in a separate box. That put an upper limit on how catchy your song could be. My next breakthrough was finding a way to make the samples aware of each other, so they stretched and flowed together. And suddenly the samples sang and swayed.

Now to get the right samples.

To trigger the right states.

★

A traditional sample was no good: it was just a slice of everything playing at once. The brilliant piano run you wanted, plus the shitty vocal and tinny drum machine. So we had to strip out the other instruments, then repair any damage. Even with most of it automated, it was painstaking work, pulling a clean Robbie Shakespeare bass line out of an old Grace Jones track.

But TB was getting interested now, despite himself, because his mathematical model of the pop song kept proving my naive theories right, instead of wrong. We dug into the research that showed different kinds of music triggering different physiological reactions. But the data quality was surprisingly poor. Most studies treated the music as a crude generic input – it was 'classical', or 'pop', or 'rock'. We needed much, much more detailed, fine-grained data.

So, he accessed a virtual brain, in the École Polytechnique Fédérale de Lausanne, and we demoed our samples on it. Did our own research.

And, bam. Yep. Oh, it was beautiful. The right beats, frequencies, certain sequences of notes, switched specific areas of the brain on and off like we'd pushed a button. So, okay, songwriters had always done this stuff. A key change, coming into the last chorus, makes the listener's heart beat faster. But their approach was hit or miss, if you'll pardon the joke. Intuitive. They didn't really know what the hell they were doing. With this data, we could automate and optimise the process. Build the perfect pop song from the ground up.

Up until now, I'd had to deal with resistance from TigerBalm. He had exams, and strict parents, and this was taking up a lot of time. I mean, his real name was Cicero, which gives you the whole family picture. Also, like a lot of black middle-class geeks, he'd rejected accessible music along with the whole hip-hop-and-basketball stereotype. A serious dude, Stockhausen and bleeps. But, now, as we finished analysing the samples, TB changed his mind so suddenly and totally I thought I heard the static crackle in his hair. It was like a hard reset.

'Okay,' he said. 'You're right. It works. So, let's build the ultimate pop song.' He pushed back his chair and started to call up samples on his other machine. 'A mathematically perfect three minutes. We can back-engineer it from all this data. Just reverse the algorithm. Instead of putting in the song and getting a read-out, let's set the read-out to maximum pop, select samples and tracks that meet the criteria, optimise their relationships, and output the song.'

So we did it.

And, you know. Holy. Fuck.

We listened to it. And then we listened to it again.

I was shaking by the end of the second play.

I tried to be objective, break it down. Okay, there was some Paul McCartney in there, some Tupac . . .

But mostly I just wanted to play it again. It made me

feel fucking incredible, I thought I was going to have a heart attack. Like poppers.

Did I feel this good because I'd helped build this song, or because the song would make anyone feel this good? TB was lying on his bed, laughing hysterically. We need civilians, I said. We need to check . . .

My brother was visiting. I pulled him away from *Halo 4*, and into my room. A good test subject, with no positive bias towards the song, because he was really pissed with me. I'd had to unplug him to get his attention, and he'd been a few seconds away from getting his last Xbox Live Achievement. (*Killing Frenzy*, for those who are interested.)

I put my good Sennheiser headphones on him, and hit play. My fingers were trembling. After a few seconds, I started to tidy the floor behind him, to give my hands something to do.

Three minutes later, he was punching my shoulder so hard that I dropped a Rolling Stones 45 and it rolled under the bed. He kept saying oh my god, oh my god, shaking his head, grinning. He put it on continuous play and started listening again.

TB was watching my brother on Skype.

It's a serotonin reuptake inhibitor, said TB.

Like Prozac?

Like cocaine.

★

We listened to it till we got sick of it. Took a week, but eventually it burned itself out, like a fever. As I was coming down off it, I thought: but what if you didn't get sick of it?

TB did the research. There was an area of the brain that changed, after a couple of hundred listens. It got chemically saturated, and nausea set in. You couldn't listen to that stimulus until the brain had recovered. And you weren't as vulnerable to that stimulus, afterwards, ever – you'd been vaccinated.

It looked like we were up against a natural limit. I started to think about that.

★

Well, it wasn't perfect. The perfect song should stay perfect, no limits. But meanwhile, as a test run, we released it into the wild. Which had some peculiar consequences.

For the duration of the fever – when they were listening to our song fifty times a day – nobody bought other songs. The music industry took a big sales hit.

They should have just toughed it out – people weren't going to listen to our song for ever. But the record companies were jumpy because no one had claimed responsibility. I mean, it was the most popular song on earth for a while, and it was free, and they didn't know who'd done it. And their legit sales were being hammered. I think they thought, what if they do it again? And again?

So, they freaked. They lobbied government, the security agencies. They wanted our song treated as a virus.
They wanted its release treated as domestic terrorism.

TB had a friend, a former hacker, who worked for
some new, bullshit, cyber-intelligence agency in Maryland. He warned us a serious shit storm was coming.

We stopped processing our data on stolen server
time. I'd been using a hacked Siemens corporate account that used the big Amazon Cloud server farm near
Hamburg. TB had been using his dad's passwords to
authorise time on some completely underutilised De-
partment of Defense subcontractor's farm. Too easy to
trace it back to us. We needed to crunch our data off-
line, and in-house.

We needed more equipment.

TB borrowed, from his so-much-money-he-didn't-
give-a-fuck uncle at Goldman's. His dad would have
coughed up, but he didn't want his dad to get suspicious.
Especially given that his dad was in the D of D.

I went and asked for my shitty old job back. They
were renovating a street of Plattenbauen, across from
my old school. Replacing the crumbling concrete balconies, gutting the 1970s interiors, one big ugly building
at a time. No job for a geek with coder's muscles. The
other guys were nice, mostly, but we had no common
ground. They believed what they read in the papers,
and what they read in the papers was football and tits. It
was lonelier than sitting in my room. When I'd earned
enough, after three weeks, I quit with a fake back injury

to protect my Hartz IV payments, and ordered some equipment from Broiler.

For weeks, I worked on blocking that little neural safety circuit. Jamming the switch in the 'on' position.

And then I found the combination. A Fela Kuti beat, with a modification of an AC/DC riff. And, let's say, a secret ingredient. As they went in and out of phase, they set off harmonics. And the harmonics caused a regular, slow physiological reaction in the hippocampus, a chemical pulse that flushed out the toxins which normally built up and triggered the switch.

You couldn't get sick of it.

When we tested it on the virtual brain, everything lit up. EVERYTHING. It was as though we'd found the right frequency of strobe light to trigger an epileptic attack. We ran the song on fast forward, a hundred times, two hundred, five hundred plays. The gimme-more area stayed lit up, even though other areas were burning out all around it. 'That'd hurt,' said TB, studying the depleted brain. Six hundred plays. A thousand . . . Still triggering the desire to press play.

'Shit,' I said, after a while. TB said nothing.

Another area burned out, somewhere at the base of the neocortex.

The virtual brain crashed. We closed it down.

We didn't talk for a few days.

★

Then Broiler got hit by the Warsaw Express, crossing the tracks near Alexanderplatz. He was being chased by store detectives from Media Markt. Three flash drives down each sleeve, and some new Intel chips I'd ordered shoved in his underpants. Someone filmed it. It was up on Vimeo for a while, before it was pulled. Flopping and twitching on the tracks, his legs a few metres away.

We played 'It's Friday, Friday . . .' at his funeral, he hated that song.

The day after the funeral, TigerBalm's friend in Maryland told TB that a law was being fast-tracked specifically to target runaway pop songs. ISPs were to treat them as viruses, with massive fines for facilitating transmission. The law could be through within weeks, tacked onto the latest big cyber-security bill aimed at China. And the main intelligence agencies had made a joint request to add us to their top-level threat list, which meant they could throw everything at us without warrants. And that request could be approved any time. It could have been approved already.

No warrants.

No trial.

No MIT for Cicero.

'We're screwed,' he said. 'It's over.'

'Fuck them,' I said. 'It's not over.'

That night, we rebuilt the perfect song from the ground up, and released it.

It fucked up Pakistan first, which we weren't expecting. But it exploded across Facebook there while everyone was still asleep in Europe and America.

We watched the figures climb. And climb. And climb. It was beyond exponential.

'People are just looping it,' I said, awed. 'They can't stop listening to it.'

'And they're telling their friends. ALL their friends,' said TB.

And then it started to spread across Europe, time zone by time zone, as people got up, and connected. We couldn't go to bed, it was awesome.

And then America woke up.

It spread so fast it triggered some latent National Security Agency cyber-defences we hadn't even known about. The NSA bots tried to auto-kill it, but we'd clumsied them by putting out three versions, one a decoy, easy to kill, two with some really misleading meta-data and a fake intro, so it looked like a legit release. Warner Brothers, because we didn't like Warner Brothers. The NSA bots started taking down legit songs, and got flagged as hackbots, and neutralised.

The crazy thing was, we hadn't actually listened to the perfect version ourselves. We'd built a mathematical model, and given it access to our database of stripped-out perfect song elements, and it had assembled the song with the new bass line, the new riff. We'd only run mathematical tests on it, to see had it built right. It hadn't occurred to us to listen to it. We were working in a very abstract realm those days. Beyond theory.

'Maybe we should listen to it,' I said.

'Fuck no,' said TB. 'And then sit here like drooling monkeys for the next week, listening to the same song?'

But every action has an equal and opposite reaction, and the reaction to this was going to be earthquake-sized, and aimed at us. We hadn't covered our traces enough to hide from something that big. We spent the next few days in our rooms, scrubbing our histories from every server we could. But scrubbing leaves traces too. We were like two guys running backwards in the snow, rubbing out our footprints, always making new footprints . . .

*

For a while, the Internet slowed down. All of it. While everybody linked, liked, streamed, copied, downloaded, forwarded, posted, plussed, burned and listened to, listened to, listened again to the one perfect song.

*

And then the world slowed down. Multitasking is bull-shit. If you're listening to a song that rewards total atten-tion by getting you high, then you are not concentrating on your driving, on your job, on your kids. There were a lot of accidents. A *lot*. Economies ground to a halt. I mean, with the first version, people had stopped buying music. With this version on a permanent loop, people had trouble doing the fucking shopping. After a few days, the saturation was so total, it began to interfere with itself. If they weren't using earbuds, people could often hear several versions of the song at once – from a neighbour's iPad, a shop doorway, a taxi's open window, a ringtone – which lowered its effectiveness.

Besides, even a junkie, if he gets hungry enough, will eat. Routines bite deep. But it was like wading through molasses. Whatever they did, while they did it, they were listening to our song. The perfect song. Everybody, all the time. We followed it online, with the sound switched off, as it moved from being a novelty item at the end of the news round-ups to being all of the news.

People had worked it out way late. Well, okay, the Americans and the Chinese tried to kill it from day one, but in a lot of countries the song was just considered an irritating novelty for a long while. Too long. By the time countries started treating their local epidemics, it was already a global pandemic.

After a while, it plateaued. People were able to get to work, they remembered to pick up their kids, the song moved to the back of their consciousness. They were listening to it all the time, but their minds were now managing to run workarounds, to get things done. Also, the amount of serotonin in circulation was dropping. Not that it was being reabsorbed – that was thoroughly blocked – just that the old serotonin was breaking down a little, and people couldn't keep up the rate of manufacture that the song demanded. They weren't worthy of the Song.

The song was perfect, and they were merely human.

The days went by.

★

It got harder and harder to stay clean. Dad didn't cry any more. He just moved the hi-fi from the living room, upstairs to his bedroom, and played the perfect song on a loop. I hadn't told him it was mine. But I'd put in stuff from when he and Mum were happy. The Puhdys, and the Rolling Stones. When he turned it up loud, it leaked into my room, and I'd have to wear earplugs.

I spent a lot of time talking to TB on headphones, but that was dangerous. The net was suffering outages, breakdowns. Everything was neglected, everyone was distracted, all the usual invisible repair that keeps the world revolving was getting half-assed. If the sound cut out in the Sennheisers, I'd hear a bar of the song from Dad's room, and I'd sweat with the need to hear the whole thing, while my fingers fumbled to crank up some counter-music. It nearly pulled me under a couple of times.

★

I left the house, playing Gaga through my buds, loud. Headed for my old school.

They'd just started renovating another building. Good.

There. Dozens of old mattresses, piled high in one of the skips. It looked like the guys expected some cartoon character to fall out of the sky.

I lugged them home one at a time, and soundproofed the room.

★

You cannot stimulate that much serotonin for that long without a major crash. A wave of depression swept around the world.

And then one day there wasn't any bread in the shops.

It was like the stories Dad had told me, about the last days of the DDR.

★

We were talking quietly in the dark on Skype.

A blast of light from behind TB, as a bunch of exhausted, depressed Special Operations troops kicked in his bedroom door.

I threw myself off my chair, and rolled under the bed as my door was kicked open. Simultaneous raids, shit. I stared at a Rolling Stones single lying among the dust balls. Tried not to sneeze. 'You Can't Always Get What

You Want.' B-side to 'Honky Tonk Woman', I thought reflexively, and could see the graph of all the analogue relationships between the parts. It started to go around in my brain, the section at the end where the choir kicks in. No, you can't always get what you want . . . But if you try sometimes, you might find . . . You get what you need.

My room must have been smaller than they'd expected, or they were too adrenalised, because the two stun grenades they threw in bounced straight back out off the mattresses on the wall, and exploded among the second wave of soldiers. Under the bed, my ears rang, but I could still hear.

Boot, boots, boots . . . My guys swore in thick Bavarian accents. Not soldiers, of course. GSG-9, double shit. TB's were American, SEALS probably, I could still hear them through the Harman Kardons. High level co-operation. Trouble deep.

They hauled me out and snapped on the plastic cuffs. Yeah, Grenzschutzgruppe 9, in full protective gear, plus noise-cancelling headphones. Fit fuckers. Two of them kicked me around a little, while the others unplugged everything in the room and bagged it. Ripped the mattresses off the walls, looking for whatever. The bass end of the perfect song came through my wall, from my father's room. I could hear him singing.

They kicked in his door and the song got louder, and then cut off as they ripped out the wires, but my dad sang on.

I needed to hear the whole song. The need was so strong I almost got sick.

My father tried to sing the perfect song, but the music was gone.

There was a thump, a grunt. My dad stopped singing.

All the doors were open. A breeze moved through the house, and dust whirled out from under the bed in a little spiral.

Outside, more supercops shouted, and a car squealed to a halt, the perfect song blasting from its open windows.

It started so simply. A line from my mother's favourite song, a line from my father's.

The guys who'd taken off their headphones scrambled to get them back on, and dropped me. I lay on the floor. The song spread through me, as layer after layer kicked in. It was like being lifted higher and higher, on waves of warm honey, towards the sun.

It felt like the one time I'd tried heroin, with Broiler. We'd fallen asleep in each other's arms, in his room, listening to 'The Dark Side of the Moon'.

And now the song, sample by sample, fired up the memories that came with each song. It was like fireworks, no, stronger: lightning, illuminating scene after scene from my life, there she was, my mother. My father. Broiler, summer, Christmas, my first kiss, faster and faster.

As they dragged him out into the corridor, my father started up again, his voice weaker now.

I strained to see him, to hear him. They kicked him. A grunt. He stopped. I pushed myself along the bedroom floor towards the door, towards my dad, towards the music, with my feet, like an inchworm. Three sets of black boots stepped in front of me, blocked me. I heard my dad clear his throat, say my name.

I spat blood on a boot.

'Fuck you,' I said. 'You can't stop the music.'

We began to sing.

Saturday, Boring

Lisa McInerney

That she wanted to have sex with him wasn't a conscious decision. It wasn't something she had to approach from different angles, like a nugget of truth suspended in a pyramid of excuses. It wasn't something she had to sit down and think about, one foot underneath her and her heel pressing a reminder against the place she'd soon be inviting him to rest. It wasn't even something he'd prompted, breathing the suggestion into her ear as valiant fingers traced intentions across her shoulders and down her spine and in the sunken warmth between her breasts. It was just there one day. It just popped into her head like a Looney Tunes light bulb. She was in town with her best friend and they were listlessly thumbing through T-shirts in Penneys when she said:

'I think I want to have sex with him.'

'What?' said her friend. And then, for effect, 'You what?'

'Why is that a shock? Why shouldn't I?'

'I didn't say you shouldn't,' said her friend. 'Did I say you shouldn't?' And the T-shirt she'd clutched like a bad metaphor slid off its hanger and onto the floor.

'So, like, you only said *You What?* because you didn't hear me? You did, yeah.'

Her friend's back made a disapproving block as she hunted for the rogue T-shirt underneath the rack.

'Why shouldn't I want to have sex with him?'

'You can be with whoever you like, girl.'

'I know that.'

There was a pause, heavy as a teacher's footfall, heavy as the connections her mother made when there was Trouble draped over her daughters' frames like flashy ball gowns. She glanced around as she waited for her best friend's back to transform back into her best friend. There were shop assistants with dark shirts and glazed eyes, and harried mothers shouting *Come here! Get!* at loud children called Dylan and Siobhán, and other fifteen-year-olds, too, maybe even fifteen-year-olds who had just decided they wanted to Do It with their boyfriends and were waiting through a similar hiccup for their best friends to say that was fine.

Her best friend rose again.

'Does he know?'

'No.'

They returned their attention to the rack in front of them. Her friend danced her index and middle finger over the brittle, plastic limbs laid out like suspension files in a cabinet marked *Saturday, Boring*. 'You know you've only been going with him three weeks,' she said.

'Nah, I didn't know that at all.'

'Yeah, well, is all I'm saying. I mean, it'd be grand if you weren't going with him but this way you have to put up with him afterwards, you know? And what if it's not good?' Her best friend had recently allowed a Shanakiel boy called Rory unreserved access and he'd made an utter hames of it. He'd pawed and scraped and huffed and ignored her afterwards. There was no mystery to her lack of enthusiasm for repeating the process, even by proxy.

'I don't care. I still think I want to.'

She wondered if she could trace this sudden longing back to something. A moment, a word, a glance. Was it a longing at all? She didn't ache for him or anything as explosively stupid as that. It wasn't a longing; it was just a want. Short, sweet, stocky. An extra, something that snuggled against the fabric of who she already was, like it was totally at home, like it wouldn't make a fuss if she never called on it or fed it or gave it its due.

He was in the same root class as her in school. They shared a few subjects, the useless ones, like Religion and PE, and English and Irish, too. Not Maths, though. He was in the Honours Maths class. Whatever alien language it was made total sense to him; he didn't have to think about it. It was just there for him and missing for her, one of the differences between them.

It was the differences she loved. And not just the obvious ones: that she was a girl and he was a boy. Obviously she loved that, the fact that he was taller and broader and deeper and stronger and all of those rough physicalities he carved out space with. But it was also the fact that she was yappy and cheeky and sharp and brave, and he was quiet and thoughtful and prone to speaking in lyrics, as if every second sentence had been mined raw from somewhere previously untapped. As if things he said and did were as often brand new as they were rehashed by routine and habit. And in that sense he was different to everyone, she thought. Now she was close enough to study and pry and she was sure he liked that, too.

It had begun to happen just a few days previously. It was April, and they were just back in school from the Easter holidays – two weeks of suspicious sunshine and warmth that prompted a premature rush on super-market sunblock and a spate of old women's warnings. Strip ne'er a clout. Strong possibilities of colds in your kidneys. She'd stripped off anyway. There had been al-most a whole week of shorts and dresses and two days hot enough for the beach, two days with him, where she'd watched him watch her with a kind of dazed rev-erence neither of her grandmothers had ever thought to prophesy. What do you do when a boy looks at you that way? When there's no threat, just flashes of awe and an unfamiliar timidity that's a million miles away from the boy he is in the schoolyard or on the street? When you want him as he wants you and every long look brings you closer to that war-torn future every grown woman strides loud-mouthed through? Sex. Betrayal. Turmoil. Confession. Kitten heels.

They were back in school after that bare-skinned, bare-faced Easter. The bell signalled the end of one class, the teacher left the room, and he stood up, across from her in the front row – he was always made sit in the front row – and stretched his arms above his head. His shirt rose with the stretch, over his waist exactly as her gaze designed it. Just an inch or so. A lazy flash of skin between the white hem and the wet-stone grey of school trousers, and just a hint, the slimmest black line of whatever he was wearing underneath, and she saw and felt smugly possessive. Greedy, in the way greed wants to show off, to swan and smirk and stuff itself while hungrier eyes watch and covet weakly. That quick and careless flash of skin, a part of him that only she could touch, right then, if she wanted to. Hers. Like he'd lost that sliver to her. He saw her watching him and neither of them smiled. *That's it*, something might have said to her, a voice of aeons from a place she'd never known she'd want access to. *That's it. It's happening*.

That might have been the source of today's sudden certainty. Maybe it took that long to translate it. But she wasn't sure.

Her best friend said, 'Will he know he's the first?'

'Not unless I tell him.'

'Will you tell him?'

'Why should I?'

Her best friend shrugged. 'He might be nicer about it then. Or he might be worse. You don't know with fellas.'

'Why does he need to be nice about it?'

Her friend rolled her eyes. 'You want it to be nice,' she said.

She wanted it to be nothing – she just wanted it to happen. Perhaps later she'd stick some stipulations on it. That it must be gentle, or fast, or candlelit, or semi-clothed in case someone walked in on them. She'd have to think about it. 'Yeah well,' she said. 'I trust him to make it nice, don't I?'

'Do you?'

'Course I do. I wouldn't even be thinking about it if I didn't trust him.'

That was it, laid flat. Experience, her friend's whittled weapon. But experience without trust couldn't compete with even the greenest craving.

'You know it hurts,' said her best friend.

She shrugged.

'It will,' said her friend.

'You know it can fit a baby's head.'

'And you can know that all you like but it still hurts. Trust me.' And she mirrored the shrug and pushed her tongue under her bottom lip and into a pout and then she said, 'Do you trust him not to blab afterwards?'

'Yeah.' She was the only person he ever blabbed to anyway. He'd told her everything she'd ever asked for and more besides, his eyes wide as if to warn his flapping mouth that he needed to stop giving away so much of himself because there'd be nothing left to hold court over soon. He told her about the battles his father dragged him into, and the hours of the clock he most missed his mam, and why he didn't care what teachers said, what guards said, what social workers said, what anybody said except her. Her mouth and, deeper and more truthfully, her body.

'They always blab,' her friend said.

'He won't.'

They drifted away from Summer Wear and further into the store, following a course marked out by pastels and Special Offers. The intercom crackled. A woman droned an order for someone to pick up a phone call.

'Will you be his first?' said her best friend.

'I don't know.'

This was something she didn't want to think about. She had made her decision and she didn't need it marred by the thoughts of his body being charted territory. Of course it was, though. There was a girl right before her; she was sixteen and a friend of his cousin's and the whole school – what had sounded like the whole school to her burning ears – had talked about it. That a sixteen-year-old girl in Transition Year would have any interest in a then fourteen-year-old young fella was something worthy of long, whispered debate and, depending on the gender of your selected protagonist, awe or ridicule. So there must have been sex. Sixteen was a milestone.

The sixteen-year-old had been shelved with staggering speed, but that, she knew, was down to her making her own intentions known to him, not because of sex too freely given and poisoning his interest. She wasn't sure exactly what it was he loved about her that he didn't love about the sixteen-year-old, but it was gratifying. Not just gratifying. Wonderful. Amazing. Head-swellingly magnificent. He loved her. He'd loved her for months. All she'd had to do was shrug and smile and he was hers entirely. She trusted him for that. Did it matter if it was to be her first time and not his?

Yes.

But there was nothing she could do about it.

'You're as well off, like,' said her friend. 'He'll know what he's supposed to do.'

'Like he wouldn't know anyway.'

Boys always knew. It wasn't something they were told in science but you didn't need to teach the absolute truth. Boys just knew these things. They were much closer to instinct than to cop-on so they were ready for it at their very first quickening. Boys never said, *Hold on*. Boys just flaked into it like hormonal juggernauts. Boys were lorries.

There was a part of her glad of this and a part of her that still wanted him to be unsure and clumsy.

Her best friend said, 'You're going to have to tell him to be ready and stuff. He'll have to get Things.'

'Don't be stupid. If I tell him, he'll *know*.'

'Oh yeah,' said her friend. There'd be no room for error or mind-changing or delaying the scheme of things if having sex was something he expected. It had to be a surprise, a feeling that the opportunity was just a gate she'd shyly left ajar.

'Then you'll have to get some,' her friend said.

'Oh, I will, yeah! He'd think I was a slut.'

'Well what then?'

'Maybe he'll have some.' She'd have to trust that he'd know, on some level, what she wanted from him. There was so much she could already tell him with a look, or a stroke of his hand. Or his back. Or that vertical line she liked to draw just above his belly button. Just below.

They were closing in on the lingerie section. 'I should buy something,' she said. 'Like, something cute. Not sexy.' Not blatant.

'Something just for him?'

'Yeah.'

'What if you wear them and nothing happens?'

'It'll happen.'

She chose a matching set: a bra with light-blue pin-stripes and a white, lacy trim, briefs to match. There was a thong too. She had no problem with thongs; you couldn't wear anything else under a tracksuit bottoms, otherwise there'd be a map drawn on your bum for any-one's mind to wander. But for this occasion it seemed wrong. Too obvious. And having sex with him was something she'd decided to do but she wanted it to be something he did to her. A thong just wouldn't work in that scenario. A thong would tell him she'd thought about it.

Her father was still freaked about the advent of thongs on his washing line. She was the middle of three teenage daughters, and she knew her dad was worrying himself grey about what they got up to when he wasn't there to shepherd them. He didn't know she had a boyfriend at all, and she needed to keep it that way for as long as she could.

She carried the underwear to the checkout. As they were queuing, she considered picking up a few of the last-minute extras the clever people at the shop lined the path with – fake tan, lip balm, false eyelashes – but she didn't have the coins to throw away on a mask, not if she wanted McDonald's and ice cream after, like every other day marked *Saturday, Boring*. The girl at the till shouted, 'Next please!' and raised neither smirk nor eyebrow when she placed the set on the counter but it might have been as obvious as a flashing siren strapped to her head; she wasn't sure and she didn't know if she was being stupid and insane and pinning meaning to things that didn't need meaning.

She picked up the bag from the counter and her friend said, 'Like, this isn't the first thing you've done with him, though.'

She didn't reply until she was safely away from the shop assistant. 'You think you'd keep it down?' she said.

'Like she's your mam.'

'Still!'

'She might tell your mam. She might announce it over the intercom. *Hello, is there a mammy here who owns a blonde wearing Cons and skinnies and a purple Adidas top? She's buying nice knickers. She's up to something.*'

'You're very smart,' she said.

She might tell her mam herself, the way she inadvertently told her every wilful snippet by letting it run rampant across her treacherous face. *What are you up to?* her mother would say. *What are you at?* Like a toddler taking revenge by scribbling on her parents' bedroom wall, she thought that she might even want her mother to twig it.

Not so with her dad.

He would be in the sitting room when she got home. He was a logistics manager down in Ringaskiddy and he usually did Saturday mornings and then came home and sprawled for the afternoon, in so far as a wiry bag of nerves could sprawl. Only the minimum required area of his arse would be on the couch, the rest of him poised like a jack-in-the-box over the balls of his dainty feet. Her dad had been designed for maximum efficiency. She got her small frame and short temper from him.

'You shopping again?' her dad would say, and she'd swing the bag loosely, so that it didn't show the form of the illicit gifts inside.

Her dad was funny, gobby and confrontational. He didn't like change and so he dealt with everything new in the wrong way – he flung threats about until the walls he'd kept around his girls were slimed with the trails of sinister promises that slid into filmy pools on the floor. He would never be able to tell what she was up to. And this made her kind of, a little bit, inappropriately for this *Saturday, Boring* . . . sad. Not crying, keening, snorting sad, of course, but enough to prick the corners of her eyes. She didn't want her dad to know what she was thinking; she wasn't sad because he couldn't read her mind. She was sad *for* him.

Her dad had been a boy once and boys lived their whole lives having their decisions made for them by girls, whether they knew it or not, whether they wanted it or not. Her dad would vow that mountains be moved before he'd allow a rival male get any sort of foothold in the conquest of his daughters – especially the middle one, the glinting little blonde who was most like him – but it would be to no avail. He could do nothing about this. He could swear and dance his tantrums but he couldn't stop progress, and this was how she was progressing, this was where she was going – straight to another dominion, and it was nowhere her dad could follow.

Her friend asked again. 'Have you done *anything* with him yet?'

More than once, she and her friends had pored over the glossy magazines with their tales of biological audacity and invading alien life forms. 'How to Blow His Mind in Ten Minutes.' 'Sex in Enclosed Spaces.' 'What Your Favourite Cocktail Can Tell You About His Cock.' There was so much to learn and so much expected of her. Waxing. Buffing. Bleaching. She had cautiously concluded that the hints and tricks and stern provisos were all nonsense. She couldn't be certain. She was afraid to wax and unsure where to buff and the idea of bleaching anything made her want to run to her mam and bury her head in her shoulder. It had occurred to her that the women in the glossy magazines were maybe being devious in their reverse psychology. That the entire genre was written and run by smirking nuns. None of it corresponded with the feeling deep in her belly and the impatience that caught in her throat when she was pressed against his chest with her hands in his back pockets.

She didn't really want to have to tell anyone what had happened between their first kiss and this afternoon's realisation. She wanted to have sex with him and she didn't want there to be a set process. Things just happened when they were together and every small gesture was theirs alone and may as well never have been attempted by anyone before. Just like his words, his actions were newborn and yet as ancient and innate as breathing.

One nana, her dad's mother, used to say of wily children that they had been 'out before'. Maybe that's how it was, between them. Old and new at the same time. When she was with him she didn't think of the sixteen-year-old who'd treaded the same ground only a couple of weeks before. She didn't think of the boys she'd been tangled up in, the ones who had botched their invasions in the dark corners of Youth Club discos. The ones with whom she'd had biting kisses. Languid, slimy tongues. One awkward hand job, where any enthusiasm she might have had was scuppered by the fact that his jeans zip was all the way up and there was no room in there for her hand to move at all.

'Well?' said her friend. 'I promise I won't tell anyone.'

They'd had two hours together last night. The Junior Cert was coming and her mam and dad were see-sawing between hardassery and judicial lenience, and on this occasion the lever had come down in her favour. She'd texted him and galloped out to meet him at the corner of the big green outside his estate. It was relatively private. There was no clear view from any of the houses around the green, and a wall and a parked car made the borders for their world. Because it was dark they hadn't said all that much. Talking was for daytime and night-time was for clawing advantage from.

'Hand job?' said her friend. 'Blow job? Cos you have to start somewhere or it'll be like a total shock to dive in totally.'

'We've started somewhere,' she said.

'Yeah, but where?'

'Doesn't matter where,' she said.

'Why won't you tell me?' said her friend. 'If you're ashamed of it already you can hardly keep going.'

'I'm not ashamed of it,' she said. She just didn't want to share. And that was a strange realisation, too. She actually didn't care whether or not her best friend thought it was fine. She'd just wanted to say it. *I want to have sex. I want to go there. I want it to be him.* To make it real and solid and to have the whole world slow down its revolution so as to make space for her.

'Be that way so,' said her friend.

'It's just between me and him, is all.'

47

'That means you've done nothing.'

Her friend waited for a reaction to her thrown gauntlet, the accusation of frigidity she'd cast between them. She'd be waiting a while.

'Are we going to McDonald's so?' said her friend, after the clock struck.

'D'you know what? I think I'll leave it. I'll go study a while.'

'Study?'

'Junior Cert's coming, isn't it?'

'That's what it is, yeah,' said her friend, bitterly.

It felt like something had snapped and broken. Some parameter she only noticed in its absence.

She wondered if he felt the same way. If he noticed the horizon shifting. If he sat at home now wondering why the sky was that bit bigger. If he was playing with his phone in his hands, waiting for her text explaining where this new space was opening from, telling him that she was ready to go with his instinct if he'd just learn a little from her cop-on.

Her friend said, 'When are you going to do it?'

'Maybe later. Maybe in a few days. You can't put a definite on something like this.'

'Tell me after, though.'

'Duh.' She wasn't promising anything. 'I'll see you Monday anyway,' she said.

For a second her friend looked like she was going to cry. Like she was seeing her off to war. She shifted her weight and her shoulders jerked and she said, again,

'Tell me after,' like a goodbye, because they both knew there'd be no full story after, that at most there'd be a quick concession to the act that had passed and the loss of that last burden of eleventh-hour childhood. They were still friends but what was friendship now?

The realisation spread across her shoulders and anchored her to the ground. Her friend turned to leave and as she watched her trudge away she pressed her palms flat against her belly and she was Home, and happy for it, and suddenly old as the sea.

Tiger

Michael Harding

I was glad to be back in Castlebar, behind my own door, talking to the cat. I'd spent the day in Sligo trying to tell Maureen that I had prostate cancer. It was Philip's eighteenth birthday, and I was amazed that she actually put on lunch and invited me, and I suppose it wasn't the time to be talking about my health; but I knew I had to tell her sometime.

I said to Philip, 'You're a grown man now,' as we munched on T-bone steaks that Maureen had cooked on the barbecue machine outside, before it started raining, at which point we abandoned the patio and came back into the sun room and finished our meal there. 'T-bone for the young man,' she said, gushing at Philip, who is seven foot tall and flaunts dreadlocks that go all the way down to his backside and he walks like he's trying to balance something on his head.

'I'm proud of you,' I said to Philip. There was no reply to that. His face said, so what. Nor could I get a moment with Maureen on her own, so in the end the prostate never got mentioned either.

I stopped the jeep three times on my way back to Castlebar to piss in the bushes on the side of the motorway and when I got inside the apartment in Angle Court, I undressed and then sat on the toilet, trying to piss, as the bath was running. The cat was in the doorway. I sometimes wonder does she notice when I'm naked, or does it disturb her.

There's a downside to everything, including living alone in an apartment; for one thing, cats, or any pets, are not allowed, and I'm obliged to hide Tiger 2's existence. But a definite plus is that the water tank is insulated in a hard green shell, so that the water stays hot all day.

I thought Maureen didn't like cats, until I was leaving and she insisted on keeping the one we had at the time. It was a long-haired white queen with some black marks. We called her Tiger, because we thought she resembled a Siberian Tiger, and she still looks down her nose at the world from a sofa in the sunroom above Lough Gill, even three years after I was banished. So once I had moved into the apartment I went out to Animal Rescue and found an uninspiring tabby in a cage and paid €10 to cover injections and took her home in a cardboard box and called her Tiger 2.

I didn't buy the apartment in Castlebar. I'm renting it. But it's my space. Completely my space, and I can lie soaking in the bath as long as I like.

In the distance I can hear Lana, the Polish girl, playing with her little dog, out in the courtyard. I can hear the occasional slamming of a door upstairs, where an American woman with a cute little button nose lives, with her Irish boyfriend, a big red-haired boy, and who as far as I can make out sells drugs. They drive a black Hilux, and one night there was a squad car in the court-yard with blue lights flashing and two female guards knocking on their door for half an hour. I knew they were inside but they didn't budge till the guard was gone. Like Lana, they too have a dog; a little brown mutt that shits through the grill of the balcony directly above me.

Pets are not allowed, but Lana, who is about seven, and has brown eyes the size of chestnuts, is always careful when she lets her puppy out for a run. I think he does his toilet in the underground car park, which nobody uses except a few boys who sometimes climb over the gates from the street and drink alcohol down there.

At the table in Sligo my son Philip said, 'You're very quiet today, Dad.'

I said, 'I have nothing to say.'

'You should try to talk about something,' he said. 'The silence is deafening.'

He's got very snotty in the past three years since I've left. It's because she spoils him.

'What's up with him?' I asked her when he was in the bathroom.

'Maybe he's angry because he lost his father,' she said.

'He didn't lose his father,' I said, 'his father was put out.'

'I didn't put you out.'

'I say you did.'

And the boy returned and said, 'Jesus Christ will the pair of you shut up. For fuck sake. Some birthday.' The room was very silent for a long time after that so I tried to broaden the discussion and be fatherly at the same time.

'It's funny,' I mused, 'but silence is an important part of my life now.' There was another long pause. Her face looked like a wall. She must have thought I was going to bitch about being alone in Castlebar. 'What I mean, Phil, is that silence is the thing I work with. All the time. Especially in the theatre. Silence is often where real communication begins. I find that very interesting.'

'Jesus,' Maureen said, 'you only ever do voiceovers. You hardly get a single job in any year on the stage. And don't call him Phil.'

Then we were all silent again and I tried to look out the window at the lake with as much dignity as I could muster.

It's about an hour and fifteen minutes from the house on the hill above Lough Gill to Castlebar. I drove without putting on either a radio or a CD. All the way home I went, in silence. Just to prove something to myself.

Years ago, when I was in secondary school, there was a gang of boys who roamed the corridors and basements, and shower areas, and the toilets and landings beside the boarders' dormitories, always looking for younger boys to terrorise. Stopping little first-years for questioning. Demanding cigarettes, information, radios. Humiliating them with orders; come here, stand there, don't look at me like that. They shoved big fists into little tear-stained faces, and pushed heads down toilet bowls, and not a single teacher stopped it. No one chastised them; far from it, the bullies were usually good on the football pitch and so were praised by everyone.

I saw people go through life struggling with alcoholism, depression and anger just because they had been treated so brutally. Some committed suicide. One fellow jumped out a window on Christmas Day. And another walked into a lake. Another dived off a balcony in Bulgaria. I suppose I was lucky, because I wasn't a boarder, and so I didn't get the worst of it. Although I never togged out for football after the incident in the basements. On Saturdays I'd go fishing instead. I'd get a line and reel, and a little Voblex bait, and I'd toss it into the brown unknown of the lake at Foxford. The surface was often flat in the afternoons, with a cloud of midges hovering above, and a glorious silence blanketing the world, except for geese squawking on the far shore.

The fish didn't like the baits. They looked at me with open mouths bleeding from the hooks. I tried battering their heads off the stones, to finish them off, but that gave me an uneasy feeling, so usually the fish lay dying at my feet for ages. And sometimes they didn't bite at all, which made me angry.

'Bite! Yis fucken bastards!' I'd hiss.

My hands gripping the rod too tightly. Pulling the line too suddenly. And then the bait hooks would get lodged behind stones in the water, and I'd tug the line until it broke and so my Voblex would be lost, and I would curse the world and cycle home in a rage.

Maureen and I broke up in June. I arrived in Castlebar on Bloomsday and during that summer I would stand on the balcony all evening, listening to the arguments going on in other apartments around me. My wife used to say I was insensitive because I never touched her in a gentle way, and I was never spontaneously affectionate. That's what she said. And I would say that I didn't understand what she was talking about, and she'd say—

'There, you see? That's what I'm talking about.'

When the bones of three steaks had been tossed in the waste bin and the three of us had made it through the chocolate cake and a pot of tea I said I'd head off. Philip said, 'I'll see you to the car.'

We stood outside looking at my jeep and we made small talk about the size of the engine, because he had never seen it before. Then we fumbled to engage in a kind of hug, but it was a terrible piece of acting. Even when he was little it wasn't something I ever mastered. I suppose it's just a family trait. My father rarely hugged me. When he did, the bristle of his chin felt as rough as sandpaper. He had spectacles as monumental as the headlamps on a tractor and he was very old when he married. Beneath his grey suits he wore long johns and flannel vests, and all his teeth were false.

There's no open fire in the apartment. But I don't miss it. I have an electric heater with one of those glass fronts that gives the impression that it's a real coal fire inside, with a pathetic flickering light that even the cat knows is not a flame. The sun was shining when I signed the lease in June of 2006. The auctioneer was a boy in a light-grey pinstripe suit and a pink shirt and grey tie. I asked a lot of questions, and he looked constipated. I suppose he was used to stitching up East Europeans in small apartments with paper-thin walls and no fire doors, and wonky washing machines, without being asked too many questions. It was a warm day and the thought of a fire never crossed my mind. The sun was shining on the floors of imitation wood. The sofas were clean and crisp. There was a French window in the main lounge, which opened and allowed the occupant to lean on a railing, much like a balcony, although one was still standing in the room. It felt like a balcony. I still call it a balcony. And from there I can see children playing in the courtyard in the afternoons. I can see an old woman in the apartment directly opposite mine at midday eating her lunch. And I can see the Lithuanians every morning in the third-floor apartment to my left, watching television as they take their breakfasts. Cartoons. Always cartoons. The constipated boy in the grey suit and the pink shirt said the lease was for one year. Then we could sign another agreement he suggested. 'And no pets,' he said, as if I was a child. And already I've been here five years.

So I have a tray for Tiger 2, and she never gets out. I sit drying off at my electric heater after a bath, and she sits on the rug staring at me, and I stare at a photograph of my son on the mantelpiece. He's wearing a mauve jumper too big for him and he is pushing a wooden horse on wheels through the snow. It's the only picture I like. I think he looks lovely at that age, in the snow, and full of joy. Philip once asked me what I would like to do when I got old. I was reading the newspaper on the patio at the time. It was a Sunday morning and Philip was about eight. I said I think I'd like to just sit here on the patio and look at the trees when I'm old. I didn't know what to say. I saw old men as remote objects of pity, passive animals, sucking pipes, holding the wall as they walked down streets, or gazing into ponds in public parks where they sat for hours on benches, or sipping glasses of Guinness in the corner bar, or strapped to wheelchairs at the doors of various nursing homes, while white uniformed women attended like angels beside them. That's what I thought of old people ten years ago.

But age creeps up on all of us and then the imminence of death astonishes us. I have to admit that when I think about it now, there's nothing I'd like more in old age than to kneel in the back pew of a quiet church mid-morning, when the rituals are over, and the great empty vault smells of incense and wine and flowers and polish. I would beg someone to forgive me. Anyone. But I may not be able to enjoy that consolation since the Church is now so disgraced that all the buildings will probably be Omniplex cinemas by the time I'm seventy-five.

I was astonished when my father died. I didn't know where he went. It was as if his presence evaporated into thin air. As if the world he inhabited and which mattered so much to him turned out to be an illusion. When he was gone there was no world. It was just things left behind to be gathered in plastic bags and dumped in the rubbish. All those medicine bottles. And the radio. The clock. The slippers. The suits in the wardrobe. The bottle of Maalox for his stomach trouble. Every detail of a sick father's room became meaningless when the suffering was over and he was no more. And when I meet old schoolmates now we talk of nothing else but blood pressure and prostates and urinating in the night, and the need for vegetables to keep the bowels in good order. We're all terrified. But there's not really much of that you can share with a young man.

At my son's first holy communion there was a bishop in such glorious vestments that he reminded me of a peacock. He stood on the steps of the cathedral puffed up with compliments from mothers in white hats, and I almost envied him his flow and confidence and brazen might. But the last time I was in Dublin I saw him walking down O'Connell Street in an old coat, fallen and graceless, his eyes watering, and nobody to bid him the time of day.

Before leaving my son's birthday lunch, I gave him money stuck in a card. The wife smiled at me. For a moment I felt she actually approved. We were in the middle of those hideous T-bone steaks which I didn't dare comment on. That's when it started to rain and she turned off the barbecue machine and we went inside and sat at the long wooden table I bought in Ballina fifteen years ago, an old antique that she always maintained was full of woodworm, though I noted that she still has it in the house. Not that I would have wanted it. The apartment is far too small for that kind of table and besides, when I first hit Castlebar I began eating out at lunchtime and for about six months I spent the evenings in bars trying to meet new friends, until I finally realised that I was too old to have a future.

And for a few days after Philip's eighteenth birthday I felt strangely attached to the cat. I even let her sleep on top of my duvet, which is not a good idea, because of all the hairs. And then on the following Monday, I got the letters. One was from her solicitors and the other was printed off a computer on blank white paper with her name signed at the bottom. It was full of the usual clichés about moving on and having found someone else, but the solicitor's letter was the real deal. Vellum paper, gold letterhead and a few cold phrases about their client's interests. So I waited until the following Sunday before calling her. There's still a faint residue of silence in Sunday mornings and I thought it might be a good time to catch her. I didn't want an argument. So I called her but the answering machine came on and so I just left a message.

'Hi,' I said. 'It's me. Just wanted to let you know that I have the letter and that everything will be fine. It's whatever you want.'

There was a long pause. I presume she was away for the weekend with her painter friend. But I could imagine the kitchen in all its detail. The hum of the oil-fuelled Aga cooker. The tick of the clock that marked every breakfast and dinnertime when Philip was growing up. The wok from Cyprus and Angela's coffee pot. Even Philip's tin whistle is probably still in the knives and forks drawer. I wanted to say I think I might have prostate cancer, but the silence was choking me, so I put down the phone. There was a time when I used to walk around that house on Sunday mornings and think how lucky I was; a chicken in the oven and two firelighters underneath six turf briquettes in the open fire grate of the lounge and the sound of my little boy crying in the bathroom as Maureen lathered his head with shampoo. Cloudy days with wind blowing and rain from the west, and the gorgeous long-haired white cat in my lap. Not that I miss the open fire. Most of the heat went up the chimney anyway. But I do miss the cat. And I don't think it was fair that Maureen got to keep her; no matter what the little fucker in the grey suit and the pink shirt said. Pets or no pets the cat should have come with me.

Godīgums

Keith Ridgway

He fled back to Dublin with his tail between his legs.
Which was the phrase he used, in his innards, repeatedly.
The words – the very words *tail*, *between*, *legs* – had come
to him on the heels of the idea, the idea of returning,
like a house-dog. Yapping and delirious. The vertiginous
idea – the fear – and its pawing drooling house-dog, the
sick little puppy of retreat, its bark. *Tail. Between. Legs.*
It followed the words *Dublin*, *return*, *humiliation*, *flight*. It
chased him through his panicked consideration of other
options, other possibilities, each of which was rendered
redundant and dropped, one then the other then the
next, by the giddy imperative of the words *home*, *Dublin*,
tail, *legs*. And his tail and his legs had been so often
invoked in this frayed and sweaty – unbearable – month-
long internal turmoil of the innards that he had begun
to believe – to see himself – as a creature with a tail –
a literal tail – and to hate his accommodating legs, and
his awful, implied, retreating arse. And he could not dis-
lodge the picture from his mind. A man. With a tail.
Between his legs. A fault and aberration, a monster made

of failure. A wretch of those sunken rooms. A misbegotten glitch, a derailment. A beast on the tracks. There was a whole language for his failure, a rich and picturesque imagery and lexicon of abasement, and he was flooded with it. And he wondered in his misery whether such a thing as a tail between his legs could be disguised, made use of, passed off for some sort of newly acquired cockiness, a thrusting appendage of success, potency, coming home with a hard-on that such a tiny place as Dublin could never satisfy or deflate. He decided not to tell his family. Certain that this would lead inevitably to him bumping into them at every corner he spent money that did not exist on tattoos. This was panic. Clutchings. As the ink was painfully pricked first into his forearm, then his shoulder, his inner thigh, and finally his left wrist, it occurred to him that tattoos would fool his family only if he bumped into them while naked, or in the event of his death and facial disfigurement. Did your son have any tattoos, they would be asked. Certainly not. So if this was not then, as it turned out, a disguise, what was it? He slumped and looked at his skin, his tail. This was a way of making his absence appear if not longer then deeper than it had in fact been. If he met his family he would pretend a mental collapse, a death, a murder perhaps, an earthquake. Anything but the tail. Or something at least that pinned the tail to him, that made of it an injury, an assault, not this self-generated, self-grown tumour of his own inability, his misfiring. He considered shaving off his beard but decided that what he needed

now was the illusion not of youthfulness but of experience. He had his right earlobe pierced twice, his left
once. The day before travelling he had his hair drastic-
ally and innovatively cut, aiming for the fashion of the
place, the fashion he had spent the previous year rolling
his eyes at. But something went awry, midway, some
combination of the trainee barber and his own instruc-
tions, and the discomfort of sitting – perching, like a
boy on the plank, like a tumorous goatherd – on such
a preposterous tail. He emerged onto the street looking
like something shocking new, something newborn into panic, slapped and scurrying into the crowds with his
head alight and the Devil's finger hysterically prodding
his perineum. The journey exhausted him. The whole
journey. The journey to his miserable hovel, the last of
it, the journey through the nothing night, the journey
through the air and over the land, and through the sick
of the sea. His belongings implicated him in something
banal. He took refuge in toilets at every opportunity –
in stations, trains, airports, on ferries and their termin-
als, and sat for as long as he could bear, considering his
tail. Its prominence, its tumescence, its stench. He tried
to love it. He tried to find its loveliness, its purr. He
savoured it and searched for ways of harnessing it. Of
turning it. No! Of wagging it. Of altering, appealing, the
condemnation of the phrase. Of putting it behind him.
But the journey was long, and nothing in it worked. He
stared at his hair and his scabby tattoos, and he wrestled
with his story and he tried to hide his tail, and the sea

disgorged him. Dublin looked like it should. The same
at first, then hideously different, then interestingly so,
then the same again, just as he had left it, as if he never had, as if he had merely slept late. It showed no sign
of recognising him at all. Sullivan lived in the south of
the city centre, near the canal, and he went there by
way of buses and he was lost three times before he was
finally weary enough to call for directions, and his accent was a sudden mess against the ones in the street and
the one on the phone, and he didn't know what to do
with it. What a ridiculous-looking building. By a cube
of stale water. Everywhere the wind smoothed out the
grey flannel sky, and there were little birds, and taxis, and
bicycles, and people, groups of people and couples of
people and solitary people, and there were balconies and
the wind and kerbs and cobbles and lamp-posts and the
air full of misremembered things, and everyone stared
at him, everyone stared, and he grappled with his bag-
gage while his tail whipped his chest and he felt that if
he did not find a small room soon he would be wrestled
off the quayside – a monster taken by a monster, a blur
of tentacle and splash – and he presumed himself dead
already, back in Dublin and dead in the water. Sullivan
was furious. Not at the imposition, but at the haircut.
You look like a fucking culchie. You look like a fucking
culchie TD. You look like a fucking Fianna Fáil culchie
TD. From 1978. It was all the rage, Michael told him,
in other places, and Sullivan scowled and ran his hand
through it and wondered if he could do a quick fix with

the old clippers. And Michael realised with a wallop that this was the first test, the first tug on his tail, and he pulled himself out, dripping and spluttering, of the sulk into which he had momentarily sunk. You won't fucking touch it you backward old shite what would you know about hair you've never been further than Bray. At which Sullivan smiled for the first time and gave him a proper hug and kissed his neck and flicked his earrings and opened a bottle of wine. Five years, he said. You've missed all the fun. And barely a fucking word, Michael. You know? And Michael nodded and summoned sadness and placed a hand on his old friend's shoulder. I am no good at writing Sully, you know that. You know me. No good at distance. No good at staying in touch. Too many distractions. Too much. But you were always . . . and he placed his other hand where he thought his heart was. Sullivan looked at him, and sniffed, and nodded. Alright, he said. Alright. I missed you. I missed you very badly for a while. And Michael felt his tail coil round his middle and creep up his back and over his shoulder and around his neck like a noose, and he went and found a seat to sit in and he looked out the window at the low city and he tried to find his throat. I missed you too, Sully. But barely a word, I know. Barely a word. And he looked at his old friend and he thought, he seriously thought, for a moment, about putting his hands up, taking his shirt off, coming clean, showing and telling. Here are my bruisey tattoos, here is my tail. I have fucked it all up and I don't know what I'm doing. And he was tired, and his body ached, and his earlobes throbbed, and his hair felt like the wrong hat, and he looked at Sully and he moved his lips, and he was about to say, about to say . . . But Sullivan stopped him. Oh well, he said. You're back, you bastard, and you're welcome, so forget it. What's past is past and I'm glad to see you. And his tail slipped down again, and he smiled and raised a glass and nodded. I have so much to tell you, he said. You won't believe a word. So they sat together in the grey sky and they drank and talked and listened. And he described the way it was, or the way it wasn't, by way of the way it wasn't, adjusted for the way it might have been, or might at least be believed. A complicated formulation this, taking the baseline of the truth, which he must obscure at all costs, which he did obscure, utterly, with a fiction, a cloak over the tail, impenetrable but nevertheless pretty plainly a cloak – which would lead inevitably to Why are you wearing a cloak? – and which he therefore had to in some way acknowledge, which he did, by drawing attention to it, even going so far as to point to the bump where the tail was, saying that it looked like a tail, isn't that what it looks like Sully, look at me, penniless, homeless, sitting on your chair and drinking your wine with my tail between my legs. So that the tail might look like something else. Something mysterious. A love, a sorrow, something that had happened. And the words he dreaded were, You haven't changed. The dread words. And Sullivan didn't say them. Instead he took what he was given and nodded and laughed and frowned

66

and seemed to show no doubt. And the details came and came, and Michael arranged them and rearranged them, and slid them around into shapes that seemed like living. And he was tired, he said, and therefore vague, and then specific, and then vague again, and there were things he said he could not talk about, and things he said he could not remember now, and things that sounded like triumphs but which he minimised and waved his hand at, and things that sounded like disasters, which he – and this, he realised was the way to do it – which he lingered over, regretted, live and learn, Sully, you know? Live and fucking learn. So he had been now, he discovered, a worker in theatre, and television, and he had lived for nearly a year in a city he had in fact visited for a week, and he had spent most of the past two years living, he was startled to learn, with an older lover, a television producer, but he didn't want to talk about that, not now, Sully, Jesus, I'm only off the boat, I'm knackered, and I'm just back for a little while, out of curiosity you know, check on the family, change of scene, and I may stay a week or I may stay a month, and I'm grateful for the spare bed but I'll get something else in a couple of days and leave you in peace, no that's generous of you, Sully, but I'd rather get my own place, Dieter might visit, Dieter, yes, Dieter. Little Dieter I call him, I don't know why, he's not little, anyway. I haven't changed, Sully. I haven't changed. I haven't changed a bit. And Sullivan looked at him, and cocked his head, and thought about that, and said nothing, and Michael took another wine and laughed lightly at the music Sullivan had available, and mentioned some acts that Sullivan had never heard of, one or two Michael had never heard of either, given that he plucked the names out of nothing, out of half-understood conversations, out of the rags of his memory, out of panic. I haven't changed, Sully. What's that? said Sullivan, seeing the inky hook of a long G crawling onto his wrist. Oh that one. I just got that one. That's one of the new ones. What do you think? Sullivan held Michael's wrist and pushed his sleeve up as if looking for tracks, and he examined it, and gave a low whistle. What does it say? HONESTY. In Latvian. And you have others you say? Ah a few. You pick them up. Over the years. Like a fool. I've made mistakes, Sully, you know? It hasn't been all fun and frolics. I've fucked up royally a few times. Older and wiser. And Michael went on like this for a while, rolling out allusions to events he had yet to make up. Triumphs and disasters. Minimise the one, exaggerate the other. Hint at its opposite through misdirection. Sullivan listened and smiled, and looked at his wrist, and asked to see the others and was told no, not now, I'm cold, Sully, what sort of summer is this? And he made a subtle and terrible show of himself. I haven't changed, Sully. Ah you have a bit now, to be fair, Sullivan told him. You have. And Michael found his bed then and fell into it and slept for thirteen hours, dreaming of the past and all that it could be.

He stood in the street, smoking. He hadn't smoked in years. It was, it seemed, still in him, still something he could do. So he took the first cigarette he was offered, in the belief that it would be suspicious if he didn't. Ah sure they all smoke over there, I left mine in Sullivan's, thanks, thanks very much, I'll go get a pack in a minute. And days later he was still smoking, and buying the things, which were expensive to the point of absurdity. He stared at the change in his hand. He thought maybe he'd given a smaller note than he'd thought. Absurd. But the next time, it was the same, and he stared at the change in his hand and laughed at it. It was the money was absurd, not the smoking. The smoking was civil-ised. The money was a joke. His tail told him so. The State, he decided, was using cigarettes to devalue the currency, and he told people so, and they laughed and he smirked and everyone felt terrible clever. He bought boxes of twenty for a while, wondering at himself, and he sweated in the street in the evenings, smoking, as it was often warm, but he was unsure which way the sweat was coming – from the climate outside or the climate within (and he loved this little metaphor, as he loved these days all metaphors, and the grand metaphor, the Great Metaphor, which he thinly sliced and imparted to all, a host and sacrament (you see!) and celebration of all that was due to him having reached the age he had so unintentionally reached, with nothing to show for it but a tail) which was a fevered tussle (the climate with-in, that is) between terror and embarrassment and the urge to talk and to not stop talking, not for a minute, to devalue the tail through the furious display of the tail.

The over-wagging of the tail. Look at the tail. Look at it! It does not exist! For this was the key he had found in his pocket, or rather in Sullivan's pocket. The key to returning with his tail between his legs. To laugh at the Devil. To say the Devil's name. To declare him with a smile, and to counter him with intelligence, with contradiction, with laughter. Show the tail to the tail detectives. He met them all head-on, his knowing look met their knowing looks. Old buddies. Old friends. Old lovers. Jokers and clowns and earnest little fuckers. All of them eyeing him like he was something that they'd seen before, and it was always languid, with the chin up – Back, is it? And he fucking held their gaze. Back it is, back alright, broke and broken. With my tail between my legs. And there was always, sure enough, a pause. But he held them, he held them all, and they all fell eventually, they all dropped those chins, and the smile went full on, and Michael would laugh with them and slap their shoulder and he'd buy them a pint. Money, he decided, covered most holes. And Sullivan too. Look at me, Sully, chased out of it, back to Mammy, the eyes fallen out of my head. Will I take you out to dinner? And it was as easy as that. Say it. Just say it. And contradict it. And he piled the money onto a credit card from a bank he had never been able to pronounce the name of, and he knew that somewhere a few thousand miles away a little counter was clocking up, and he didn't like that metaphor, but what can you do? Life is what's important. He spoke and he recounted and he told them

all about it. I was there for two years, then there for
six months, then I was everywhere for a while, then I
moved in with Dieter, no that was after the stint at the
radio station, and my time in the theatre company, and
no, Dieter is in his forties, well, his fifties then, what
does it matter, you people need to drop the ageism, and
no, no, I don't think my accent has changed at all, what
are you talking about, I'm the same as the day I left.
He switched after a while to roll-ups, they were cheaper, a little. And he switched then to pouches he bought
on the streets, Mary or Henry, which tasted either like
steel wire or laundry, but it was cheaper, and he was
rattling through the money like a runaway train, and
Sullivan smiled at him, half smiled, and wanted to see a
picture of Dieter, and Michael couldn't find one. And
apart from Sullivan – Sullivan and his big eyes and his
hugs and his kindnesses and the long hours of listening
as Michael stroked the tail – the people he was talking
to were acquaintances who felt no entitlement to pin
him down on any of it. He told someone he'd spent a
night in jail in Bucharest. And he spoke, regretfully, as
if of a terrible time, a terrible mistake, of the amount of
drugs he took over a six-month period in Copenhagen,
though he'd never been to Copenhagen, and he told
everyone this, and asked them to keep it to themselves,
and he would cheer them up at the end of it, listen to
me would you, wounded creature, back home with my
tail . . . ah here, I'll get you another. And he sometimes
stroked that tail obscenely. He'd seen some raw times,

some shocking things, and it was good to be back in this quiet little city where no one had any money and no one had a clue. The truth in him shrank. It shrank and it shrank, and he lost it for days on end, obscured by the clutter of these stories, and the stories were so much more comforting, and fuller, and they seemed fairer too, they seemed closer to him, to what he was, to him as a person, and they were not all to his advantage, and he punished himself with some of them, for balance, for justice. He deserved them. And they were beautiful and cruel and complicated, these elaborations. He saw in his listeners' half smiles their appreciation of the close calls, the humiliations, the sorry state of his tattered progress, which had stuttered but was progress, was something, was a life, was a life in particles, in anecdotes and characters and things that had happened. He was a tour manager for a Ukrainian punk band on a debacle through France and the Low Countries. He had slept with two sisters in Warsaw. He had been beaten half to death on a train through the Carpathians. He hinted at drug money. He'd lived with a couple of rent boys in Hamburg – sweet days those, the sweetest. He'd driven a taxi in Berlin. This last one he dropped as soon as he'd said it. Ah no, I didn't, my German is terrible. But I had a lover who drove a taxi in Berlin. The stories he told me. I'm sure he made most of them up. Born liar, trouble, I got out of it pretty sharpish. He stayed away from his family, though he thought he saw his sister once, crossing Dawson Street in a rain-shower, and that was like a dream that he suddenly remembered. The furtive Christmas visits, three of them in five years, he didn't mention them. He claimed not to have been back once, and thought he could get away with that. He claimed a family rupture for convenience, though there was none that he knew of. He claimed the time of anyone who vaguely recognised him, who fell into his orbit. He declared himself broke and bought everyone a pint. He declared his tail between his legs and he made new friends and he slept with some of them and he was proud of his tattoos though everyone had them here, or something like them, and more of them, and everyone had already slept with everyone else here, and certain inconsistencies in his metaphors were showing. Here.

He ran, Michael did. You have told this one before, Michael, darling. I have? You have. Is it not worth hearing again? Maybe, for the variation. He ran. He ran down his minutes. He would step outside for a cigarette so that he could gather himself. And if no one joined him he would step back in again after two drags to hear what they were saying. Nothing. Dieter, did I tell you, the kindest man I ever knew. A beautiful man, a loving caring man. But I couldn't bear to see him fail, his health, after the operation, I couldn't bear it, and I know it's selfish, and I know, I know, he calls me every day, and I miss him, Jesus I miss him, but I can't, I can't . . . I'm sorry. And he found tears for Dieter. Remarkable, true tears. Poor Dieter. I'm a bastard and I know it and I don't deserve a thing.

He delivered the invocation one night to a woman he'd been to college with – apparently. He said it to her under a full moon on Dame Lane with a pint in his hand and a pint in hers, and his roll-up burning a sour taste of scorched bone onto his lip. Tail between me legs, he said. And she regarded him, and exhaled towards the heavens and sighed a little sigh and said, Sure we all have our tails between our legs these days. Whether we're coming or going. That's the truth. And if you don't have your tail between your legs then you're going nowhere, and you might as well lie down and die. And it turned out that she was off to South Africa the next week. And she did not think she would be back. And he wondered was there anyone listening to him at all.

It was Sullivan, nearly a month in, who caught him in the bathroom staring at himself in the mirror, at his tattoos and his collapsed hair, weeping like a child.

What is it?

I can't remember.

You're hurt, aren't you?

I suppose I am.

It's your heart, am I right?

What else is it, ever?

And there is no Dieter, and there is no television, and there is no Copenhagen, and there is no Berlin taxi driver or Hamburg rent-boys.

No.

So. It's alright. It really is. Come here. Tell me the story. Tell me the real story.

No.

And he stared at what was written on him, and wept for what was written through him, and he had no idea what he was at all, or what he was at all.

The Second-Best Bar in Cadiz

Andrew Meehan

I left Ireland to escape mince, in search of properly ripe fruit, but in time I have discovered that the diners of coastal Andalusia, despite a stated fondness for seafood, have no interest in foods like sardine ice cream and are impatient with destination dining of any kind.

I shave my face in the green darkness of the bathroom in Oscar's – which is not yet a destination restaurant, however much I want it to be – then move to my papery chest. Because I am going out again. I am going to meet Nacho, who will be returning from a pick-up. Most nights we go to his bar, Puntillitas, and drink and do drugs and sometimes, when I can get Viagra, we make love. Most of the time he has somewhere to go or has had too much cocaine, but I will certainly see him sometime before morning, even if we have parted as though that is it.

Nacho is a typical Gaditano (whatever that means, from day to day) and I am not. However, my apartment near the cathedral does have one of the biggest terraces in Cadiz and I work nearby. My life is a postcard and yet

I have fostered a dependence on products and especially pills to get me through any kind of normal situation – exercise, sex, breakfast – until now, when it has become impossible to regard any kind of situation as normal, even a drink with my boyfriend. Even cooking, which I chose as a career because it contained the promise of impressive people, regular money, perfect discoveries in foreign locations resulting in awards and enticing invitations. And because being a chef means I am not The Man with the Plastic Fork in the Emperor Inn in Castlebar. I do not hear from Nacho and so drink vodka alone on my terrace.

Nacho keeps leaving the same message. It is 5 a.m. and calmly I make it clear that I am looking forward to seeing him tomorrow. I assume that his bar with the palm-warm *manzanilla* will still be there tomorrow. Now he is at my door and he has been sampling his own wares – usually coarse, pink, pure MDMA – and is smiling so much that he may dislocate his own jaw. He is a tiny, stout skinhead with a spider's web creeping from his elbow all over his arm and when he is not high he is lugubrious to the point of being sinister. His bar is near the market but he lives in a house near Puerto de S— that he passes through just two or three times a week. Tonight, he has not been home.

Unreliable time-keeping aside, Nacho is a kind, superstitious man with unquenchable curiosity about the strangest things – geology, gambling – and an unsolvable disinterest in most others. He enters deep trauma at the thought of anything happening to any of his family and fierily worries that one of them may outlive another and is therefore irrevocably concerned about his own drug intake. Amongst other things, he is convinced that he is about to have a heart attack and die before he has finished tiling the fountain at his house in the country.

I'm laughing – this is usually funny – until Nacho upends his fist and thumps his breast, swallowing uselessly, pleading with me, somehow, before pouncing on my vodka. Now he rolls around the mattress like he is trying to wipe something off himself and onto my sheets, groaning, and reaches for the bedside drawer where I keep the Valium, which I sense are beyond him in some way. This is exactly what I wanted to avoid to-night.

'I've changed the sheets,' I say. 'Can we do this in the other room?'

'Fucking fuck,' he says.

Of course, he is exaggerating, but it is effective, and I am now willing to agree to whatever point he has wanted to make. What I am not expecting is Nacho to lose control completely. This is unpleasant and if I am not mistaken could be a lose–lose situation. I strong-arm him through the sitting room where I manage to prevent him from barfing onto my explosively white carpet and steer him towards the kitchen and, eventually, after some argy-bargy with the fridge, to the terrace, which is drenched in the cooling perfume of honeysuckle. After another frenzy, he begins to soften and calm.

'I want to get some sleep tonight,' I say.

'Fucking fuck,' he says.

He is not the type to analyse things. We kiss dolorously before he goes off to get more coke. He promises to return and customarily he doesn't, so I manage some sleep before I have to prepare for work. I take my tea to the terrace and stay there longer than normal (I allow myself ten minutes per morning), listening to the cathedral bells and working on my plans for Oscar's.

Nacho, heart attack avoided, is where?

I am now in a hurry to get to work and so do what I have to do – there are just the two of us in the kitchen so I will make the bread, gut the fish, skim the stock – before Oscar joins me; though, unexpectedly, I take a detour via the *churro* stall near the market. I sit stupidly on a tiled bench near some roadworks. I can picture it, if today is like any other day: Nacho half-asleep beside some eighteen-year-old, partially clothed and unable to do anything about it, thinking about the dust and piss on the floor, about me, unaware that I am considering a future without him and may soon be gone from his life completely. This is a good idea but a new one and something I must develop further.

After a few minutes a man I recognise – a tinker – sits down beside me. He is carrying a small sack of chickpea flour and is keen to discuss last night's famous football match. He does not seem to mind that I do not care for sport, and seems happy to lead the conversation in between mouthfuls of flour.

Until the explosion. From nowhere – my brother Johnny.

It is rarely necessary to tell anyone here how I came to be in Cadiz; no one is ever that concerned where the man frying the hake comes from, only that their meal is superior to any other meal on their trip (our few customers are tourists), but the silly, dull, compromised story of my journey here has a lot to do with Johnny.

Too long ago to be specific, around the time I was beginning my studies in architecture in Glasgow, Johnny was in the habit of sending me postcards from Munich and Istanbul and then Munich again – a regular circuit. One card suggested I pick a European city where Johnny could join me and treat us both to a weekend of beer-drinking and hell-raising. It didn't take me long to decide on Paris – I had it all planned. I intended to visit the *hammam* at the mosque where I would meet a man, attempt to make love with a man and attempt to explain this to my brother who would make very little of it before communicating it casually to our parents who would extend me their best wishes before wiring me the money for the deposit on an apartment.

I don't like to tell people what actually happened – jail, where Johnny ended up with a bang – and the effect it had on our parents, who acted as if they were the ones caught with heroin somewhere outside Dubrovnik and were themselves sentenced to seven years in a German prison, in as much they both entered an indistinct funk from which they have not returned.

I start to take Johnny in. His tabby hair is fading to a military-looking grey that is accentuated by a brisk and appealing buzz cut. He's wearing ripstop combat shorts and his feet are spreading all over a pair of translucent pink pool shoes so that it looks like he has just come from a nightclub or the beach.

'Where's my big John the Baptist welcome?' he says. 'Aren't you supposed to kill something to celebrate my return?'

'You're getting your parables all mixed up,' I say. 'Give me till lunchtime and I can organise a beheading.'

'We'll skip lunch if you don't mind. Is that tuna cock for sale over there?' he says, helping himself to a dough-nut. 'I think someone tried to sell me a fried eye.'

'No they didn't.'

'I had better food in Ulan Bator.'

'Not to mention prison,' I say.

A gust from the building site covers Johnny's dough-nut. He hands the dusty parcel to the tinker who has been enjoying our reunion, shoulders his rucksack and flops into the market, beckoning me to follow him. I am not expecting anything unique or memorable to come from today (not from Johnny).

'Little bit rough for you here, no?' he says. 'Or is this the kind of place where you pay people to piss on you and beat you up?'

He hops from stall to stall helping himself to fruit as I give not-with-me smiles to the stallholders that I know. It doesn't occur to me, as Johnny is filling his pockets with apricots, that I haven't seen him in fifteen years and that my hell-for-leather flight from home was made from blame for myself but first blame for my unlucky, dumb big brother. It has occurred to me many times that the reason I am not an architect but a chef – albeit not The Man with the Plastic Fork in the Emperor Inn in Castlebar – is down to not going to Paris.

I was in Hong Kong in a relationship with a beautiful boy so I didn't encourage contact upon Johnny's release. I was cheffing in hotels bigger than hospitals, in a casino built into a canyon. When I heard that he was living in a bus in the countryside in Portugal I didn't care, though one night, with most of a bottle of Ketel One inside me, I contacted him there. I was going to book him a ticket the second I got off the phone, call one of my contacts at the Shangri-La and get him a rate. I intended to lose the boy for the weekend and the brothers would drink beer and raise hell. When it came down to it we were brothers and we could rely on each other.

But I didn't book the flight or call the contact at the hotel (the beautiful boy took his own sweet time to disappear) and have had no further contact with Johnny until now.

We escape the market, walk along Calle S— and bump straight into Nacho, who has seen us before we have a chance to evade him. He pulls me right inside Puntillitas with the skill of a kidnapper. I prefer somewhere that allows light but this is Nacho's idea of a perfectly mysterious little shithole: a hot, concrete-floored cavern with cancer-ward lighting, rancid hams, ashtrays like salad bowls, toothless whores applying ointment underneath disturbing and camp holy pictures, a sweating fridge full of rusty tins of Russian salad to be consumed straight from a ladle. There is a large *Superbad* poster behind the bar.

Johnny won't allow me to talk my way out of there and seems drunk before the first glass of *moscatel* is drained. It is nearly ten and, naturally concerned about Oscar's, I depart making sure he has money for drink. (He has lots.)

I close the restaurant's preposterous church doors, a huge edifice concealing a good acre of spindly greenhouses sagging with misuse, not to mention the womb-like dining room only a failed architect could bear. In the spooky courtyard I drink coffee under a photograph of a phantom façade and decide that the problem – today – with Oscar's is its owner's infuriating comfort in its failings.

I want to make a proposal to Oscar. I put this in a letter. I consider the opening carefully. 'It's time to plan for the future and plan carefully.' No. 'Please give me the opportunity to be part of the future.' This is a better start. I describe the kind of dishes I would like to see on the menu: game sushi, four types of heirloom beetroot, ambitious desserts like molasses and Tic Tac soufflés. I take time over the letter because I want Oscar to be my friend and perhaps my lover once this is over.

Oscar came to Europe from Argentina in the 1960s

to take photographs of wars. Not finding war in the south of Spain he specialised in buildings and people in disrepair. Dead birds in muddy puddles. He also photographed weddings.

A few years ago, whilst unhanging a brave but unloved exhibition of photographs of decaying geraniums, Oscar had a conversation with his then wife from which I suspect he has not recovered. He opened the restaurant shortly afterwards – a place that takes Spanish classics and improves upon them, and though it has been open for less than two years, it has been shaped by a way of life that he has formed over forty years. He is a slippery man. He acts like we are friends though it is certain we aren't. I have scarcely any relationship with him, except that he is my boss and a man who, because of his moods, is forever preoccupied, as though he is totting up a sum having realised a previous error that is now impossible to correct.

I make no mention of what happened in his life. This is because I am unable to consider properly what happened with his wife; if they were happy just beforehand or caught up in something that is now foggy but was important at the time. Oscar, apparently, could not accept that he was not a war photographer, though he has admitted to closing his shutters on anything as dangerous as a New Year's Eve firework. The conversation concerned his refusal to pay attention to his (failing) marriage, his too-huge-to-contemplate dreams gainsaid by an empty gallery, the photographs bubble-wrapped and leaning against a wall, and Oscar standing, baffled, before them. This is not something he has told me himself (I heard it from a regular customer), since we are not in the habit of discussing anything intimate. It is also possible this is not something we will ever discuss, as I gather from another customer that the restaurant has been discreetly put up for sale. My letter should change that. I envelope it and head for the kitchen with my coffee.

He arrives around noon, carrying a pile of courgette flowers that he won't discuss when I suggest we stuff them with air-dried chicken skin. He stands by my prep station and grumbles, his particular linen chef's whites already crumpled up like tissue paper. I sense that Oscar's grumbles are enormous and cannot be confronted. Somewhere along the way he has decided that I am not the person to engage in important confidences, conversations that might distinguish a moment like a silvery, orchestral score. Instead we discuss the evening's menu, divide up the duties and decide, since there are no bookings, that it is all best left for another day. He places the courgette flowers to one side and suggests we might both take some holidays.

My day has been eventful but does not feel like it has begun. I stroll back to Puntillitas, letter written and course almost set. I notice Nacho at the rear of the bar – his silly expression lets me know I am interrupting some fun. A bottle of vodka sits beside possibly thirty empty bottles of beer. Johnny appears to have lost a tooth since

I have seen him this morning.

'What happened to your mouth?'

'What happened to yours?' he says.

Johnny looks like someone you would avoid after dark. He rotates his jaw and continues in an urgent tone whilst smuggling something into Nacho's palm. At the bar a fat man dances with a bucket of *boquerones*, and my brother, crooked but exaggeratedly clear, calls for silence.

'I would like to thank you, Nacho, for this auspicious entry into Spanish business life. I intend this to be the best bar in Cadiz. That's impossible. This is already the best bar in Cadiz. The second-best bar in Cadiz, then. Definitely the best cocaine in Cadiz though.'

Nacho has climbed onto his chair. He looks like he would like a smooch and I try to nuzzle him a little but in fact I am not in the mood. It has become that kind of day. Now Johnny declares that this bar is the reason he is in Cadiz: I don't think that it is. That he thinks Cadiz is crying out for another Irish bar: I doubt it very much. That he has already made the arrangements: no way. He pours some vodka into a beer glass and lowers it, as if he is commemorating some kind of deal with himself.

'I suppose you've been working on your business plan?' I say.

'No need,' says Johnny. 'Your boyfriend is my business partner. But you can be my first customer.'

'And when is this bar opening?'

'When? Whenever.'

'It's opening in here?'

'Here, yeah. Wherever.'

'And you're doing what?'

★

I expect to see Johnny at some point later or in the morning. I don't. And not a word from Oscar about my proposal. I spend the afternoon at the beach, where I see that a racy-looking bunch of language students have come, in all likelihood, straight from the bars on Paseo M—. I half-expect to see Johnny among them. I can picture him pulling a litre bottle of Cruzcampo from one of the ice bins and helping himself, happy as you like, to a skewer of prawns from the makeshift barbecue. He would fit right in. This would not surprise me; however I do not expect to see Oscar wandering the shoreline, sandals in hand. He takes a slug from a bottle of water and throws the empty into the surf. It's clear to see that something is going on, that he is in the mood to be left alone, but that is not what I do.

I walk beside him and suppose that a beach is not the most ideal place to be so out of sorts, the tinkling seas a reminder of what is no longer before you, your mind drawn to better times and the certainty that they have all come to an end. But you have to be sad somewhere.

Oscar abruptly throws his sandals into the surf and begins kicking water into the air so that it falls on us as if from an aspergillum. He turns his face to me and I see that he is crying. His tears seem inappropriate in the sunshine, as pointless as a sing-song. For his sake, I wish that he had stayed at home this morning. Of course, I attempt to hold him – only I clumsily clobber my forearm into his chin, breaking some of his tooth. Oscar springs backwards into the waves and, this is something I will never forget, spits some tooth into his hand and laughs like this is the funniest thing since that house fell on Buster Keaton.

'What are you doing here,' he says, as we walk back to the restaurant and I wait as Oscar checks that, once again, there are no bookings and the day can carry on with no particular purpose.

*

Nacho can't stop talking about Johnny's idea. My brother is Irish and must know a thing or two about bars, after all. However, my thoughts narrow to a single notion that at once widens, until I am back in the kitchen composing my future. I suggest we take a walk to Parque G— and look for a quiet bench to have the conversation that might get complicated but without which we have no chance of progress. Instead, we spend the rest of a long, tedious afternoon on the terrace with only flashes of good humour (due to Nacho's pouch of sparkling powder) and ending in yet another humid failure to perform in bed for both of us.

And so we visit my brother's new bar. Johnny welcomes me at the door with a ceremonial sweep of the arm and, instead of the fat man dancing with a bucket and calling out for his saviour, I find a room that has been transformed into something casual and unshowy in a way that I like. Already Johnny is dispensing glad tidings from behind the bar and friendly people I don't know sit on crates piled three high. Springsteen yahoos happily from the stereo. I take Nacho's hand and scare him with kisses to which, to my surprise, he responds. It begins with that. There are no quiet corners so we go to the alley where someone has placed the *Superbad* poster. He unbuttons my shirt and kisses my smooth chest, shaved now to the point of self-abuse; I start to believe that we are experiencing the rebirth of our relationship. I do not doubt the sincerity of his feelings for me. I am in his arms. I touch his face. We return to my postcard apartment and make love on the carpet – beside a solid lump of something like wallpaper paste – with an intensity that is not expressible as love; it is too guiltless for that. It is closer to a refrain of hunger and confusion. Afterwards, I put some fish in the pan – it is that lovely and that simple. There is a little more action before we fall asleep.

Oscar's has never opened in the daytime – Oscar, for his own reasons, decided that Gaditanos don't eat lunch – but the next day my boss is there before I am. I remain in the darkened restaurant from where the scantly lit kitchen seems holy or at least surgical. He is manoeuvring carrots and cutting at them in strange stabs so that I know that this will be for a perfectly lethal braised beef-cheek dish: the complex puddle at the bottom of your plate reacting with your mouth so cheerfully that you feel magnanimous and start making plans to keep your own cattle.

He doesn't acknowledge me but begins pouring sherry onto some vegetables and then adds some other vegetables, including the carrots, to a pan of browning meat. It is important to prepare this dish in two, three, four, five pans, which allows the flavours to develop separately; the complexity comes later, with time. But I am confused. This dish is not on the menu in summertime, though it is one of Oscar's particular favourites, and I find myself unexpectedly disapproving of his choice, given the daunting heat outside. I should leave him to it, but as I have an urge to make him like me, finally, I approach and begin peeling shallots. He will appreciate this.

'This will be the last meal I cook for a while,' says Oscar. 'So it is a staff meal.'

I toss the onions into a hot pan and peer at them as if they need to be scolded, whilst Oscar decants the reduced sherry into the pan containing the softened vegetables and meat. This is normally conducted in silence; which is how he prefers it. He reaches under the counter, produces a parchment paper lid which he places gently onto the surface of the stew. He looks confused, though it occurs to me that I should be confused. He invites me to smell the pot before he places it in the oven. I lean in and notice something new: his heavy breathing. He nudges me out of the way and opens the door of the oven – the air there seems cooler than the air in the kitchen.

Oscar steps out of his chef's jacket, adding an old-fashioned soapiness to the evaporating-wine air. There's something heart-warming about his gymnast's forearms, his hairless skin almost glittering in the kitchen lighting. He wanders around looking for a clean jacket and I can't think of what to say and when I come up with something about the apricots my brother stole at the market, Oscar doesn't acknowledge it, buttoning up a new jacket whilst considering my onions at close quarters. (These will be added to the beef cheeks later.)

'Please invite your brother to share this meal,' he says.

More even than the French waiter at La R— on Polk Street, or the tiny but all-seeing monk at the monastery in Wales, or those barnacled brothers on the boat to the Aran Islands, Oscar has a hold over me. It has little to do with sex, the distracted, hapless and sad way I go about making love now – not that I ever sizzled. His expression makes it clear that this is just a casual dinner, don't assume otherwise, and this is what I expect for the rest of the afternoon.

★

My brother – part-fucked, toothless and happy – walks down Calle S— towards me, hauling a shopping trolley containing a piece of wood the size of a surfboard. He's babbling into what I think is one of Nacho's mobile phones and doing his best not to look excited. Some people passing by have an idea that Johnny is a visiting theatrical when in fact he looks like an asshole and Nacho, behind him, I can see now, looks as disreputable as can be. I am not even sure he knows it's me. I play with the idea of dinner tonight. I consider mentioning it to Johnny, since I am feeling unusually happy and somehow feel responsible for his well-being, since he is nearly paralysed by whatever Nacho has been giving him and would make himself right at home at Oscar's or anywhere; but now I consider the message this will send to all concerned. Johnny finishes the call and explodes into laughter and a healthy attempt at an Irish jig.

'Don't ask me how I do these things,' he says. 'Don't ask me because I won't tell you. But I did it.'

'Fucking fuck,' says Nacho.

'You did what?' I say. Now I am concerned by Johnny's disrepair and burning breath, the cabbagey pallor of his skin.

'The man from Guinness just happened to be in the area.'

'This is Cadiz?'

'Quality control is very important to them. We'll be pouring filthy black pints before the day is out.' Johnny hooks his arm around my neck, his pool shoes making a sound like a flapping salmon, so that I can see the proud and gaudy lettering on the sign in the trolley: *Foley's Bar, Cadiz*.

92

This bar, everything to do with it and what it means to Johnny – and, I wonder, him to it – is something I would rather ignore as something ridiculous but easy to bear, like someone singing the Hokey Cokey in between courses of a tasting menu. His life choices, the choices that led him to a German jail, and now to an Irish bar in a town no one but me seems to regard as a destination, are the reason I don't take my brother seriously and he has never had a problem with this.

'Wait till you see what we've done with the place,' he says, panting like a spaniel.

'Since when?' I say.

'You'd be surprised what you can do when you put your mind to it.'

'I have to see this,' I say.

I sense something, though, and become timid as we turn the corner to the old Puntillitas, whose rankness has been replaced by minimalism and restraint, in theory. I understand now what Johnny – and, somewhere in the background, blasting Pogues records at distortion levels, Nacho – is trying to achieve with this place and I hate it. My quasi-boyfriend, with confidence that only intermittently betrays his drunkenness, climbs the ladder to erect the sign for Foley's Bar. I stand at the bar, lean backwards as if to stretch my spine and study the greasy ceiling, turn a full turn and take in the Celtic mural Johnny has applied to the bare walls above the tile-line.

'You've written what all over these beautiful walls? A poem?' (This isn't to say that I am not a sentimental man and don't love poetry and dip in and out of it during the dark times, just like the next man.)

'*The Great Hunger*. You sent it to me when I was in prison. It's perfect. This is an Irish bar.'

'It was just a bar yesterday, and a perfectly good one. And something else entirely the day before that.'

Johnny whoops and fires a bottle of beer off a wall, so declaring the place open for business. But I do not believe that this is a real bar or that Johnny has sound intentions or that any of my momentous plans, once I have had this dinner with Oscar, will not come true. In the real world, this would not count.

I am about to leave for dinner with Oscar when a woman enters: she could be their first customer – a stiffly nervous youngster whose skin has the clarity of good veal stock, whose mobile mouth and calculating eyes I recognise from somewhere, someone else. Her brother.

This is Caridad. Nacho throws her an apron. There is work to do. I try not to squint or stare too much, but I enjoy watching my brother and his new girlfriend – my boyfriend's sister! – work alongside each other. They have a lot to take care of. She unpacks cases of beer and he hauls in more from the store. It's not long before he has everything out on the bar, pouring shots of rum and putting them before Caridad, who accepts them as if she has little interest in alcohol but cannot bring herself to tell him so. I observe my brother duplicate his girl-friend's hazy gestures, something I invariably did for him

94

when we were younger. When I look carefully I see that he is following the lines of her lips as she speaks; mouthing rosaries of his own. I wonder if he has been given the gift of love that I long for? Nacho turns on some Horslips and the Spaniards start to dance. Up onto the bar goes Johnny and I slip out of the door quickly in case anyone tries to stop me.

The air in the street outside the restaurant smells of tired oil. It always does. One of our neighbours has a stall where she fries the troublingly young fish she serves to other neighbours in paper coned like a magician's hat. Out here, it feels like Oscar's doesn't exist. I push the door and find the courtyard empty except for a few dancing daddy-long-legs, the familiar purplish-mucky light – the first moment of expectation and uncertainty experienced by all visitors to this place; a restaurant that offers little assurance to the intrepid diner that you have arrived somewhere. *You Are Here.*

The dining room is lit and just a single table is laid with Riedel glasses and red wine in a decanter. I imagine Oscar did this before reuniting with his beef as it braised under the parchment lid; the unforeseeable transformation that always makes him smile like a child. He may be downstairs, choosing another wine, the only unknown element of the dinner that awaits us. Empty, the dining room looks like very little, which is fine with me. This is never the issue.

Taped to the oven door is a note in Oscar's hand, familiar to me from so many lists and reminders. It is written on the back of one of his geranium photographs. I focus on the flower instead of the flat, sorrowful words, whose intent I miss at first go. His tone is indecipherable and the news, once I have read the letter several more times, is as routine and lifeless as the butcher's block against which I am leaning. Oscar's is now closed and has been sold and Oscar has already left this pitiable place for Buenos Aires, not to return. The note ends with an invitation to eat the meal and drink the wine; this is his gift to me. I am The Man with the Plastic Fork in the Emperor Inn in Castlebar. I drink beer after beer standing at the fridge until I am barely able to remove the casserole from the oven and spoon some into a cup, to get myself into the dining room and the table, where I notice that, instead of a napkin, the cutlery is resting on my unopened letter.

The Ladder

Sheila Purdy

On the eighth floor of Virtual Processes & Systems Corporation you hang up your jacket in the staff kitchen, kick off your runners and get into your Crocs. The water boiler has to be filled and switched on to have the water scalding by the time the catering girl comes in at 8.30 a.m. You use the linen cloth on the crystal tumblers, holding each one to the fluorescent light checking for finger marks, giving a good rub. You take them on a tray to the boardroom. The rule is a tumbler and two bottles of sparkling water beside each crimson blotter on the big table; the delft goes at the far end of the sideboard. Then you switch the air conditioning to high and close the door.

After you've hoovered under the desks, you have a few minutes, so you put on the kettle.

With the mug in your hand, you sidle out the back way to the seating area for a quick smoke under the tree. The morning sun gets between the buildings and shines on the ornamental paving and the grasses. Overhead, a crane towers, a heavy chain swaying idly from its arm.

You sit for a few minutes and watch the chain, and after a drag or two, you put out the cigarette in the sand box and save the second half for later.

Vera, your supervisor, comes into the kitchen at a quarter to nine. With her back to you, she flicks through the catering daybook beside the phone on the worktop, and picks up the pen.

'Annie?' She folds back the pages. 'Kylie's called in sick. I won't be able to find anyone else.'

She turns and looks at you.

'Have you another skirt?'

You have on the little animal print you got in the sales.

'Never mind, this meeting starts at ten. You'll have to do as you are.'

She examines the book again.

'Tea and coffee for seventeen. And remember, these men haven't got time for talk. Don't get in their way.' She writes something in the book. 'If you do well today, we might see about moving you up a grade.'

Her iPhone dings. She touches the screen and moves towards the door.

'And Annie?' She keeps walking, keeps looking at the screen. 'Don't offer Mr Jackson any milk. He's lactose intolerant.'

In the two years you've been here, you've never done more than clear the big table, wipe out the execut-ive fridge, empty the bins, line up the leather blotters, straighten the velvet swivel chairs. You've never done

any serving. There's not much time and you're not supposed to go down the fire escape to the shops, your PIN
access is for cleaning purposes only, but it's the quickest
way so you go. In the Spar, instead of John Player Blue,
you buy a pair of Barely Black for €4.95, Microfibre
with Cotton Gusset, and a packet of Silvermints.

In the eighth-floor ladies, you stop the hand dryer
that seems to have been running all night. You get into
the tights, balancing on one foot, putting in the other,
getting hotter as you do it. Your skirt feels short, you
tug it down, and pull to make it longer but it's a hopeless skirt, the fabric has no stretch at all.

Now you fill one tall flask with tea, two with coffee,
and another with boiling water – the way Kylie does it.
You wheel them on the gold-plated trolley. No one is in
the boardroom. The digital display on the plasma screen
on the left-hand wall blinks 9:40. The tumblers seem
to sparkle under the star-lights high in the ceiling. You
place two oval plates on the near end of the sideboard,
one full of hot croissants, the other piled with apple
and cinnamon Danish delivered fresh from the deli next
door; beside them, the butter, the jams, the marmalade,
and the cutlery you've rolled in white serviettes. You
can't think of anything else. You don't know what's supposed to happen in a boardroom when the men come
in – you should've asked Vera what happens, exactly, but
she can be short sometimes. There's the option of giving Kylie a bell at home, only she'd tell everyone, and
anyway she's sick. The trick is to get through the day

without turning red or breaking anything. There's time to nip out to the top step for what's left of the fag. It'll be all right, you tell yourself.

When you get back to the boardroom the air-con is off. Two engineers in T-shirts are working at the floor boxes with pliers and screwdrivers; beside them, on the carpet tiles, green and red insulating tape and coils of wire half rolled out. Some of the floor boxes you use for plugging in the hoover, they're left wide open, cables spilling from the one nearest the sideboard. The pastries have been moved, the two plates stranded slantwise on top of blotters; everything has been pushed out of line. Even the plush chairs are swung in all directions, and the trolley is blocking Mr Jackson's chair. The plasma flashes 9:49.

'What's all this? Mr Jackson's meeting starts in ten minutes.'

They don't answer.

You walk to the nearest floor box, and, with your foot, flick the lid up and over. It clangs down, bounces a little, shuts flat. A loose copper cable catches your ankle.

The younger one jumps up.

'Hey, we're busy here.'

You wait with your hands on your hips like your mam used to do when she meant it. You surprise yourself.

The wire picks at your tights. You bend down and get rid of it.

'Right so, yeah, okay,' he says, 'we moved the plates. Laptop is going here.' His hand is on the sideboard and he waits for a comeback, then he points with the pliers.

'We're patched to that box, it's the only one we can work off.'

The other engineer lifts his head.

'Basically, love, we need the sideboard. End of story.' He scratches his head with the tip of a screwdriver and goes back to work.

There's no other surface for the refreshments. And only minutes to redo the room. You feel hot, you need to go out, need to figure out what to do.

Outside the door, you bump straight into Angela Burns, Mr Jackson's PA. She's getting the morning mail.

'Sorry,' you say. You step to one side, wrench your skirt down as best you can. You spot a hole in the tights.

'Annie, I've been looking for you,' she says.

You cross your legs, lean back against the wall.

'I was in the boardroom.' Your throat's dry. 'Getting it ready.'

'I know, don't worry, the meeting's put back to ten thirty.'

She goes to the water cooler and pours a drink from the blue tap and hands it to you.

'Come upstairs,' she says. 'There are technical difficulties with the live presentation. The engineers are working to resolve it.'

As she walks, she works her way through the bundle of letters, reading.

The ninth-floor corridor is dimly lit with hidden lights; the smell is fresh flowers and cigars, or raw wood.

The walls seem higher, and the sound of your Crocs gets lost in the carpet.

In her office the desk phone is ringing. She lifts the receiver and beckons you to follow, pointing to the turquoise seat. You tuck your legs and smooth your skirt as best as you can. Her big clean windows look down on the city: in the distance, there's Tallaght, but you can't make out Fortunestown. White shelves are stacked here and there with pale-coloured files and boxes in pastel pinks, blues, mauves. All the files are labelled with words and numbers, perfectly lined up, like in an IKEA catalogue.

At the end of the call she replaces the receiver without making a sound and then stays quiet for a moment.

'I've arranged for a table to be brought to the boardroom. It's not ideal but I know you'll do your best.'

She looks at her watch, a pretty watch with a white patent strap and gold face.

'There's not much time, I know, but redo the flasks. The coffee has got to be hot.'

As you leave her office you keep looking. If you do well with the serving, you might get a chance. It isn't too late. You just have to serve. How hard can it be?

There's a busy feel to the eighth floor with people pushing past, bustling, late. You race to get to the trolley, the flasks. You must wait in the corridor while the new table is put on its side and pushed through the boardroom doorway. The engineers still haven't left.

The water boiler is almost hot again, so you scald out the flasks. You take a damp cloth from the draining board and a white tablecloth from the drawer.

In the boardroom, the engineers are soldering wires with a short hot rod. It's the smell of your da's workshop on a wet Saturday. You wipe the table, push it against the wall and spread the tablecloth so it hangs down evenly. You move the pastries and cutlery, straighten the blotters, tidy as the files in Angela's office, and swing the swivel chairs back into place.

By 10:22 a.m., the flasks are redone and ready in the boardroom. A third man has joined the others and all three puzzle over a laptop. You lift the last flask into place on the side table and you are about to shine it with a soft cloth when a great laughing cheer sounds: 'Lads, we're up 'n' runnin'!'

They gather all their things and start to leave.

Quickly you pick the bits of tape, the wire, off the carpet tiles and check the bins. You spray a quick *tsss* of Glade into the room, put the air conditioning on 'blow' and leave the door wide open.

With a couple of minutes to tidy the kitchen before the meeting starts, you clear the worktop of dishes and cups, reload the dishwasher and rinse the sink with Spring Fresh Domestos. The last thing is to take the jug of milk from the kitchen to the boardroom.

You're at the fridge when the phone rings.

'Annie?'

It's Vera.

'Mr Jackson's PA, Angela Burns, I believe you were talking to her this morning?'

'I was up on the ninth, in her office.'

'So I heard. Angela has offered to serve the refreshments herself this morning. You're off the hook, so to speak.'

You close the fridge door.

'Mr Jackson's on his way down. Is the room ready?'

'Ready? Yeah, it's ready.'

You're done. You go down in the lift to the basement and back out for a smoke. The windows of your office block mirror the other buildings opposite. The sun has moved on. You sit back under the branches. The leaves make shadows on the concrete at your feet. There's no wind to ruffle the leaves but they have a sound of their own just the same. You stretch your legs and feel the ladder getting longer, running on down past your ankle and under the sole of your foot. You think about Angela Burns, her office, your skirt, the cost of the tights. It's not enough to get an opportunity, to be presented with a chance. You have to be ready. Ready when the chance comes. You smoke and stay out as long as you can get away with. Then you stub out the butt, crumple the pack and go back inside.

Barcelona

Mary Costello

They had not long arrived in the city. They had driven all day on the motorway, over high bridges and around wide sweeping bends, with cars speeding past and trucks bearing down on them and only a low metal guard shielding them from the ravines below. The drive had terrified Catherine. She had kept her head down. Peter had not seemed to notice, or hear her when she asked if they could please get off the motorway.

Their hotel was on a narrow street off the Ramblas where Picasso had once lived over a jewellery shop. They walked out into the bright shopping streets, and parted company for a while. Catherine strolled around, in and out of expensive boutiques with gleaming tiled floors and semi-bare rails. Through La Boqueria, the covered market with its trays of tongues and hanging hams. Now and then she stood before a shopfront or a billboard – the colours of Spain, of Miró, everywhere. The afternoon sun beat down. Once, she caught sight of Peter up ahead and ducked into a shop. She found a café down a side street and sat outside with coffee and a cigarette. Sometimes she thought she could live on cigarettes alone, silently, deeply inhaling, letting thoughts gather, coalesce, then purge themselves in the exhalation.

Later, together, they walked in the shade of the plane trees on the Ramblas. The birds, locked up for siesta, were silent. Rabbits and tortoises too. *Canarios €14. Pico de Coral €20. Isabellas €25.* Arrival in a new city often reminded Catherine of her youth, the pining for home she would feel on Sunday nights as her bus approached the city and the orange lights up ahead bled into the horizon. Now her mind was crowded by details of the day, the drive, the week ahead. It was their fourth anniversary, and this trip, this city, had been Peter's choice. She knew he wanted it to matter, to mean something to them afterwards. Setting out that morning, she had brought up Lorca, whose poems she had taken with her.

'He was from Granada, or near Granada,' she said. She looked out the window at the orange groves, the scorched headlands, the limpid day. 'He was murdered by the Fascists in the thirties. It's still a sensitive issue here.' Peter shrugged. Before they joined the motorway she took out the poems. *In the dark wake of your footsteps, my love, my love.*

'They never found his grave,' she said. *See how the hyacinths line my banks! I will leave my mouth between your legs, my soul in photographs and lilies.*

She would have preferred Granada. She would have liked to have found the mountain road near Alfacar where Lorca was shot and buried. 'He was chasing *duende*,' she said. 'That's what he was after.' She looked at Peter. 'Do you know what *duende* is?'

He shook his head. 'No. Tell me. What's *duende*?'

She was surprised to find herself doing this, making him feel less, under par. He was proud, accomplished in his own field – the law – and generally peaceable. She was in a strange mood. Lately she found herself growing dismissive, impatient, employing at times a withering attitude towards him.

'It means soul,' she said. 'The dark cry of the soul, the terrible sadness that seizes the flamenco singer.' He was staring straight ahead. 'The grief and hardship in her voice,' she said.

She watched him search for a reply, for some comparison he might offer. The singer falls into a trance, he might say, like in *sean-nós*, or old women's keening. *Yes*, she'd say. The kind that goes to the marrow, he'd say. *Yes. Yes.* She waited, but he offered nothing. 'She is haunted by love,' she continued. 'Deranged by love, and death too. There's always death.'

They were approaching the motorway then. She found her mind veering off into an imagined conversation. After a while she turned to him. 'Why do couples always make love – desperate frantic love – after a big row?' she asked.

★

They wandered around the port and then along narrow streets, stopping now and then to gaze up at the buildings. A spaniel came out of a courtyard and sat on the footpath, calmly looking at her. They walked for a long time. They did not know where they were going. In a doorway a teenage boy stirred and looked up at her with deep-set, familiar-looking eyes and she was filled with a mild panic that he might speak to her, say her name even.

They returned by different streets and came upon a procession of altar boys carrying a cross and banners and priests wearing robes and pointed hats like the Ku Klux Klan. At the rear, a brass band played and uniformed young men rode on horseback and she thought there was something haughty and triumphalist in their bearing, something in their perfectly sculpted features and flawless olive skin – the whole spectacle, in fact – that chilled her. Peter smiled and raised his eyebrows as if to say, *Okay? Enjoying this?* He took out his map. 'That used to be a bullring,' he said, pointing across the street. 'There's still one in use, not far from here. We should go, before they outlaw it.'

Later, in a restaurant, he brought up the bullfight again. 'Seriously, we should go. There's one on Sunday.' She shrugged. She thought it was a test. They were drinking Rioja. The restaurant was crowded, buzzing with talk. He had ordered *codorniz*, quail, and when the waiter arrived and put down his plate the scrawny little bird toppled over. Just then a woman at the next table let out a sharp laugh that startled Catherine. Peter righted the carcass and tapped on the breastbone. He peeled back the skin and teased a morsel of moist dark meat from the ribcage and raised it to his lips. She turned away. A terrible piercing loneliness entered her. A scene from a book, from years ago, surfaced. *Justine.* There were lovers – maybe a love triangle – and hazy bedroom scenes and beyond the window the heat and bustle of a North African city. A camel collapsed from exhaustion on the street outside and men with axes came and hacked off its limbs and carved up its flesh, while it was still alive. What she remembered, especially, was the pained puzzled look in the camel's eyes, and the eyes moving as its limbs were cut off. The eyes still moving as the head was hacked off.

The woman at the next table laughed again and Catherine looked at Peter. She began to picture the walk back to the hotel, the bedroom, their nakedness. She had had the feeling, setting out that morning, of going someplace, and now she had ended up somewhere else, somewhere that made her more homesick than ever.

Peter was smiling, holding out a small red box. Inside were earrings, amethyst.

She frowned. 'I didn't get you anything.'

'I don't want anything.'

She began to remove the earrings she was wearing and put on the new ones. He sat, quietly regarding her. He would soon want children. When she tried to picture a child it was her sister's child that always came to mind.

Amy. A beautiful, pale dark-haired little girl. Radiant with innocence. Catherine felt a strange closeness to this child that she did not feel towards the other children in the family. As if she saw Amy as she might have once been herself – a clean slate, as yet unblemished by the world – and had singled her out for saving.

She fingered the earrings. She looked at the couple at the next table. When we are young, she thought, we have enormous hope, we expect that someone – a man bearing love and mystery and new ideas – will come and help reveal us to ourselves. She looked at Peter's waiting face. He was no longer mysterious to her. She watched him talking sometimes, eating and drinking with gusto, bouncing through life on the stable ground beneath him and she was struck by the distance that exists between people. How everything, the details of everyone's hidden life, far exceeds anything we can possibly imagine. And how for brief periods one can live at a different pitch, an extreme pitch, and then, when it has passed, return to the middle way again. Without anyone else ever knowing. No one bound her to secrecy, and she thought now that people do this – *she* did this, she kept things secret – so that they can reimagine their lives when lived life is not enough.

On the way back to the hotel he took her hand and she walked blindly beside him. She would have liked to have said something about the religious procession, the boy in the doorway, the drive that morning, them – their union. She thought there was a thread of messages on the streets, maybe even in their footsteps and in the tides of their silence, to be unriddled, but she knew that to voice such a thought would make her appear cold and remote, signal a drift in her.

In the hotel room Peter switched on the TV and flicked through the channels. Then he patted the bed and said 'Come here,' in a warm open voice. She came and sat on the bed. He put his hand on her shoulder and she felt its lovely weight and closed her eyes for a few seconds. 'Are you tired?' he asked. She shook her head. He began to kiss her neck. 'Let's watch something,' he whispered. He stopped kissing her and surfed the pay-to-view channels and then paused. A couple was having vigorous sex against a wall, the man driving hard and fast into the woman. Then the scene froze and the menu appeared on the sidebar. Peter took out his credit card and leaned towards the keyboard. He had always been keen to use porn. Everyone does, he said, and she supposed he was right, but it always left her feeling empty, and a little sickly, as if their love-making had been communal and he had shared her and her private raptures with others. She watched him type in his card details. Certain remote memories had a way of returning unexpectedly, and as he tapped the keys she began to remember a night out from a time before they were married. She had not known Peter for long and they were in a late-night bar with two of his friends. There was a DJ and a small dance floor and footage from old black-and-white movies being projected up on the wall behind Catherine

– clips of Laurel and Hardy, Charlie Chaplin, a flapper in a beaded dress doing the Charleston. Then suddenly one of Peter's friends laughed and Catherine glanced back at the wall. The Charleston girl had stripped down to her bra and knickers and was doing a kind of belly dance, wriggling her ample hips and jiggling her breasts, her nipples covered in little tasselled cones. Then she turned around and bent over, exposing her backside in cut-away knickers. Catherine looked away. Peter gave a little whoop, then leaned in and said something to his friend. When they laughed – a low secretive laugh – Catherine felt her heart sink. She looked into her drink. If she were a different woman she would have got up and left, but even then Peter had become the hub of her life, the one to prevent the drift. The friend laughed again, a guffaw this time, and Peter turned away to conceal his own contorted face. When she looked up the dancer was still there and, instead of knickers, a little triangular flap – a snatch or scrap of animal pelt – hung over her genitalia, attached to a thin band around her hips. She wriggled and shook, and the little flap, as if part of her, wriggled and shook too, and lifted, and something struck at the heart of Catherine and she burned with shame, as if she herself were up on the wall, naked, with the little female flap flapping and hopping and lifting, and Peter and his friends standing there, convulsed with laughter.

He moved the cursor over the menu and clicked. Two naked girls with enormous pumped-up breasts appeared, writhing on the screen. Catherine turned to say something but then his phone bleeped and her gaze drifted off and came to rest on the novel on the bedside table. She felt a sudden longing to return to it. To the promise of solitude, private and illicit, that it held. To the strange gaunt creature at its heart: a silent disfigured man, pushing his mother out of the city in a makeshift wheelbarrow, and then, after her death, wandering the desert, surviving on almost nothing, his mind growing emptier by the day. She had found herself worrying for him, as if he were real and in her life. Suddenly, at the thought of him, a jet of pain shot down her left arm, enfeebling her. How had she found kinship with such a man? Why was she flooded with feeling for him?

Peter moved up on the bed, propped himself up on the pillow and then tugged at Catherine to follow. The TV scene changed and a man and woman entered a ship's cabin and began kissing and clawing and tearing each other's clothes off, then panting and moaning exaggeratedly. Catherine assumed the language was Spanish. She read the subtitles, single inane words, and remained unstirred. The moaning and limb-thrashing grew louder, more phoney. She felt Peter grow impatient. He switched channels, began to surf for a different film. She got up and stood at the window, and he did not try to stop her. She leaned against the window sill and waited, not knowing for what. The memory of the motorway returned, the great hulking shadows that closed over them, the monstrous trucks thundering past as they all careered downhill. In a second everything could end. She closed her eyes, began to envisage the plunge, the fall into the gorge, and when she could no longer bear it she threw off her seat belt and climbed to the back and flung herself on the seat where she lay face down and motion sick for the rest of the journey.

She turned towards him. 'I got a fright last night,' she said. 'I woke up in the middle of the night, choking.'

He threw her a glance and made a face. 'What?'

'It was a kind of nightmare. You didn't hear me?'

He shook his head, then lowered the volume. 'Why didn't you wake me?'

'It was you who was choking me.'

He hit the mute button. 'What are you talking about?'

'It was . . . a half-dream, half-real. I thought I was at home sleeping in our bed and you crept in to get something and you whispered, "Shh, go back to sleep." And then there was a thumb pressing down on my Adam's apple – hard, really hard – and I couldn't breathe and in a second the pressure surged up inside my chest – and I knew I was going to burst and my heart was going to break into pieces . . . and I said, "Peter, Peter, stop." I said it urgently but in a nice voice too because I knew you didn't mean it, you hardly knew you were doing it . . . I had to wake myself up to save myself. I knew I was only a second away from dying.'

She turned away. She could feel his eyes still on her.

'Why are you telling me this? What does it mean?'

'I don't know . . . Maybe you've silenced me.' She half smiled. 'Have you put a gagging order on me?' Then, after a moment, 'Do you remember, once, I told you about a boyfriend I had when I was nineteen?'

He shook his head.

'I did, I told you. I told you a little bit. His name was Luke.'

'The animal boy,' Peter said flatly. 'What about him?'

'I kept him a secret from everyone. I didn't tell you that.' Peter raised his eyebrows. 'It wasn't difficult,' she said. 'I had my own bedsit. He used to sleep late, watch TV while I was at lectures, smoke dope sometimes . . . He never knew his father. There was just him and his mother growing up, and sometimes foster homes . . . '

'What made you think of him now, tonight?'

'I don't know. The restaurant . . . The quail, maybe.'

'*Jesus Christ.*'

'Did I tell you how I met him? Maybe I did. He was giving out leaflets at the entrance to Stephen's Green – with pictures of awful animal experiments, you know, monkeys with their heads drilled open without anaesthetic, mutilated kittens, circus animals . . . And the word *vivisectionist*—'

'Jesus, Catherine,' he groaned. 'Not this old hobby horse again.'

'I remember seeing that word and thinking it was a bit like *abortionist* . . . Do you know what he told me one night? He said he was happy only once ever in his childhood. It was a summer's evening and he and his mother were sitting in her flat as dusk fell. Just the two of them . . . hardly speaking . . . with the light fading . . . and the sound of kids playing drifting up from the yard below . . . '

She looked at Peter. 'He saw it all, you know – the abattoirs, the transport trucks, the slaughter . . . It tormented him – the Devil's carnival, everywhere.'

'Oh, *please* Catherine! Not this again. Do *not* equate the life of a cow with the life of a human being. Six million human beings.'

The sound of muffled voices carried from the next room. She was aware of naked limbs moving on the screen. 'When I was small,' she said, 'I used to hear my father getting up in the dark on winter mornings and going out and loading up cattle for the factory. He had reared them, you know, he'd looked after them every day . . . They walked meekly up the ramp onto the trailer for him.'

Peter swung his legs out and sat on the edge of the bed. 'They didn't know,' he said. 'They're not capable of comprehending any of that.'

'They're capable of suffering.'

They looked at each other. He would always outwit her with words, with logic. Then his shoulders seemed to slump. 'He put all that into you, didn't he?' he said sadly. 'All that animal business.'

She turned her head away. Suddenly she felt far from home. She thought of her rooms, her chair by the window, her little garden.

'He used to steal from me,' she said. 'Just little things – CDs, gift vouchers – to get money for dope . . . I didn't say anything . . . I couldn't.' She shook her head. 'At least when he was stoned – at least then, I thought – he might forget, he might get some peace.'

She had been incapable of tearing herself away from Luke. She had felt his silence as a kind of deprivation. And yet she almost wished to return to those times, to the fidelity of being she had felt then, the streaming across into each other, the mornings spent in bed when a thought that might have been his became hers.

Peter's chest was rising and falling rapidly. Suddenly he flared up. 'You were a mug, Catherine, that's what you were – a mug.'

The sound of thumping music floated up from a bar and faintly vibrated in her. She thought of the tourists on the Ramblas, the birds in their cages, wings twitching from thwarted flight. She wondered what her life meant.

'What happened?' Peter asked in a quieter voice. 'You dumped him, I hope.'

'No. He just stopped turning up. I think he was ashamed . . . I searched the city for him, knocked on doors till I found his mother's flat – she was sitting in a dark room watching TV . . . I hoped he had run away – on the UK news sometimes I'd see protesters outside animal-testing laboratories and search for his face in the line . . .

'Eventually I went back to my old life, my old friends

. . . And then, ages later, I got a call from his mother's neighbour. A builder had found him in a narrow gap between two buildings at the back of Capel Street, badly decomposed. He'd been missing for nearly two years . . . He must have climbed up there one night when he was drunk or stoned, and fallen off. Or maybe he jumped . . . '

She used to imagine him drifting in and out of consciousness, the footfall of strangers on the far side of the wall. His brain winding down after death. Everything deeply and terribly wrong. She went to her parents' house in the country for a while and lay on her old bed in the evenings, conjuring up his final hour. It was always night time, and he would stop on the street, tilt his head as if discerning a cry above the din of traffic, then glance up and catch a glimpse, an apparition – of what? A cat perched on the roof's edge, or a man – himself, his own form – silhouetted against the sky? And then his footsteps running around to the back lane and the vertiginous climb until he could go no further and he stood on the roof, eyes drilling the dark as if trying to pierce the secret of what he might become, and something at his centre – his will, his life force – beginning to disappear, dissolve, silently implode.

'I had this thought one night,' she said. 'This notion—' She hesitated, uncertain, her words seeming weak for the task. 'It struck me suddenly – like lightning – that he had done it intentionally – that he had sacrificed himself for the animals . . . Maybe he thought they'd know – somehow they would know – and be consoled . . . ' She looked at her husband's face. 'You have to understand,' she whispered. 'He changed my heart.'

They were silent for a long time. All day she had been waiting for something to deliver her, wanting the day to end gently.

'Tell me something,' Peter said then. 'Imagine . . . imagine there's a fire, and you can save only one thing – me or your dog. Who would you save?'

'Peter . . . please.' She began to cry. 'You're being silly now.'

'I'm serious! Just picture it – imagine it. Who would you save?'

The image of her beloved dog, Captain, near the end of his life, appeared before her, raising his head, his misty eyes, rising on his stiff old bones to come to her when she entered the house. She thought of a fire, and Captain running through the rooms. And Peter.

'Answer me. In a fire, who would you save?' His eyes were penetrating her.

'I'd save you both,' she whispered.

'Not allowed! You know the rules. *Choose.*'

She took a step away from the window but there was nowhere to go. She thought of her father's cattle locked in the shed the night before their journey, sensing something – the approach of an awful dawn. *Yes, a holocaust*, she wanted to say. And we are all complicit. And I am complicit too – because I say nothing, I do nothing. But she could not say it – how could she say

these things? What words would she use? How could
she say that when she saw her father walking into his
barn in springtime with a tin of rat poison in his hand
that a vision of such catastrophic, such apocalyptic, pro-
portion loomed before her – of rats, legions of rats,
gasping, dragging their swollen bellies on the ground?
Crazed running rats. Females shedding the contents of
their wombs on the concrete floor. How could she say
such things? How could she ask if the terror of rats is less
than that of any other species?

'I cannot help it,' she said. 'It's what I see. And it's
getting worse – I see it everywhere . . . in sheds, in fields
. . . their waiting. And at Christmas when your mother
lifts the turkey out of the oven and bastes it and prods
it with a skewer till the juices run clear, I think of her,
and my own mother too – good women, full of human
kindness – as executioners. And everyone around the
table feasting on this poor corpse – and Amy too, sweet
Amy, growing more tainted and tarnished with each bite
– and all I feel is shame, and I sit there thinking, *Are they
all mad? Has the world gone mad? Or am I the mad one?* Am
I, Peter?'

He was staring with wide open eyes. For a second
she thought she glimpsed a hint of mercy in them. But
then a look of bafflement, or dread, began to take hold.
She turned away and felt herself sway. She was almost
dreaming now, with everything swimming before her.
Peter was right – Luke had put this into her. He had
left her afflicted. She saw him again on the roof that

night, hardly a body at all, his gaze cast down for a long time, but then his senses slowly sharpening and heightening until every sound reached him distinctly, and he became alert to something – a dawning, a dizzying realisation that he was coming into something that might never again be his – a slowly turning earth, the opening of a vision, a vista, a promised land – the face of a father, a beautiful serene mother, a vast plain with all the beasts of the earth, wild and tame, assembled there, and in the air a note, a song, the sated sound of immortal longing rising from the tongues of birds and beasts and inanimate things. She closed her eyes and became momentarily free. She had the feeling of being there on the plain with him, called to follow, suffused in a beautiful phosphorescent light.

After a time she stirred and turned her head. Peter was sitting in a chair now – she had not felt him move. On the TV a man was silently rearing up on a woman, his face twisted in ecstasy. Peter was leaning forward, staring into a corner with desolate eyes. He put his head in his hands. At the sight of him something in her shifted. She began to perceive the damage she had done. She crossed the room and put her arms around him. She kissed the top of his head. She lifted his right hand and pressed it to her breast, urging him, willing him, to take hold, and for a moment she felt a give, a fleeting submission, in him. But then, as soon as she let his hand go, it fell away and he let it fall, and it swung for a moment and then hung by his side, pale and limp and indifferent.

The Mark of Death

Greg Baxter

From the top of Franco's building in the seventh district
we watched the city in a gold, quivering blaze gnash
itself into the smoky and loud paralysis of lunchtime.
We: Franco, me, and Sylvia. Franco hasn't worked in
months. He was so broke that he was wearing little rusted saucepans for house shoes. He was an electrician,
and there wasn't much work left anywhere – not in offices or houses. His mother had died in winter. If he
didn't make the rent this week, they would turf him
and he would lose the view. He used to say, Even if I
lost both my arms, it wouldn't be much worse than it is
now; what do I need arms for? Sylvia was a hopelessly
happy schoolteacher who had decided it was her destiny
to cheer him up, except she had no money, and that was
really all that could have cheered him up. Nevertheless –
or perhaps I mean to say inevitably – they became lovers. I had come by with a bit of money to lend and a few
drinks, and to try and convince Franco to dump Sylvia
and come with me into the city and find some normal
– slightly unhappier – girls. But she wouldn't leave us

alone. She kept saying, And look at the cathedral! And look at the city hall! And look at the castle! As though she was not up on the roof once a week. When Sylvia suggested that we go see the new exhibit at the museum of modern art, which was not very expensive, I thought, No no no! But I shrugged and when Franco agreed, I took the empty bottles and put them in a bin and thought, Why not? What's there to lose?

Over the few days preceding that one, I had taken on the kind of look a man gets – they say (I have heard) – when his death is imminent. The mark of death. I saw this in myself one morning, in a mirror, after I had brushed my teeth. It took some time to figure out, but in the end it was unmistakable: it was no longer my face. Not entirely: it bore the strange sign of a fate that cannot be avoided. So, I immediately thought of Lermontov (I was quoting him before I remembered him), and for these few days I have had dreams and waking dreams in which a man comes and whispers in my ear: You're going to die soon! I believe in the predestinative power of the imagination, so I called work and told them I was dying, and wasn't coming in. My boss said to have someone contact him when it was . . . he searched for a word . . . *over* . . . to arrange a collection in the office for a gift for the funeral. I cleared out my bank account (there was not much). I sent all my belongings to my mother, so she might distribute them to my cousins. I did not tell my mother I was dying. I told her I had become religious. I should have said I was dying, because now she is chasing me around the city.

I go around now exclaiming things to myself, as though I am not a real human being. I, sitting in my armchair at home, listening to slow piano music, exclaim: O life! O life!! O *life*! As though I ever lived a second worth an exclamation. I spent so much time in cinemas and in the office, at concerts, or on holidays, in bars, cafés, on roads and streets, in aeroplanes, in museums, in trains, looking at the sea, in houses, looking upon streets and roads in rain and snow and sunshine, in all the apartments I have dwelled, and rooftops I have stood upon, on highways, on water, in buses and streetcars, and many different countries, and in bed, but I have spent so little time in my own mind – so little time in the vast and slow universe of thought – that nothing I achieved or experienced had meaning. And now there was no time to correct it. O Life! What an unfathomable and fast darkness you became! What will become of my thoughts when our association has ended? Are my thoughts worth so little that when I am gone, they are gone, or are my thoughts the thoughts of all men, and in that way men and women are no more than vessels for ideas that exist externally in the universe, like matter, or divinity, or a lab experiment?

We left Franco's building and argued over the best way to travel. The options: walk ten minutes to the underground and arrive five minutes from the museum, or wait ten minutes for the bus and arrive at the front door of the museum but make a dozen stops along the way.

Only a city dweller understands the terrible unanswerab-ility of such a conundrum. In the end I don't remember which we took. The city life is a life of continuous for-getting – like seizures: gaps in time that are filled with great activity and motion. These moments are filled with thousands or tens of thousands of individual angles of perception like ever-rearranging ballistic lines through space, and they have flashed and exploded and expired before you, and you have banished them to darkness. Just as now, at this moment, who you are and what you are thinking is the multi-forked ballistic trajectory of your life, and it is tumbling into the amnesiac darkness of the crowd that surrounds you.

Franco and Sylvia slowly and without any words at all created a very severe and acrimonious argument. I sensed that Franco either suddenly did not want to go to the museum, or that something Sylvia said or did had inspired a little bile in him. Sylvia's response – she was cheerful, but she had feelings – was to be hatefully dis-appointed with him and very interested in me, and this enraged Franco. By the time I paid for everybody's tick-ets, Franco and Sylvia refused to look at each other.

The museum was crowded with tourists – especially young men and women in shorts and flip-flops and backpacks, taking photographs of the coat-room lady, the museum shop, the guards, the lifts, and themselves in front of the toilets. They also took photographs of the exhibit.

The man said to start at the top – Étage 8 – and work

our way down. Franco immediately said to me: I'm doing the opposite. Sylvia said to me: I'm doing as the man says.

So we separated. I went with Sylvia, as the man had suggested. Franco went to the bottom floor – Étage 0 – which was four flights below the ground level. I was happy with this arrangement, because Sylvia was not a bad person when Franco was gone. Franco tended to be a miserable person all the time. I loved him, of course, but preferred not to be around him too often. As soon as we were in the lift, Sylvia and myself, I knew we were not going to make it through the day without having sex. She was very pretty – or rather she was prettier than many of the girls I had slept with. She had brown hair that was straight and cut short over her eyes, and brown eyes, and she was more interesting than Franco. Why had I always considered her such a dullard? Was I always in love with her? Is that the reason I despised her? I decided to stand close to her and reveal that I hadn't much time. But the doors of the lift opened, and suddenly the eroticism of the tight space released into the dark and vast open structure of the building – the lifts, which were glass, rose through metal scaffolding, and all around them was open space, and the black-grey walls of the central structure. From the top, you could see the bottom. I looked over some rails and saw Franco staring up at us. He waved, and I waved down.

I have seen everything I ever wanted to see, and it amounts to little more than extreme pessimism. What is

mune, since we had no destination. Franco said: I want to go home. I have no money, and I will feel humiliated if you buy me anything else. Suit yourself, I said.

He got up to leave, and, to my surprise, Sylvia got up as well.

You're leaving? I asked rather desperately.

Franco looked at Sylvia. Sylvia sat down in a mood that expressed dejection and rage and incomprehension. She was, I realised, very in love with Franco. But I could now see that her optimism was in ruins, and Franco was smashing it to smithereens, on purpose, to finally get rid of her. Wasn't this my original plan? But now I was with Sylvia, and in love with her!

And there it was! There! The mark of death upon Franco's face! How absurd! He threw a small bag over his shoulder and took out a music player and some earphones and when he was entirely ready to go, he looked at himself in the mirror. Then he looked at Sylvia, who was no longer looking at anything, with something like sympathy, and I no longer knew what to make of anything. I only knew that Franco was going to die soon, and I was going to die soon, and this was how we spent our final hours – bickering, drinking coffee, going to an exhibit, trying to dream up interesting conversations.

As soon as Franco was gone, I said to Sylvia: Would you like to come home with me?

Yes, she said, with some embarrassment.

I am in love with you, I said.

She said nothing.

I am in love with you!

At my apartment, I undressed her the moment we entered. I threw her clothes down in the hallway and pulled my jeans down and lifted her legs around me and penetrated her, and she moaned, and I told her I loved her again. She said, I love you too! I love you too!

What did it matter? The end of the world was coming. The evening had arrived, and on our walk home the air had dropped a few degrees, and we had kissed under many large trees, and looked very deeply at each other – I had never looked in the eyes of anyone at all, and here I was, fearless, as though I had a soul that existed in my eyes, and her soul was alive inside her eyes. I got her into bed. She cried for a moment, but wiped her eyes and forgot why she was crying. She was, I suppose, about my age or a little younger – around thirty – and I felt that our combined hours on earth were scattering excitedly and twirling in the air like useless cash – cash from some other country, or from long ago – that some old man with half his wits might throw into the street below him to no one, so that after the hysteria he must go downstairs, outside, and gather up the coins and bills and carry them back to his apartment.

O life! What a swift and bewildering odyssey you became! What a delusion! My hours, scattering down upon the street like confetti – to the sound of Sylvia making such terrific cries, and my own stupid grunts, and the bed making noise like a marching band – take them! Take them! Take them! Anyone! This is my life! I give it unto the city of mice suits and traffic and rooftops and horrific, obvious art! I beg you! Pick something up!

The street below remains empty. I ask Sylvia if I may come inside her. Yes, she says. Yes. Yes. Yes.

A little while later there is a knock on the door. At first it is soft, but it gets louder and louder, until it is banging. We both think it is Franco, so we say nothing. I begin to tremble. Sylvia does not. I sense relief in her. Then my mother screams into the apartment through the door. Answer the door, she screams. I know you're in there!

She knows you're in here? asks Sylvia.

She's probably having me followed, I say. She thinks I've joined a cult.

My mother has brought a man from the university – a professor of classical philosophy – though he is quiet and shy. I think everyone immediately understands that I have not joined a cult, and so he feels somewhat out of place. So my mother and Sylvia and the philosopher and I have an awkward cup of coffee in the kitchen – and now the city is dark – and no one says anything of substance. On three separate occasions the philosopher says, This is lovely coffee.

I knew you were going to say that, I tell him, each time, and he shyly blinks and arranges his spectacles on his face. My mother coughs. I wait for the phone call to tell me that Franco has shot himself with a revolver – it must be a revolver, something from the war, a war – that

he has undressed himself and walked to his roof, and absorbed, corporeally, the irrelevance of his unhappiness or
jealousy or disillusionment upon the curved and twink-
ling body of the city – a city that does not even exist: it
waits to exist; it always waits – it is a city in the future.
But no call arrives. My mother says to Sylvia, That's a
lovely jacket.

Sylvia looks at her jacket. This? she asks.

My mother says: It's very nice. It's sensible.

I'm a schoolteacher, says Sylvia.

That's nice.

Yes.

And above this scene of ravening, bewildering, but
sympathetic domestic effort the city is upside down in
the sky. It is the expression that the city wears, like a
face, but without features – pure but diminished light.
And how far could a man travel beyond that light before
he touched the very wall of inexistence.

Summer's Wreath

Éilís Ní Dhuibhne

Next thing, I was pregnant.

My mother lost no time in shipping me off to an island in the North Sea. Her plan was that I would give birth to this baby of mine far away from civilisation, i.e. in a place where English wasn't spoken and nobody knew anyone worth knowing. Or anything. What was going to happen after the birth hadn't been divulged, but I suppose she planned to find somebody to adopt this baby, or to foster it, or otherwise palm it off on somebody far outside of the family circle. I didn't have any plans of that kind myself. To tell the truth, I found it impossible to imagine this baby of mine – what it would look like, how it would sound, or what colour its eyes would be, or its hair. (Do they have hair?) I couldn't even imagine its sex, although on the whole, if I thought about it at all, I assumed it would have to be a girl. Because how could a woman like me, a *girl*, alone on an island in the North Sea, without a man at her side, have a boy baby? It would be like having a frog, or a seal, or a tortoise. I wouldn't know what to do with it.

My mother paid Frau Holle well (that's what I called her; she had another name) to look after me. Which she did, up to a point.

For instance, she gave me a room under the rafters in Rosenhaus, her thatched cottage, and it was oh such a sweet room, with pink flowery wallpaper on the sloping walls, muslin curtains on the delicious little window, and a green reading lamp that shone like a fresh leaf on the desk. There *was* a desk. That was the great thing! My mother and Frau Holle acknowledged that I would need one, even as I waited for this baby of mine to be born. The desk was under the window, and had a view of a stone wall. This was no common wall, mind you, but a garden wall, ancient and crumbling and draped with a tangle – no, a jungle – of nasturtiums. Orange and yellow petals, a few deep wine red. And those great green dinner plates of leaves that a frog could sit on, if he were so inclined! (The cottage itself had tight pink roses trained to clamber over the porch; like obedient little ballerinas they circled the door and vied with each other to win the prize for Most Fragrant Flower.) When I opened the window of my room (I opened it most of the time, because it could get very hot, up there under the thatch) a sea breeze, like fresh oysters, wafted in, and mixed with that was the scent of the roses. I have never been in a room that smelled more delicious.

Frau Holle kept a few guests, *select*, in Rosenhaus; she also owned an inn, or a café, or something of that kind, in the village. Her husband was the innkeeper but Frau

Holle wore the trousers (well, most of the time she wore a dress that looked like something you'd see in a pantomime: a heavy sack of a skirt bunched over her big bottom, a black bodice laced up the front over her big bosom, and a white lacy blouse billowing over her big red arms). Herr Holle spent all the time at the inn. I never saw him, but took her word for it that he existed. Frau Holle joined him after lunch, and stayed till eight or nine. As soon as she departed for the inn, at one o'clock, Rosaleen came in to clean.

The first thing Rosaleen told me was that she could ride a bicycle and the second was that she was double-jointed. She could also hold a cigarette between her big toe and her next toe and smoke it. 'Gas, isn't it?'

(Another gift she had was that she could wriggle her ears.)

The third thing she told me was that she came from Dublin. So how did she end up here on this island?

'God alone knows!' she laughed. 'How did you?'

I didn't point to my belly, because it wasn't showing yet, I believed: I'd always been plump, and this worked to my advantage now.

'I'm writing a book,' I said, in a quiet voice.

Rosaleen didn't ask what sort of a book I was writing, or anything else. She just nodded, and maintained a grave silence for a moment or two, as if she thought writing a book was a worthy but undesirable activity, on a par with going on a religious pilgrimage, maybe, or being in hospital undergoing treatment for some chronic and unsavoury disease. Then she changed the subject.

She was a sort of housekeeper for Frau Zimmerman – she, too, kept a few select guests. Everyone on the island kept a few select guests, during the summer months, according to Rosaleen. Loads of people wanted to stay in this gorgeous place, it was so healthy, it was so safe for the youngsters.

Rosaleen's cleaning of Rosehaus didn't take long – 'Sure it's too clean for its own good already' – and in the afternoons she took me to the beach, and sometimes in the evenings she asked me if I'd like to come out with her, to a café. Not the café in our village, the Holles', but another one, in the next village, the main town on the island, where the boats came in. It was about three miles away and we cycled there. Frau Zimmerman owned a bicycle, which Rosaleen was allowed to borrow whenever she needed it. She suggested that I ask Frau Holle for a loan of theirs. I didn't bother asking. I knew she'd think it was dangerous – my father had never let us ride bicycles in case we'd fall off and break our teeth, which was a euphemism for our maidenheads. No need to worry about that now. I took the bicycle without asking.

I met Floryan at the café in the town. He knew a friend of Rosaleen's – she knew everyone. This wasn't something I noticed, at first: in so far as I thought about it, I took it that she and I were special friends, and that this had come about due to her good nature, and contingency. But as time went on I saw that Rosaleen could make friends with almost anybody.

After Floryan was introduced he focused completely on Rosaleen. This annoyed me; I hate being left out, even though I didn't think him in the least bit attractive, that first night – he wasn't very tall, but he was very thin, and his hair was so fair it was almost without colour at all – that very fine flat hair which children on the island had, like bleached sea grass. Maybe if he hadn't ignored me I'd never have taken to him. But he did, completely. I might have been invisible, sitting there at the corner of the table while he and Rosaleen engaged in the kind of animated chat that is first cousin to flirtation; their eyes met often. He had large washed-out blue ones, and hers were brown, those sparkling eyes which always look as if they're laughing. They could enchant you before you knew it.

He bought her a beer. That was another thing: Rosaleen ordered beer, like the German women, like a man. Never wine, never a cup of coffee and definitely never an ice cream.

Rosaleen remembered my existence when he was at the bar.

'Kathleen, darling, what will you have?' I didn't like her calling me Kathleen, but she forgot, when she'd had a beer or two.

I glanced at my empty dish – I'd had an ice cream, strawberry.

'Lemonade, thanks.'

I didn't drink alcohol then. It wasn't because of the

baby, I just hadn't started on alcohol, as yet, in my life.

Floryan came back to the table and seemed to see me then for the first time, although we had been introduced an hour earlier. He asked me where I was from, always the first question, and then what I was doing on the island, and, because I wanted to impress him, I said I was writing a book.

'What variety?' he asked. Another surprise. If anyone got this far, their next question invariably was 'What's it about?' (Which is not a bad question, but it's not one I could answer, then, or ever.)

I told him. Short stories. In fact I'd started a novel but at that moment, talking to him in the warm, dark inn, I decided to turn the novel into a short story.

He knew what a short story was. Guy de Maupassant, Edgar Allen Poe, Turgenev, and some other Russian I'd never heard of were mentioned, in a waterfall of words, oddly assembled. I was charmed. Nobody on the island ever seemed to read a thing, not even a newspaper, and here was Floryan, who had read everything, in Russian and German and English and Polish. Soon he mentioned that he too was writing a book. More than one. He'd already published reviews ('several reviews, many, many' is what he said) and some essays. But now he was writing a *Bildungsroman* and a collection of short stories and reviews.

'All at the same time?'

'I have so many ideas, they flow out.'

He tapped his head, to show me where all these ideas

were, waiting for their chance to escape.

He wasn't from the island at all, or even from Germany. He'd been born in some place in Poland which I can't remember, his mother had died when he was six years old. He'd attended university in Kraców, had studied Russian and German and English (and several other subjects) and was hoping to find a niche in the German press and then a publisher for his novel, as yet unwritten.

'To publication, that is the way,' he said. 'The newspaper. Get it known, your name, then they will like you, like honeybees after you, oh yes they will be.'

I believed absolutely everything he said. He seemed to be immensely knowledgeable, wise, and canny. He knew a lot about everything, but especially about the literary world.

All this advice he gave me while Rosaleen was busy chatting to a friend of hers called Dagmar, who sat at the bar among the men. I noticed this because I took a fancy to Dagmar's clothes: a black smock, and a velvet beret, and a red bow loosely tied around the neck of the smock. I decided I'd try to get a dress just like that – the smock would hide me, but that wasn't the only reason I desired it. It'd make me feel like a writer, even before I dared call myself one . . . easier for me to become what I wanted to be. I believed, if I copied Dagmar's style, wore a big pretentious smock instead of the white muslins and the soft merino gowns I had from home, I'd write better.

Rosaleen came down and gave me my lemonade. It was delicious, cool, served in a champagne glass with the edges dipped in sugar.

'You're doing fine!' she winked at me, and went back to Dagmar, with, it seemed to me, a bit of a swagger, a swing of the hips, which gave me pause. I had a look at them, their backs, Rosaleen's and Dagmar's, Rosaleen chunky, in the bottle-green blouse, the brown knickerbockers she always wore when she was out, and the other lanky, in her flowing artist's smock. Even their backs seemed to be chatting to one another. Spine to spine, hip to hip.

*

The sands of the island were fine and golden and immense; they stretched on and on, out to the milky North Sea, which was miles and miles away, and you couldn't tell where sand stopped and sea began or where sea stopped and sky began. Water, sky, sand all blended into a picture that could have been painted by Monet or one of those French painters; you saw where the inspiration came from when you screwed up your eyes and gazed at the vista.

And behind, the little fringe of spicy pine trees, and behind, the fields of corn, high, waving. The narrow blue roads and the children and grown-ups cycling along them on their bicycles with enormous wheels. Horses too. Once, a motor car, its hood down, its brass accoutrements gleaming, like winking eyes. (How did they get it onto the island?)

We lay on a rug under a pine tree. Me and Rosaleen. Nearby was a café – a café was always nearby, on the island. At this one, more a stall than a proper café, you could get *pommes frites*, and frankfurters, and hamburgers. Also coffee and ices. There were wicker chairs and tables, striped parasols. Everyone dressed in blindingly white clothes. The children in navy sailor suits, or white knickers and navy jerseys. Sandcastles, tunnels, towns built on the sand.

'I'm meeting him again,' I said, referring to Floryan. All our conversation was about people we knew, or that Rosaleen knew and I had heard about. They were endlessly fascinating to us. Frau Holle, Frau Zimmerman, Dagmar, other friends of hers. What they did – painted pictures, kept guest houses, rented out horses or bicycles – what they looked like, what they were feeling, who they liked and who they didn't like. Who they were married to, or had been married to, and who they were in love with now.

'Be careful, lovey,' she said. She blew a smoke ring. 'You could get yourself into big trouble.'

'Yes,' I started giggling, and then so did she, and we giggled and giggled till we couldn't stop, so that a mother in a big black straw hat, shepherding her children down to the sea, glared angrily at us, as if we were giving them a bad example. (The children ignored us; concentrated as they were on tumbling along, they didn't even hear our giggles, which were in any case all mixed up with the symphony of voices on the wind, and the screams of the seagulls, and the distant whispering of the waves as they began their long journey towards the coast, towards us – a trip which was just starting, very very slowly, now at the turn of the tide, and would gradually speed up until, before high tide, those gentle waves would gallop like a herd of furious wild animals into the straight line of pine trees that separated the genteel and gentle island from the untameable ocean.)

★

We were sitting on his bed. There was nowhere else to sit, in Floryan's place, which was a hut with a red tin roof, one tiny window looking out on a high fence, a narrow bed and a tea chest for a table. (It had the advantage of being not far from the baths where he worked as some sort of assistant or guard.) It was down a lane – the island was all lanes. You turned off the promenade at the big chessboard, where men shoved the pawns and bishops and castles around all day. The promenade was a place of pomp and splendour, bandstands, parasols of red and yellow, but this lane was dreary, not a bit like Frau Holle's. No roses or nasturtiums, just depressing little shacks with a few hens scratching the lane outside the front doors. I don't know who lived there, apart from Floryan. He made no apology for the squalor of his quarters; he accepted them as a natural, temporary, necessary step on his road to fame as a great writer. Sometime in the future, quite soon, he'd be rich and famous. As soon as I saw his shack I realised that right now he had no money at all apart from whatever he earned at the baths. ('Not much', Rosaleen knew the sort of money you could earn at these summer jobs, as you learnt German or wrote your book, or otherwise prepared for your brilliant future. She didn't have any of these aspirations herself, actually, so it wasn't all that clear to me what she was doing here.)

We'd been with friends of his, in a café, talking about literature, but really mostly about ourselves, our hopes – especially Floryan's – who we were sending our stories and articles to. Afterwards, because it was late and Rosaleen had disappeared, he asked me to stay with him. He'd sleep on the floor.

He didn't have a spare blanket. Not that I could see. There was nothing in the hut. His good blazer was hanging on a nail, on the wall, and a few clothes were piled on the tea chest, neatly folded.

He shrugged. 'It is all right.'

That was like him. There was a bravery in him, a lack of fussing about what he regarded as trivialities. It was as if he was so concentrated on his real work, of reading and writing, that all these effects of the present, the menial job at the baths, the shack, the poor little thin bed, were shadows in a dream from which he would wake up, in the palace that was his birthright. Nobody in Wellington was like that. Or in London. Or even in Germany, where the young men were more sure of themselves than in England, and less sissyish. It must be a Polish thing, I decided.

I pulled off my smock – I'd already got an artist's smock and a black velvet beret; I'd decided against the red bow – and kissed him, and we slept in the narrow bed. I was pregnant anyway, so there was nothing to lose. He knew many tricks, most of them new to me and quite good. And this was what I expected of someone who was an assistant at the baths, someone who was ready to leap into the water and pull people to safety at any moment, someone who could sleep in his clothes on the hard floor, and who could also speak four or five languages. Sex was just another one which he knew fluently, much better than the father of my baby had.

★

Rosaleen tickled my shoulder.

'Your shoulders are like two nice mushrooms,' she said, gravely.

I pretended to be offended, but I wasn't really, and she went on tickling, then stroking, for a few moments.

We'd been in swimming. Now we were sitting on a sand dune, in our wet bathing suits. It was a hot day.

'You should swim in the nip. It's a shame to cover that gorgeous body.'

She was sitting a few feet away from me, on her own towel. She didn't have a proper bathing suit, like mine,

144

but went in in not-very-white knickers and a plain shift, which now clung to her chunky midriff. Her chest was flat as the strand.

'Yes, well,' I didn't know what to reply to this.

She turned to me and her eyes were back to normal – laughing. Mocking?

'Have you slept with yer man?'

I nodded.

Rosaleen stopped stroking my shoulders, to my regret. It felt very pleasant because her hands were warm, much warmer than Floryan's. He had poor circulation, maybe because he was so thin, or because he spent his days pulling invalids in and out of freezing cold baths.

So then I told her about the baby. She probably guessed about it anyway, since my stomach stuck out in the wet bathing suit. (I was almost five months gone.) It was a relief, that somebody else knew, apart from Frau Holle. Also, it was a relief, and a surprise, to find out that Frau Holle hadn't told the whole village.

'Aren't you sick?'

'No.'

'Were you?'

'A bit, at the start.'

'You need to look after yourself, young one!'

'Frau Holle looks after me!'

'You shouldn't be riding that yoke,' she nodded at my bicycle. 'You could do yourself an injury.'

She tickled me again, but in a different way.

★

Floryan gave me some stories he'd translated from Russian to German.

'You could put these into English,' he said. ' A good way to learn a language, translating is good.'

'Well, yes. But I'd rather write my own stories.'

My own stories. I sat and wrote for two hours in the mornings, at the desk overlooking the nasturtium wall. A lot of the time, I looked out the window, at the orange flowers, the huge leaves on which the morning dewdrops slid around, disconcertingly dry-looking, like beads of mercury. The flowers bowed and moved, looked as if they were alive. If I stared for long enough I could see pictures in among the leaves: the party we'd held when I was a child, in our lovely garden on Tinakori Road, our summer house at the cove, where my friend Edith and I played on the sand, swam far out into the warm sea. Sometimes I would stop looking at the pictures on the wall and then words poured out of me. I could work away like a little black spider. But I felt I was producing cobwebs, hanging like woolly broken threads from the ceiling. The perfect web had as yet failed to materialise. I was a bad little spider.

I could talk to Floryan about this and he could listen attentively and with understanding, for up to three minutes at a time. After that his eyes would glaze over and we'd talk about what really mattered. His writing. The work which he knew would be great, just as he knew mine couldn't be. You're wrong there, Mister, was what I thought. Floryan preached equality – he believed in the suffragettes' cause, for which I'd no time at all. Who wants to vote? Such a bore. But he couldn't allow a woman to get the better of him. He negotiated a fine line between encouraging and debasing me, all the time. I forgave him; he was one of those men who had to be best, at everything.

'Have you heard from *The New Magazine*?'

I shook my head.

I'd heard from nobody.

Not from *The New Magazine* or *The Old Magazine*, or *The Blue Magazine* or *The Pink Magazine*, or *The London Magazine*, or the *New York Magazine*. Not even from *The New Zealand Magazine*, where I'd only want to be published as a last resort, anyway.

Nobody cared enough about my stories to even answer my letters.

'They do not read them even,' said Floryan, consolingly. 'Your name, not know it, so they say, she is nobody, waste no time. Poosh! Down the basket.'

He knew everything there was to know about the mysterious habits of publishers, but it didn't seem to help him much. Nothing was getting published, although many important editors were considering his submissions, and he expected to receive offers and commissions from Berlin, Paris, Moscow and Warsaw, among others, at any moment. I hoped he got a bite from at least one of them. If somebody took one of my stories, it would be as if I won a doll at the funfair. It would be fun, a luxury. Whereas for Floryan getting published seemed to be a matter of life and death. (Daddy's banker still sent me a cheque every month; there was that.)

'So, translate. This fellow, he is good, learn something from him will you.'

'Such as?'

He had to think for a while, as people often do when they praise some writer's work. What *is* so good about it?

'Atmosphere. Mood.'

We were walking along the prom. Floryan had dressed up, in his striped blazer and white trousers, his straw boater. Oh he could look like a beautiful boy doll when he tried!

'*I'm* good at atmosphere and mood.'

Actually my stories were more atmosphere than story. That's what was wrong with them. One of the things.

Floryan screwed up his eyes.

'He is . . . suggestive,' he said, and thought again. We stopped and looked at the old men playing their never-ending game of chess. He had to explain what that meant. Suggestive. 'The stories, they are like poems. More than one meaning, can you say? Hints, nuances, something.'

'Like the impressionist painters?'

'Perhaps.'

I twirled my parasol and we walked on, slowly, towards our destination. His shack. A girl on a tricycle whizzed past and there were white sails like seagulls out on the sea. It was a perfect day for a walk. I was in love with him, after all, and wanted to be with him from morning till night.

But he was busy at his job in the baths most of the time. So I went on writing, at the desk by the nasturtium window. I kept my head down. I translated the story.

It was about a children's nurse, who's really just a child herself. Her working conditions are terrible; her master is your typical Russian villain, big and ugly as a bear, always drinking vodka and beating everyone in sight. The baby cries constantly so this poor girl can never get enough sleep. She starts having hallucinations, brought on by exhaustion. She sees pictures on the wall, images from her past – which was ghastly, of course, all gloom and doom, illness and death and hunger. (Goodness, who'd be a Russian?) Eventually, tired out, driven to madness, she strangles the baby whose cries keep her awake.

It was basically a murder story, with a few grisly subplots tossed in for good measure. More melodrama than nuance, if you ask me.

But it had something. It was gripping. And full of understanding for the plight of the nursemaid, disgust at the brutality of her boss. Really it was an angry story above all, angry about the plight of the powerless, the poor. Convincing too in its description of the little girl's mental breakdown, and the weird visions she saw on the walls of the house, her prison.

I found that I worked on my translation with much

more concentration than I had on my own stories. I got lost in the story, finding the right words in English for the German version absorbed me more than finding the right words in English for my own thoughts. When I was writing my own stories I got distracted and spent hours staring at the flowers, mistaking daydreams for inspiration. But with the translation, I'd start writing at nine o'clock, after breakfast, and when I'd look up it would be almost one. Frau Holle would be getting ready to leave, Rosaleen would be coming in to clean, and the pleasant activities of the afternoon all about to begin.

Floryan admired my attempt.

'It flows,' he said. We were sitting in his shack, on his bed. Naked. How he could pleasure me! That was his real gift, maybe his only one. 'Such flow. A pity he is not known, in Europe.'

'Maybe he will be,' I said. 'If I published this translation in London, for instance?'

Floryan shook his head. A few collections had come out in German, maybe in Italian, but nobody paid much attention to them. Anyone could see that this writer wasn't as good as Tolstoy, or Gogol, or Turgenev. He'd written short stories, a few plays. Not much else.

'In Russia, much admired,' Floryan said. 'But a local writer he is, essentially local.'

And he'd been dead for five years. It was unlikely that his international reputation would grow now, if it hadn't when he was alive.

'Was he old?'

'Forty-four.' He was always precise as to dates and numbers.

Old enough. But I shook my head, pretending to be sad . . . as you do, stupidly, even about people you've never heard of.

'He might have made it if he'd lived longer?' I said.

'Who can tell?' said Floryan, and he tickled me with his long thin fingers. 'Like two fat button mushrooms, down here, did I tell you that before?'

'Two ripe peaches was the simile employed, I seem to recall.'

'That too.'

'Two ripe turnips?'

Later, he suggested something else, about the story, I mean. Since I liked it so much, why not write a version of it? I could transfer it, from Russia, to a place I knew. New Zealand, or England, or even here? Germany?

Frau Holle as the employer. Rosenhaus as the setting.

'Frau Holle, give unto her a child.'

'Yes.'

'Friedrich.'

'Friedrich the Great. A fat sodden lump of a child, who screams all the time. I can give her a few more children for good measure. Snotty-nosed brats.'

'Why not?'

'She should have five or six. Keep her out of that inn of hers.'

'Keep her off the beer.'

I did it. An exercise. Oh, it's as easy as cheese to write a story when somebody hands you the plot.

Floryan told me I should send it to one of the editors I'd been pestering. Just to see how he'd react. Mr *New Age*. What fun! I could tell him about the source later – if it came to that.

I sent it off, along with two other stories, and crossed my fingers.

There's a feeling I get when I put a story in the post, which is not quite like any other feeling. It's a bit like the mixture of hope and anxiety you can have when you meet a man you like, and wonder if you'll meet again, and what will come of it all? (Which can range from anything, love, marriage, babies, to absolutely nothing, and everything in between, and all of these seem possible, on that first day or two, the waiting day.) The sense of having finished something, of having taken the risk, the sense that you've done your bit and now it's in the lap of the gods (or the hand of some man, really, but one who is used to taking risks, who can weigh up words, the way the grocer weighs a pound of sugar, and know, more or less, how much money the customer will hand over for same, in a brown paper wrapper).

A week later the reply came.

A *reply* came! A cause for celebration in itself!

It came in the afternoon post, this reply. Frau Holle was at the café, Rosaleen had come, smoked her cigarettes, and gone. Rosenhaus was empty. I had no plans for that day.

Dear Miss Mansfield

Thank you for your submissions . . . would like to publish all three stories in due course . . . can you call in to our office when you return to London . . .

We are particularly impressed with 'The Child Who Was Tired.'

I read the letter again and again. I was in my bedroom under the thatch, lying against a heap of white lace pillows. A vase of pink roses Frau Holle had placed on the desk filled the room with oh such an intoxicating fragrance, and the afternoon sun filtered through the curtains, dappling the room. It was all gold reflections, flickering dark shadows, dancing around me like the ghosts of my past and the promises of my future. Joy and sorrow, light and shade, such a mysterious combination of feelings, I couldn't articulate them, I couldn't contain them, the light and dark were for once almost one and the same.

My stomach fluttered.

A butterfly fluttered in my stomach. Then leaped, then thumped.

The butterfly started kicking, actually, like a cross little pony.

I got up and walked to the window. And there I saw this thing. On the nasturtium wall among all the sly winking flowers. The baby. Cradled on the most enormous flat leaf of all. I could see him quite clearly.

He was perfectly formed as if from grey silk, with a round head and a fat little slug body. And in the baby's little fishy hand was a little shadow book.

This baby of mine had got hold of my stories. He had them all, in his fin fingers. This baby of mine could read, already, before he was born? What was he doing with my book?

Not reading it. They don't read, do they? Babies?

In his cradle of green nasturtium leaves the baby raised my book to his mouth. And now I could see that he had an enormous mouth. In among the yellow flowers and the orange flowers, his mushroom body, his waving fish hands, disappeared, and he became an enormous mouth, with big sharp teeth like a shark's.

He started to eat the book. My stories.

That's what babies do. Eat.

I stared, and the happiness sank down, down through my stomach into my legs and down to my feet and out on the floor, the fountain soaked down into the earth leaving just a splotch of filthy mud behind.

It came to me in a flash. What I could do. I'd go cycling. I'd cycle for hours, I needed to see the whole island, every village, every farm, every beach, every lane. Then I'd come back to my room and write about what I'd seen.

But first, the desk would have to face the inside wall. I could no longer stand the sight of those nasturtiums, of that irritating sun dancing through the curtains. I could not risk seeing that baby who had invaded the flowers, who had moved in to the garden wall. He'd drive me insane.

From now on I would face into the room, not out. It's better for a writer to face a blank wall, everyone knows that. I would focus on what was inside my head. I would concentrate, then, on my writing, without the distraction of all those evil flowers.

The desk was oh so heavy. But I had shifted furniture before and I knew how to do it. Well, the secret is the secret to almost every kind of work, which is simply this: little by little. You don't try to yank the whole thing around at once. You go to one corner, and you shove. It doesn't budge. I know this too. At first, nothing will budge. *Nil desperandum*. Shove a little harder. And on the third shove, the thing inches across the floor, just fractionally.

I knew I could keep doing this until the desk turned the way I wanted it to.

When I woke up, two days later, the desk was back in its place by the window. But I knew before Frau Holle and the doctor told me, it didn't matter.

The baby was no longer there. In the nasturtiums.

Or anywhere.

★

I didn't see Floryan for a fortnight, because I had to stay in the house. I didn't see Rosaleen either. Where was she, now that I needed her, to fetch things for me, from town, to bring me news of Floryan, to bring Floryan news of me?

'She's gone,' Frau Holle pressed her lips together.

Frau Zimmerman had given her the sack.

'She was lazy as sin, the Rosaleen. She never did a tap of work here, or at Zimmerman's. Always smoking those cigarettes and gallivanting around, drinking beer and up to God knows what. She was bad news, that one.'

Later she told me that the bicycle had been stolen.

A new girl came to clean Rosenhaus, one of the locals, aged about twelve, with the flat pale face and the flat fair hair.

So in the mornings I slept – I was very tired – and in the afternoons I sat in the garden, reading the Russian stories again. They really had something, and it was surprising that the author was not more known, but such is the way of the world. I believed I could use some of his tricks – description, which I was good at, I was like a painter more than a writer, I sometimes thought. I saw how he used description, of the sea and the sky, even of houses and streets, to represent emotions. Well, nothing new there, every child does that. Sun means joy, rain means sadness, wind means anger. He just did more of it, more subtly. More suggestively, as Floryan said. And the other thing he did, so I thought, was write about poor people, and about children, and about women, and about small shifts of feeling as if they were big important events.

'I should tell the editor,' I said to Floryan. We were

sitting in a café under a white umbrella, celebrating my success. Floryan, he knew nothing about Rosaleen, cared less – 'Gone home, maybe?' – was still waiting to hear from the most important newspaper in Paris about an article he'd submitted, but he was sure they'd take it. I was eating an Eskimo becker, a plain ice without any cream or berries, since I didn't have such an appetite any more. (I had got quite thin; I tied a wide red sash around my smock, to show off my new waist, and I'd cut my hair short, like a black helmet around my face. Everyone stared at me, when I walked along the seafront.) The sea was very flat today, dark blue, and the sky over it pale with wisps of clouds like wedding veils. The seagulls glided about languidly, looking for scraps, and the children played quietly in the sands, making neat sandcastles that looked indestructible.

'Why?' he said. 'That will make complications.'

They mightn't publish the story about the baby. They might be suspicious about all of my stories.

The band started to play.

'It is yours now. Your own, your story, you made it new,' he sounded immensely knowledgeable, wise, canny.

The tune gained momentum, like a storm gathering, or a wave swelling. But it was far far away, a whisper on the horizon, and for now the notes floated on the air like fat silver doves.

'Nobody in London heard him, never, never,' said Floryan. 'Not to be worried, my dear little mushroom!'

The Clancy Kid

Colin Barrett

My town is nowhere you have been, but you know its
ilk. A roundabout off a national road, an industrial estate, a five-screen Cineplex, a century of pubs packed
inside the square mile of the town's limits. The Atlantic
is near; the gnarled jawbone of the coastline with its
gull-infested promontories is near. Summer evenings,
and in the manure-scented pastures of the satellite par-
ishes the Zen bovines lift their heads to contemplate the
V8 howls of the boy racers tearing through the back
lanes.

I am young, and the young do not number many
here, but it is fair to say we have the run of the place.

It is Sunday. The weekend, that three-day festival of
attrition, is done. Sunday is the day of purgation and re-
dress; of tenderised brain cases and see-sawing stomachs
and hollow pledges to never, *ever* get that twisted again.
A day you are happy to see slip by before it ever really
gets going.

It's well after 7 p.m., though still bright out, the warm
light infused with that happy kind of melancholy that

attends a July evening in the West. I am sitting with Tug Cuniffe at a table in the alfresco smoking area of Dockery's pub. The smoking area is a narrow concrete courtyard to the building's rear, overlooking the town river. Midges tickle our scalps. A candy-stripe canvas awning extends on cantilevers, and now and then the awning ripples, sail-like, in the breeze.

Ours is the table nearest to the river, and it is soothing to listen to the radio static bristle of the rushing water. There are a dozen other people out here. We know most of them, at least to see, and they all know us. Tug is one many prefer to keep a tidy berth of. He's called Manchild behind his back. He is big and he is unpredictable, prone to fits of rage and temper tantrums. There are the pills he takes to keep himself on an even keel, but now and then, in a fit of contrariness or out of a sense of misguided self-confidence, he will abandon the medication. Sometimes he'll admit to the abandonment and sell me on his surplus of pills, but other times he'll say nothing.

Tug is odd, for he was bred in a family warped by grief, and was himself a manner of ghosteen; Tug's real name is Eamonn, but he was the second Cuniffe boy named Eamonn. The mother had a firstborn a couple of years before Tug, but that sliver of a child died at thirteen months old. And then came Tug. When he was four they first took him out to Glanbeigh cemetery, to lay flowers by a lonely blue slab with his own name etched upon it in fissured gilt.

I am hung-over. Tug is not. He does not drink, which is a good thing. I'm nursing a pint, downing it so slowly it's already lost its fizz.

—How's the head, Jimmy? Tug caws.

He is in a good mood, a good, good, good but edgy, edgy, edgy mood.

—Not so hot, I admit.

—Was it Quillinan's Friday?

—Quillinan's, I say, then Shepherd's, then Fandango's. The same story Saturday.

—The ride? He inquires.

—Marlene Davey.

—Gosh, Tug says. Gosh, gosh, gosh.

He worries his molars with his tongue.

Tug is twenty-four to my twenty-five, though he looks ten years older. As far as I'm aware, his virginity remains unshed. Back in our school days, the convent girls and all their mammies were goo-goo-eyed over Tug. He was a handsome lad, all up through his teens, but by sixteen had begun to pile on the pounds, and the pounds stuck. The weight gives him a lugubrious air; the management and conveyance of his bulk is an involved and sapping enterprise. He keeps his bonce shaved tight and wears dark baggy clothing, modelling his appearance somewhat after Brando in *Apocalypse Now*.

—Well, me and Marlene go back a ways, I say.

Which is true. Marlene is the nearest thing I've had to a steady girlfriend, and if we've never quite been on

we've never quite been off, either, even after Mark Cuculann got her pregnant last year. She had the baby, just
after Christmas, a boy, and named him David for her
dear departed da.

I ran into her in Fandango's on the Friday. There was
the usual crowd; micro-minied girls on spike heels, explosively frizzed hair, spray-tan mahogany décolletage.
There were donkey-necked boys in button-down
tablecloth-pattern shirts, farmers' sons who wear their
shirtsleeves rolled up past the elbows, as if at any moment they might be called upon to pull a calf out of a
cow's steaming nethers. Fandango's was a hot box. Neon
strobed and pulsed, dry ice fumed in the air. Libidinal
bass juddered the windowless walls. I was sinking shots
at the bar with Dessie Roberts when she crackled in my
periphery. She'd already seen me and was swanning over.
We exchanged bashful, familiar smiles, smiles that knew
exactly what was coming.

There is the comfort of routine in our routine but
also the mystery of that routine's persistence.

Marlene lives with her consenting, pragmatic mother,
Angie, who even at three in the morning was up and
sat at the kitchen table, placidly leafing through a TV
listings magazine and supping a cold tea. She was happy
to see me, Marlene's ma. She filled the kettle and asked
if we wanted a cuppa. We demurred. She told us wee
David was sound asleep upstairs, and be sure not to wake
him. In Marlene's bedroom I bellyflopped onto the cool
duvet; her childhood menagerie of stuffed animals was

piled at the end of the bed. I was trying to recall the names of each button-eyed piglet and bunny as Marlene tugged my trousers down over my calves.

—Boopsy, Winnie, Flaps . . . Rupert?

Now my calves are paltry things, measly lengths of pale, undefined muscle all scribbled with curly black hairs; their enduring ugliness startles me anytime I glimpse them in a mirror. But Marlene began to knead them gently with her fingers. She worked her way up to my thighs and hissed, 'Flip over.' You have to appreciate a girl who can encounter a pair of calves as unpleasant as mine and still want to get up on you.

—She's a nice one, Tug says.

A fly lands on his head and mills in the stubble. Tug seems not to notice. I want to reach out and smack it.

—That she is, I say, instead, and take another sup of my pint.

And just like that Marlene appears. This happens frequently in this town; incant a body's name and lo, they appear. She comes through the double doors in cut-off jeans, sunglasses pushed up into her red ringlets, zestfully licking an ice-cream cone. She's wearing a canary-yellow belly top, the better to show off her stomach, aerobicised back to greyhound tautness since the baby. A sundial tattoo circumscribes her navel. Her eyes are verdigris, and if it wasn't for the acne scars worming across her cheeks, she'd be a beauty, my Marlene.

Mark Cuculann follows her in. Marlene sees me and gives a chin-jut in my direction; an acknowledgement, but a wary one; wary of the fact that Cuculann is there, that big Tug Cuniffe is by my side.

—There's Marlene, Tug says.

—Uh huh.

—So is she *with* the Cuculann fella then or what?

I shrug my shoulders. They have a baby so it's only fair they play Mammy and Daddy; it's what they are. Whatever else she does or does not do with Cuculann is fine by me, I tell myself. I tell myself that if anything I should feel a measure of gratitude towards the lad, for taking the paternity bullet I dodged.

—She's looking fair sexy these days, Tug says. You going to go over say hello?

—I said hello enough Friday night.

—Better off out of it all right, maybe, Tug says.

I slide my palm over my pint like a lid and tap the rim with my fingers.

—D'you hear the latest about the Clancy kid? Tug says after a lapse of silence.

—No, I said.

—A farmer in Enniscorthy reckons he saw a lad matching the Clancy kid's description with, get this, two women, two women in their thirties. They stopped into a caff near where this farmer lives. He talked to one of them. Get this, she was – well, German, he reckons. Talked with a kind of Germanic accent, and they – she – was enquiring about when the Rosslare ferry was next off. Little blondie lad with them, little quiet blondie lad. That was a few weeks back though, and only the farmer didn't put two and two together till after.

—A Germanic accent, I say.

—Yeah, yeah, Tug says.

His eyebrows flare enthusiastically. The Clancy kid has become something of an obsession for Tug, though the wider interest has by now largely run its course. Wayne Clancy, ten, a schoolboy out of Gurtlubber, Mayo, went missing three months back. He disappeared during a school excursion to Dublin. One moment he was standing with the rest of the Gurtlubber pupils and two adult teachers on a traffic island at a city-centre Y junction – the lights turning red, the traffic sighing to a halt, the crowd of boys and girls crossing the road – and then he was gone. At first the assumption was that wee Wayne had simply wandered off, disoriented by the big city bustle, but it soon became apparent he was not just lost but missing. His disappearance haunted the front pages of the national papers for all of May. The established theory was that Wayne was snatched, either right at the Y junction or shortly after, by persons un-known. A national Garda hunt was launched, Ma and Da Clancy did the tearful on-camera appeals . . . but nothing happened, and nothing continued to happen. No boy, no body, no credible lead or line of enquiry could be unearthed.

Everyone's interest was piqued, for a while, given the proximity of Gurtlubber parish to our own town. But things go on, and bit by bit we began to care less and less.

Tug can't let the Clancy kid go. He can't resist the queasy hypotheticals such an open-ended story encourages. *What-ifs* proliferate like black flowers in the teeming muck of his imagination. Left unchecked he'll riff all evening about unmarked graves packed with lime, international rings of child traffickers, organ piracy, enforced cult initiation.

I tell him, lighten up.

—They could be lesbians. Tug says. German lesbians. Who, you know, can't have a child. Can't get the fertilisation treatment, can't adopt. Maybe they got desperate.

—Maybe, I say.

—The Clancy kid looked Aryan. You know? Fair-haired, blue-eyed, Tug says.

—All children look Aryan, I say, irritated.

Marlene's laughter, a high insolent cackling, carries down the yard. She and Cuculann have joined another couple, Stephen Gallagher and Connie Reape. Cuculann is tall, underfed and rangy, like me; Marlene has a type. She is cackling away at something Gallagher has said. Everyone else, including Gallagher, looks abashed, but Marlene is laughing and batting Gallagher on the shoulder, as if pleading with him to stop being so hilarious.

—But it wouldn't be the worst end for the lad. It wouldn't be an end at all, really, Tug says.

A waitress comes through the double doors, bearing a quartet of champagne flutes on a tray. Marlene waves her over and distributes the drinks, stem by stem, a strawberry impaled on the rim of each flute. Cuculann pays, and as Marlene drops the napkin that held her ice-cream cone onto the tray I catch the telltale twinkle on her ring finger.

—Wouldn't it not be? Tug says.

He reaches over and drops his paw on my forearm, shakes it.

—Be fucking super, Tug, I say.

He cringes at the snap in my voice. My mind, I want to say, has been enlisted in the pursuit of other woes, Tug, and I can't be dealing with the endless ends of the Clancy kid right now.

—Oh, Tug says.

He tucks his hand under the opposite armpit, like he's after catching a finger in a door jamb.

—You're in a mood and it's – he looks over, sniffs the air – it's Marlene. It's that loose cunt Marlene, he says.

I make a disapproving click with my tongue. I jab my finger at him.

—I'm easy as the next man when it comes to getting his end away, but Tug, there's no need to be throwing 'round them terms.

He leans back and his span thickens.

—I'll say whatever I want. About whoever I want.

—You really are an enormous fucking child, aren't you?

Tug grabs the sides of the table and I feel it shudder and float up from under me. I snatch my drink and lean back as the coasters go twirling off the edge. Tug sways and the table follows his sway, crashing against the concrete. People nearby yelp and jump back.

I daintily disembark from my stool, one foot then the other, keeping my eyes on Tug's eyes. His lips are hooked up into a sneer, his breathing fast and gurgled.

—I'm sorry Tug, I say.

His nostrils pucker and flare and pace themselves back to an even rhythm.

—That's all right, he says, that's all right.

He rubs a palm over the dented round of his skull and looks at the capsized table with an expression of broad mystification, like he had nothing to do with it.

—Come on, I say, let's book.

I drain the sudsy dregs of my pint and plant it on a nearby table.

Everyone backs away as we pass by, me in Tug's wake.

I know what they're thinking. Manchild gone mad again. Manchild throwing another fit. Oddball Manchild and his oddball mate Jimmy Devereux.

—Hi Marlene! Tug says cheerfully as we trundle by her table.

Marlene is unfazeable as ever. Cuculann beside her is hunched and close-shouldered, braced for action.

—Well big man, Marlene says.

She looks at me.

—And not-so-big man.

—Are congratulations in order? I say.

I lift up the ends of her fingers, straightening them out for inspection.

Marlene slips her hand from mine and covers it over with the other.

—Too late, I chuckle, I saw it. Nice aul' hunk of rock.

—It is, Cuculann says.

—Very pretty all right, Tug says.

I can feel him behind me, the looming proximity of all that mass, restored to my side and prepped to go ballistic at my word.

Marlene's bottom lip does something to the top, and she fixes me with a look that says: pay attention.

—Jimmy, I'm gone very happy, she says. Now please, fuck off.

Outside Dockery's the evening sun is in its picturesque throes, the sky steeped in foamy reds and pinks. The breeze has grown teeth. Shards of glass crunch underfoot like gravel. There are cars parked in a line along the road, and one of them is the tiny, faded silver hatchback Cuculann boots around in. It sits there bald as an insult on the kerb, a wrinkled L sticker pasted inside the windscreen.

—Look at the state of it, I say.

I wallop the flat of my palm against the pockmarked bonnet.

Tug looks at me wonderingly.

—It's Cuculann's car, I say.

—The thing's a lunchbox, Tug says and laughs.

—A pitiful thing to be chauffeuring your bride-to-be around in, I say.

—Awful, awful, awful, Tug agrees.

—Tug, are you off your meds? I say.

—No, he grunts.

He places the palm of one huge hand on the hatchback's roof and begins to experimentally rock the vehicle back and forth, the suspension squeaking in protest. Tug has never been a competent liar; his size, his physical advantage, means he's never needed to develop the ability to dissemble. You can always tell the truth, always say what you mean, if you're big enough.

—Be awful if you were to tip that thing onto its head, I say.

—Easy, Tug says.

He rocks and rocks the car until it is squeaking madly on its wheels and bouncing in place. It is parked at an angle, parallel to the lip of the kerb which is a couple of inches off the street, an angle that favours Tug. At just the right moment Tug bends down and digs his hands in under the springing hatchback's bed and pulls up with all his might. The wheels leave the kerb. For a moment the car hangs on its side in the air – I see the vasculature of blackened pipes that run along the car's underside – then Tug lurches forward and the hatchback goes over onto its roof with an enormous crunching sound. The passenger window shatters, the glass skittering in diamonds around our feet. The wheels judder in the air and Tug reaches out and stills the one closest.

—Well done, big man.

Tug is puffing, his cheeks inflamed. He shrugs his

shoulders. A car drifts by in the street. Child faces jostle in the rear window for a look at the overturned hatchback. An old codger ambles out of Dockery's, fitting and refitting a wilted pork-pie hat onto his trembling head. His loosely knotted tie flaps at his flushed, corrugated face. The codger grins yellowishly.

—How are the men? he says.

—Fucking super, Tug says.

The codger salutes us and wanders right by the wrecked car, not seeming to notice at all.

I look down and see, half in and half out of the shattered window, a brown leather handbag, its contents scattered in the gutter. There's wadded tissues, loose coins, crumpled sweet wrappers, a ballpoint pen, receipts, a roll-on stick of underarm antiperspirant, a gold-rimmed black cylinder of lipstick. I pick up the lipstick, unsnap its cap. I go to work on the passenger door. In bright red capitals I spell out my plea:

M A R R Y M E

—Shit, Tug says, and clicks his jaw. Hardcore Jimmy.

I shrug and pocket the lipstick. I pick up all the other things and put them in the handbag. I pass the bag through the broken window and tuck it into the passenger-seat footwell.

—Back to yours, big man? I say.

—Sound, Tug says.

Tug lives on the other side of the river, in Farrow Hill

estate with his mam. Like Marlene, his da is gone, in the ground ten years now. Big Cuniffe's heart burst ushering yearling colts from a burning barn. Tug's mother is a sweet old ruin of an alcoholic who spends her days rationing gin on their ancient, spring-pocked settee, lost in TV and her dead. You say hello and she offers an agreeable but doubtful smile; half the time she has no idea if you're part of the programme she's engrossed in, a figment of memory, or actually there, a live person before her. Sometimes she'll call me Tug or Eamonn, and she'll call Tug Jimmy. She'll call Tug by his father's name. Tug says there's no point correcting her. Such distinctions matter less and less as she settles into her sodden dotage.

We pit-stop at Carcetti's fast-foodery and chow down on chips as we take the towpath by the river. Slender reeds brush against one another as cleanly as freshly whetted blades. The wet shore-stone, black as coal, glints in its mucus bed of algae. Crushed cans of Strongbow and Dutch Gold and Karpackie are buried in the mud like ancient artefacts. Thickets and thickets of midges waver in the air. They feast on the passing planets of our heads.

Up ahead a wooden bridge traverses the river.

The bridge is supposedly off limits. During a spring storm earlier this year a tree was swept downstream and collided with the bridge and there it still resides, the great gnarled brunt of the trunk rammed at an upward forty-five degree angle amid ruptured beams and splintered fence posts. The bridge sags in the middle but has not yet collapsed. Instead of removing the tree's corpse and fixing the bridge, the town council erected flimsy mesh fences at both shores and harshly worded signage threatening *a fine and risk of injury/death* to anyone attempting to cross.

But the fences have been trampled down, for the bridge is a handy shortcut to Farrow Hill and, despite the council warnings, is still regularly used by estaters like Tug to get in and out of town.

As we approach we see that there are three kids playing by the bridge: two very young girls and a slightly older boy. The girls look five or six, the boy nine, ten.

The boy has white hair – not blond, white. He's wearing a cotton vest dulled to taupe and a pair of shiny purple tracksuit bottoms, one leg ripped up to the knee. The girls are in grubby pink short-and-T-shirt combinations. The boy's face is decorated with what looks like tribal warpaint – a thumb-thick red-and-white stripe applied under each eye, and a black stripe running down his nose. He's wielding an aluminium rod – it could be a curtain rail, a crutch, the pole of a fishing net. One end of the rod is crimped into a point.

—What are you, an injun? Tug asks him.

—I'm a king! The boy sneers.

—What class of a weapon is that? A lance, a sword? I say.

—It's a spear, he says.

He stamps up along the flattened fence and hops back

onto the towpath. He goes through a martial-arts display: slashing the air with the rod then spinning it over his head, fluidly transferring it from one twisting hand to the other. He finishes by leaning forward on one knee and brandishing the crimped end of the rod at Tug's sternum.

—This is my bridge, he says, baring his teeth.

—And what if we want to pass? Tug says.

—Not if I don't say so!

Tug proffers his crumpled bag of chips.

—We can pay our way. Chip, King?

The boy reaches into the bag and takes a wadded handful of vinegar-soaked chips. He examines the clump, sniffs them, then peels the chips apart and divides them between the girls. The girls eat them quickly, one by one. They tilt their heads back and make convulsive swallowing movements with their necks, like baby chicks.

—Good little birdies, the boy says, and pats each girl on the head.

They giggle to each other.

—You shouldn't take things from strangers, Tug says.

—*I* gave them the chips, the boy says, tapping his vested breast with his spear. What business do you have across the bridge?

—We're looking for someone. A boy. A little blondie-haired fella, Tug says, a little bit like you. He went away but nobody knows where.

The boy knits his brow. He steps back up onto the

fence and peers along the curvature of the river.

—There's no one like that here, he says finally. I would've seen him. I'm the King, I see everything.

—Well, we have to try, Tug says.

Leave it be, Tug, I want to say, but I say nothing. So much of friendship is merely that: the saying of nothing in place of something.

I turn and take a quick look beyond the towpath, along the way we came. A hill leads up to the road and beyond that is the squat, ramshackle skyline of the town. I hear – or think I hear – sounds of distant commotion, shouting, and I picture Mark Cuculann outside Dockery's, raging at the inverted wreck of his car. Marlene will be by his side, arms folded, and I can envisage the look she'll be wearing, the verdigris glint of her narrow-lidded eyes, a smile flickering despite itself about the edges of her lips, lips painted the same shade as the proposal I scrawled for her on the passenger door. I feel for the cylinder of lipstick in my pocket, take it out, give it to one of the girls.

—More gifts, I say. Well, let's get going then Tug.

Tug goes to step past the boy. The boy draws up the rod and jabs the crimped end into Tug's gut. Tug grasps the rod, twists it towards himself. He mock-gasps, and claws the air.

—You've killed me, he croaks.

He staggers back, and folds his big creaking knees, and puddles downward, dropping face forwards flat into the grass, arse proffered to the sky like a supplicant.

—You've done it now, I say.

I toe-nudge the fetal Tug in the ribs. He jiggles life-lessly. The boy steps forward, mimics my action, toeing the loaf of Tug's shoulder. The girls have gone silent.

—How are you going to explain this to your mammy? I say.

The boy's eyes begin to brim, even as he tries to keep the jaw jutted.

—Ah, he's set to start weeping, I say.

Tug, soft-hearted, can't stay dead. He sputters, raises his head, grins. He eyes the boy. He hoists himself up.

—Don't be teary now, wee man, he says, I was dead but I'm raised again.

He lumbers up over the fence and out onto the bridge and I follow.

—Goodbye King! Tug shouts.

As I pass him the boy scowlingly studies us, arms folded, aluminium spear resting against his shoulder.

—If ye fall in there's nothing *I* can do, he warns.

The bridge creaks beneath us. Halfway across, the thin gnarled branches of the dead tree spill over, reach like witches' fingers for our faces, and we have to press and swat them out of our way.

—So tell me, Tug, I say.

—What?

—Tell me more about the Clancy kid. About these German lesbians.

And Tug begins to talk, to theorise, and I'm not really listening, but that's okay. As he babbles I take in the back of his bobbing head, the ridges and undulations of his shaven skull. I take in the deep vertical crease in the fat of his neck like a lipless grimace, and the mountainous span of his swaying shoulders. I think of the picture of the Clancy kid, scissored from a Sunday newspaper, that Tug keeps tacked to the cork board in his room. The picture is the famous, familiar one, a birthday-party snap, crêpe birthday crown snugged down over the Clancy kid's fair head, big smile revealing the heartbreaking buck teeth, eyes wide, lost in the happy transport of the instant. I think of Marlene. I think of her sprog, so close to being mine. I think of her sundial navel, her belly so taut I can lay her on her back and bounce coins off it. We all have things we won't let go of.

The beams of the crippled bridge warp and sing beneath us all the way over, and when we make it to the far shore and step back down onto solid earth, a surge of gratitude flows through me. I reach out and pat Tug on the shoulder and turn to salute the boy king and his giggling girl entourage. But when I look back across the tumbling black turbulence of the water I see that the children are gone.

Hospitals Requests
Pat McCabe

'The November frost had starched the countryside into silent rigidity.'

That was one of the sentences, along with various other scraps and fragments of stories, that I came across in my old notebook/diary detailing a variety of aspects of my adolescence in the sixties.

Not, to be honest, that I cared what the November frost had done – any more than I did about a great deal else, ever since the bond between us had been irreducibly severed. Even at a remove of almost forty years it can still make galling reading . . . although I have to say the legal people certainly seemed to derive a degree of amusement from its contents before eventually returning it to me.

'Memories of Myrtle, Aug. 18, 1968.'

'We continue, happily, during these God-given days, to appraise one another as figures in a myth of our own construction, a hopelessly elevated amour in which valedictions from *A Midsummer Night's Dream* or Juliet or Romeo are by no means uncommon.'

The foregoing, annotated in a looping, vertiginous calligraphy, was bordered by an assortment of hand-drawn pictorial representations in Bic biro of my beautiful companion, Myrtle.

Whose father, as a general goods merchant and part-time auctioneer, sold milking machines throughout the district. This was to become a source, perhaps not of agony, but certainly of continued distress for me, throughout that blissful time when we perambulated the roads of our little home town in Ireland, my gorgeously wistful summer girl and me.

She whose coils of platinum-blonde hair were as ir-radiated, distended wonders. 'Floating, unfurling as bog cotton in the sun,' as I had apprehended it.

She was small in stature and, curiously, never wore lipstick. Not that such details mattered for, in any case, now it was over between us. 'I'm sorry, Feeney Reilly, I don't think we can ever meet again,' she was to inform me, lowering her head in that familiar bashful way. 'Would you like to buy some milking machines?' de-manded the ruffians who, as ever, stalked me going home, before cawing shrilly as they made their boister-ous departure: 'Mr Macklin's milking machines – going cheap!'

'You can have this photograph to remember me by,' she suggested later. 'Just to show there are no hard feel-ings or anything like that.'

I was grateful, to be honest, for it really was a nice print, a glossy one about three inches square, washed in vivid colours of purple and blue with her fair hair glowing vividly and her pale natural lips spreading out in a disarming smile. It was one we had got taken in the train station in Dublin – in a Kodak booth specially provided for the purpose.

Ah, Myrtle Macklin – how I tremble at the name of my long-ago summer girl. It was a tragedy I didn't think I would ever get over. And most likely wouldn't have, either – but for the arrival of dear Auntie Honey. Or 'Bunny Honey' as my mother preferred to call her.

My heart it literally stood still in my chest when I first saw her; however, little did I dream that her arrival on our humble doorstep would in actual fact effect a cure for my malady, banish my obstinate delirium for ever.

But that is what it did, for Bunny Honey set my soul on fire. 'She reads the *News of the World*,' some locals said. Effectively suggesting that she possessed loose morals. Some were even more forthright, with Harry Murtagh's wife actually declaring that she was 'a low-born good-for-nothing tramp'.

I could scarcely believe it when she showed me the photographs. Also glossy, but in shades of achingly beautiful Kodachrome amber. 'Yes, I was a Windmill girl in Soho,' she beamed proudly, and I couldn't command my eyes away from the sandal – the item of Scholl's footwear that was dandling beneath the hem of her tight-fitting black slacks, complete with foot-strap. I found myself on the verge of collapse.

★

You think that you'll forget, like I assumed I had done with Myrtle Macklin. Or 'my once-upon-a-time summer girl' which I had taken to calling her around that time. But it's not always that easy. There are forces at that age that you don't understand, and once they've taken root, established themselves surreptitiously deep inside you – well, I'm afraid there isn't a great deal you can do.

I arrived home one day – I happened to be doing the Intermediate examination at the time – and found Auntie Bunny helping my mother with the zipper of her skirt. They were discussing clubs in London which no one in their right mind would frequent – 'grubby places' where 'men and women of the worst character' were known to congregate. When they saw me in the doorway they both started giggling. My father left down the paper, coughed uproariously and hurled himself out the door.

Looking back, I suppose, that was the first time I'd noticed anything. However, nothing happened after that – at least nothing worth reporting – until what I thought of as the 'night of the stocking'. Or what Bunny herself took to describing as 'The Great Kayser Bondor Stocking Mystery'.

She was scratching her head, clearly somewhat out of sorts, when I entered the kitchen. Her great glossy beehive was shining in the late evening sun, and her black slacks might have been sprayed onto her posterior. 'I can't quite understand it,' she kept saying, 'I was sure that I'd put them in my drawer. But one of my stockings . . . why, it definitely seems to have disappeared!'

She shook her head as we sat down at the table and consumed some tea.

She lived in Margate – on Marine Parade, right on the seafront, she told me, tapping her elongated nails on the table's wooden surface.

'Everyone wears their hair up,' she continued with a smile. 'On the mainland, I mean – just like this, in the style of Kathy Kirby.'

Then she told me all about the Blitz in London. 'It could be lovely and yummy down in the tube stations where everyone gathered.' She exhaled softly as she described how reassuring and warm it could be down there. 'So yummy cosy with us all huddled in!'

I sat there, stiff, as her bosom heaved with the pink lambswool of her sweater swelling, as she regarded me, twinkling-staring directly into my eyes.

'But where could that Kayser Bondor have possibly gone?' she pondered anew, cradling her small chin on a pale moisturised hand.

Like my father previously, I was on the verge of losing my nerve and disappearing out the door – because I really didn't know the answer to the question. I was flummoxed – but those eyes kept on sparkling. 'I wonder,' she repeated, and then again: 'I wonder . . .'

At the end of the exams there was a party, and, in celebration, or so they said, they danced. Not me, just my
mother and Bunny. She had always loved Bobby Darin,
I heard my mother remark almost dazedly, huffing and
puffing as she manoeuvred our mock-teak three-speed
radiogram right out into the centre of the floor.

Bunny Honey took her by the hand, twirling together and tossing back their heads as out swept the swinging
jazz number to which she and all her Windmill girl pals
liked to dance.

'Happy we'll be beyond the sea,' she laughed, with
a little tinkle in her voice – those, of course, were the
words of the song. This time – with any thoughts of the
laughter of Myrtle Macklin my summer girl now long
since dissipated, to such an extent that their very existence might have been questionable – she wasn't wearing
slacks but lots of beads, a white skirt and with her hair
styled in a blonde French pleat. Snapping her fingers
as I looked on, listening to them have a great laugh
about a wooden doll called Lord Charles – an aristocratic dummy, a ventriloquist act, who apparently had often
played the Windmill Theatre, and even sometimes used
to sell confections from a tray, hot meat pies that were
known to be delicious, as he swept along the aisles in
his candy-striped blazer, bleating, 'Any requests? I say,
ladies, any requests? Lots of nice little juicies here!' And
who, although he was wooden – oh how my auntie

laughed! – would often help himself to a drinkie or two, the monocled cad, and was not at all shy when it came to the ladies. 'He used to leer from the wings, you know! Sloshed, I swear, as any sailor on shore leave! But at other times he could really be a dear – tee hee! O that bounder, that wicked old Lord Charles! The way he smiled with those clamped wooden teeth! Honestly!'

★

The house was deserted the next night I came home. Or so I thought. At least until I heard it – soft but un-mistaken, her voice coming again. The only light in the quiet kitchen was that visible on the old valve radio, slowly pulsing – the tiniest little green bead on the dial.

I heard her joke – would I, she wanted to know, per-haps like a biscuit? 'We used to always have one on our lunch break at the Windmill. A fig roll, I mean.'

She was holding a packet in her hands. She found a plate – even in the darkness it seemed to require little effort. She closed the cupboard and shuffled some bis-cuits onto the plate. 'Did you ever happen to hear of Jim Figgerty?' she asked me.

He was a fictional character they used to advertise Ja-cob's biscuits. On the TV it said he knew the secret of how they got the figs inside the hard brown flavoured envelopes.

I nodded and said that yes I had indeed heard of him.

'We don't have him in the UK, though, of course,'

she went on. 'No one over there would even know who he was. They wouldn't, I'm afraid, have the faintest idea. It was your mother was telling me about him. She likes to tell me everything that goes on while I'm away. Ha ha! After all, it is such an exciting country, isn't it? So much to do!' Her lips grew thin as a strand of white sewing thread whenever she said that, and I could have sworn that her eyes . . . that they had almost become hollowed out. A development which had unnerved me by virtue of its sheer abruptness.

'Isn't that right?' she said.

I didn't know. I didn't want to talk about it.

'The mysterious secret of Jacob's fig rolls,' she whispered, nibbling the small rectangle all along the edges.

The twinging green bead had faded now, and we found ourselves immersed once more into darkness. Then suddenly the door crashed open as the kitchen literally exploded into light. 'I was at Benediction,' I heard my mother say.

Being a Protestant, my aunt was under no obligation to go.

★

The light was slanting in the window of the terrace as her Kathy Kirby sandal with the raised heel hung suspended once more from her alert wriggling toes. The shade of her nails was as startling as when I'd first seen them. 'Cutex coral pink,' she whispered again huskily, 'soft enough to be innocent, sweet enough to inspire.'

Then she coughed and looked away. Before sighing and turning to smile at me, ever so tenderly, wearing an expression that seemed almost forlorn.

'Do you miss her?' she inquired softly. 'That beautiful summer girl you once had, I mean?'

'No,' I explained, as further tragedies unfolded on Raidió Éireann. A wall had fallen on six laughing schoolchildren who were there to welcome a local celebrity. Then there was the weather and sports reports, with 'the focus this evening' on Intermediate girls' hockey. After that it was the sponsored programmes, starting off with *Hospitals Requests*.

Maureen was in confinement in St Mary's Ward in St Ita's in Athlone intoned the intimate, neighbourly voice of the presenter. She'd been taken bad while out for a walk. After tests they had discovered a shocking variety of ailments. Hope you get well soon, Maureen, I heard the announcer reading from a sympathy card. Bunny smiled, shivering a little as she folded her arms. 'Imagine if you were in hospital,' she said, 'and I was the nurse. It wouldn't be hard – I mean I have been an actress. Which means that I can pretend to be . . . well, anything really.'

It was the first I'd ever heard of the film *Naked as Nature Intended*, in which she'd apparently starred alongside a number of other Windmill girls. She began telling me the story of it just as the presenter of *Hospitals*

Requests introduced another tune: the Pat Boone hit 'Love Letters in the Sand'.

Most of the picture, she went on to explain, had been shot in a car park off the Charing Cross Road. With occasional forays to the south coast, down to the seaside town of Margate. 'Ironically!' she pealed, 'the place where I live now! Doesn't that just take the biscuit? Or, should I say, the fig roll, ha ha!'

There could be no other word but 'mesmerising' as she continued to describe her participation in the feature which entailed playing the role of a shy office girl by the name of Miss Lattimer. Whose boss announced one Friday afternoon that he happened to be going away for the weekend and did she perhaps think that she might like to come? It was only on the train that she learnt that he was, in fact, travelling to a nudist camp.

After the censor had effected his cuts, she tinkled, there was only about fifty-eight minutes remaining. 'It was X-Cert, of course, and premiered at the Cannon Moulin in Windmill Street.'

Would you please play Alma Cogan for Lucy, wrote a listener, Lucy who's in the Mater Hospital in Dublin, I would be so grateful. Could I have Bridie Gallagher for my dear mother Mrs Cooney, who's been in the Bon Secours this past fortnight, came another request. After that it was The Bachelors for Imelda in Mullingar. And then The Seekers for Booboo and Mopsy who were greatly missed by their grannie and granda. And poor Mary Ellen in Marino who had polio.

Might I, at this juncture, suggest that another possible name for the author of this somewhat unfortunate testimony of regret might well be Feeney Reilly of the Overactive Retina for it has always been my blessing or curse to be in possession of what can only be described as a fiercely cinematic imagination – and now the scene she had set presented itself to me in all its breathtaking clarity, in crisp pink and crimson Eastmancolor tints, as vivid as if the businessman and Miss Lattimer were actually standing naked and preoccupied with a multi-coloured beach ball right there in the centre of our kitchen. Except that it was Bunny who was standing beside the mantelpiece, sans beach ball, but ever so slowly popping the buttons of her dove-white stiff and sharp nurse's uniform. I could just make out the lace edging of her brassiere. 'X-Cert,' she was whispering, 'are you comfortable, dearie?'

Solely on impulse, I found myself reaching out and touching her ever so gently – hesitantly, not even beginning to approach the slopes of her bosom, and certainly not directly on the breast – before looking up to see her glaring hideously at me, with her body rigid, flattened, with her back against the kitchen wall. And, to make matters worse, I began to realise she was actually crying out. 'Just what on earth do you think you're doing?' she screeched fiercely, trembling violently from head to toe. 'Just what do you think you're doing?' she demanded again.

I shrank from the ghastly scene in dread – just as

she herself proceeded to do. Shaking all over with her lips stony, ashen. Her continuing cries of protest could be heard clearly all along the length of the terrace. My expression was reflected in the window directly opposite where I stood – it was pallid, sickly, greenish. Here's hoping to see you home again soon, Grainne, piped the homespun voice of the radio announcer as another gay tune wafted out from behind the brown chevron-wave grille cloth of the varnished Pye cabinet. 'He touched me!' my aunt was shrieking. 'Huh-huh-he touched me!'

Her sandal appraising me with a hungry open jaw.

★

(The succeeding pages were not contained within the diary itself but were discovered elsewhere – in my London lodgings, in fact – by the authorities, and have ever since formed part of my official record. For my part, however, they remain what they always were – disparate uncrafted musings never intended for the public eye. Which, conceivably – that is to say, if even some lacklustre attempt to impose a shape on them had ever been made – might ultimately have been presented as a little memoir of sorts, or a short story perhaps entitled 'Love Letters in the Sand', in memory of the Pat Boone hit that gave rise to them so long ago. And which attained their, perhaps inevitable conclusion, almost forty years later, after a lifetime spent in England.)

Love Letters in the Sand; or An Old Naïve, Remembering by the Sea.

'Almost as soon as he had covered over the small ribbon-bound cache (its colours were blue and white) in a little sprinkling of the finest dry golden grains, the elderly gentleman in the panama hat experienced the most enormous sense of relief – indeed it seemed almost as though a tumour had been cut out, deftly removed from his body – smiling away as the mellow strains of the Pat Boone melody he remembered from long ago lingered soothingly in his head. Ah yes, 'Love Letters in the Sand', he sighed, tapping the lapels of his neat grey overcoat as he stood erect, setting off across the strand, past Dreamland Ballroom and the Oval Lawns. Smiling to himself as he thought of his days as an ingénue film-maker who had latterly become a devotee of the Lindsay Anderson school of early sixties Free Cinema – the centrepiece of which was his somewhat superior featurette/documentary on Margate and this very ballroom. Which, of course, like a lot of sights in this once grand seaside town, had fallen somewhat into decay. But Feeney Reilly didn't give that much thought – knowing only too well the quite extraordinary alchemic powers of art, particularly film. For him, he reflected, there was, and continued to be, even now as he himself approached his sixties, something spiritual about the dimming wall-lights of a movie theatre, an ecstasy almost, which he had experienced at its most profound, perhaps, in the 1970s when on release from his confinement in prohibitive Ireland where even simple contraceptives were illicit and the concept of abortion entirely alien. And where even a harmless little celluloid bagatelle such as *Naked as Nature Intended*, which he had happened to see in the Cameo in 1971, a laughable little romp featuring beach balls, bums and strategically placed towels, had not only been awarded an X-certificate but roundly denounced in both the local and national press. He laughed wryly to himself as he recalled the darkened theatre and the bowler-hatted man who was departing his office for a 'spot of relaxation' . . . 'On the coast, Miss Lattimer, with some friends and genial company. You don't care, I suppose, to join me?' His mousy secretary blushed violently and lowered her head, disappearing into a folder of files.

How standards change, he mused, shaking his head yet again, arranging his easel on the edge of the clifftop overlooking the bay. Ultimately, as it happened, film had proved an unsuccessful prospect for Mr Feeney Reilly, to such a degree that he had ended up making no money to speak of, even in that purportedly lucrative category of 'Continental pictures', where the blending of 'art' with 'the erotic' was scarcely unusual and in which he had laboured for quite some time before drawing on some savings he had wisely salted away and eventually opting for the pursuit of a much more realistic and certainly realisable aim: working in watercolours.

On one occasion, having discovered it quite by chance in a bric-a-brac shop, he had purchased a monster cut-out of the model Pamela Green, the original star of *Peeping Tom*, with which he was besotted, as much for its *mise en scène* as for its startling – for its time – theme and its groundbreaking cinematography. There were others, too, which he treasured and viewed repeatedly, never seeming to tire of their idiosyncratic impishness, even muted defiance. Such as Mary Millington's *Come Play with Me*. But his favourite would always remain *Nudes of the World*, produced by Arnold L. Miller and put on general release in the year 1962, after which there followed many copycats, notably, perhaps, *I, Nudist*, also 16 mm, replete with a comparable quota of volleyball nets, beach windbreakers and strategically placed towels, not to mention late-night camp meets at which the popular songs 'Hand Me Down My Walking Cane' and 'Won't You Come Home, Bill Bailey' were regular favourites, piped from a crescent of candy-striped deckchairs tenanted by city-dwellers bathed in a delirious glow.

Deckchairs of exactly the same design and pattern that he intended to include in his Margate picture, which he had just this very moment begun. Briskly drawing his brush across the canvas, experiencing an extraordinary sensation of delight and elevation that had been commonplace from the moment, effectively, that he had learnt to paint, conjuring up the simplest of images such as the frontage of municipal buildings, green grass and, as now, an expanse of golden sand and the nearby glittering sea. Although he would never have claimed to lead the field in the medium in any commendable way, rather intending – if he had such a thing as a philosophy of art – to recapture the freshness and principle of naive art at its best. His friend Kerry Mannion, an associate of many years standing and, among many other things, a ticket clerk at Waterloo Station, would have endorsed this view. Proclaiming him at one point similar to the notorious Alfred Wallis, variously described throughout his career as 'a ham' and 'limited' and indeed on one occasion as 'the world's worst painter'.

'Did you know he was plagued with voices and was given to breaking off in mid-sentence to insist that his dead wife pipe down?' he recalled him saying.

Poor old Mannion – he too was gone now, taken by cancer after going in for routine tests. He touched up the outline of the figure's scarcely formed head; a fleck of blue. And sighed. How much he owed Mannion, who had arranged a position for him after leaving the seminary, where Feeney Reilly had studied in the end for a mere three years. Before finding himself, unshackled, with all of the possibilities of London before him. It was Mannion who had introduced him to Fairleigh and Urquhart, both of them, according to his friend, and so it proved, 'remarkable talents, each in their own way'.

Urquhart had met Polanski, he told him, and as for Fairleigh, there wasn't one in the French House pub who didn't know him.

He daubed the figure's forehead with a spot of ice-cream pink, similar to the shade of Eastmancolor which he loved. 'Soft enough to be innocent, sweet enough to inspire,' he murmured.

Then paused and smiled, thinking nothing of the vehicle drawing up alongside the concrete shelter, or the discreet blue-serged elbow that appeared out the window. He merely exhaled and smiled once again, contented with the way his work was proceeding.

A Postcard from Margate, he intended calling it, proposing it as something of a gay-coloured tribute, although it was, in effect, an interior. His shoulders sagged again, and he paused as he recalled – it was Mannion who first mentioned it, a scene from the sixties movie *Catch Us If You Can*, in which Margate had been described as 'smelling of dead holidays'.

They had seen it in the Coronet, as he recalled, or was it the ABC in Soho? He couldn't quite remember, and in any case experienced no great compulsion to pursue it, considering it was, as it happened, in that establishment there had been a complaint to the management about him. By an ill-intentioned, perhaps mentally unstable, individual in his sixties, and motivated solely by bitterness. His protestations had proved futile. 'Interfered' was the word, the constant refrain that assaulted his ears as he found himself manhandled and, ultimately, quite humiliated, as he was consigned to the lashing rains of Piccadilly.

But those were ancient, of little consequence, times.

For now he was in Margate, home of the Salvation Army Band, of pipe-smoking dads and dilettantes on cliffs. He was just about to add the tiniest dab of white onto his canvas – a mere suggestion – on the elevation of an empurpled wave when he felt a somewhat reluctant hand touch him on the arm.

'We were wondering, sir, if we might have a word?'

Both men stood for a moment, implacably, before one of them turned a ghastly shade of grey. Clamping his hand to his mouth as he . . .

His constable colleague stood between him and the painting.

★

There was a fire extinguisher in startling scarlet red secured to the wall at an awkward forty-degree angle. Feeney Reilly had been watching it for some time through the six-by-four panel of glass in the door. Before his eyes lit up when he heard it again, the familiar sound like the squeaking wheels of the wheelchair that the constable had produced in the day room on that occasion, after they had driven him from the beach – it was covered in plastic, with a plaid rug underneath.

'I was wondering,' said the officer, 'do you recognise this?'

★

As always, the nurse was accompanied by a stocky mental staff orderly – a fine fellow indeed. A countryman of Feeney Reilly's, as it happened – from a village only miles from the place where he'd been born.

'So how are we today, Mr Reilly, any requests?'

Only half-interested, the orderly yawned and looked out across the concreted enclosure, where the metal sign marked 'Friern Barnet' was glazed with little drops of rain.

Feeney Reilly stroked his chin and considered his choice for a long time – initially he selected a muffin along with coffee before changing his mind. He was secreting upon his person the small glossy photograph which he had been perusing for some time, and then his face slowly began to turn pale, a development which went entirely unnoticed by his custodian. Who remained quite oblivious to the depth of the shock and surprise which, not to put too fine a point on it, was now enveloping Feeney Reilly who, admittedly, had some apprehension of what was now happening to him.

He was reminded of a story which he had read long ago – where exactly he could not recall, probably in a doctor's waiting room somewhere – recording a lady's quite extraordinary experience when, kneeling in a church and praying devoutly, she had been alerted by the gentle, scarcely audible sound of strings, the source of which proved to be an image high above her on a stained-glass window. Where a small angelic figure was plying a majestic wooden harp with such commitment that, somehow, a single note became detached from the instrument – literally being released into the still air of evening, before wafting, with an almost impossible lyrical grace, and settling softly, with an extraordinary delicacy, directly on the pew in front of the enraptured penitent.

In exactly the same manner as the lips of the photographic image had just done and which were, of course, those of Myrtle Macklin, and with whom he had been enjoying, it might be said, a passing moment of 'private theatre', throughout the course of which – under dim lights – he had cast her as the mousey 'Miss Lattimer' and himself as her bowler-hatted bespectacled boss whose mysterious journeys to the south coast had revealed something more, quite a lot more, than she had anticipated, arching like a translucent meniscus directly in front of his eyes, before coming to rest, not as the singular note of the harp had done, in a quiet corner there to remain as some harbinger of harmony, but affixed (curiously, as always, and quite incongruously in these new circumstances, with no adornment of any kind, as was to be expected with Myrtle) to a life-size cardboard cut-out of Pamela Green, but somewhat absurdly if convincingly bearing the soft plumpish features of Bunny Meers, statuesquely attired in a lace-up basque and lengthy ribboned suspenders. And from which, impairingly, now emerged the following words: 'Milking machines? No, we don't sell those anymore. But I really must recruit your enthusiasm, dearie. You see, I've lost my stocking and without it I simply don't know what to do. You know, I feel such a ninny, having permitted such saucy comportment, and in the sanctuary of my own private rooms. And how my neck hurts now as a result, O how it stings! Why you were almost as naughty, I declare it, as that incorrigible bounder, that wicked rascal Lord Charles – tee hee!'

Even when his expression deepened and turned quite pale, the orderly gave no hint of recognition of any sort, with Feeney Reilly's attention being gripped by the sudden and unexpected sight of a crook-handled and red-striped stick of rock, which – his blood ran cold as he recalled the implacability of the prosecuting lawyer, who pointed to the painting standing on its easel – rested sideways in the centre of the trolley. Bringing back, as it did, the opportunistic description in one of the more sordid dailies. In which the Scholl's sandal had been described as 'priapic'. Not to even consider their comments on the various 'randomly scattered' pieces of clothing, including the stocking, which was more of the 'support' variety than the 'Kayser Bondor'.

It was a distressing recollection and explained why he found himself changing his mind, on no less than three occasions, as the orderly proceeded, yet again, to somewhat wearily caress his five o'clock shadow.

The flushed glow of the fire extinguisher angled behind him was quite overwhelming.

'I think, after all, I'll just have a pie,' he sighed,

eventually, nodding his head, before suddenly lurching forward as a swollen blotch of emerald sputum appeared lividly between his lips and he found himself groaning helplessly as he quivered, 'Like the ones they always sold during intervals at the Windmill.'

The Recital

Eimear Ryan

It was one of those sleek, silvery wine bars: anonymous as an airport, the oversized glasses filled a third of the way.

'He's in NAMA,' Tim would murmur in my ear as we tended bar. 'That lad there was before a tribunal.' Tim knew everyone's scandal, had it boiled down to the absolutes. 'Grace,' he'd say, 'the tax evader wants another gin and tonic.'

Sometimes I wished he'd keep his voice down. I couldn't help but like the clientele. It wasn't just that they tipped well. They had presence – a tragic, shop-soiled charisma. They told great stories. They'd been powerful men, once.

I'd dropped my CV into the bar because of the piano that sat squat and dusty in the corner. I'd hoped they might hire me to play. When Tim offered bar work instead, I didn't hesitate. I needed a reason to get out of the house, away from my sister's reproachful looks.

Not that Jen ever let up. Often when I got in from work she would materialise in the darkened living room, warning me not to wake Ruán.

'Could you not get a different sort of job? One with more civilised hours? You know, something in an office.'

I thought of the early morning rush, of girls in pencil skirts and chunky white runners stalking grimly to work, their heels in their handbags. 'No thanks.'

The piano, I soon learned, was little more than an expensive prop. I was forever running over to it with a cloth to wipe the sticky wine-glass rings away. The bar was fine as a stopgap, a 'just' job – *And what are you doing at the moment, Grace? Oh, I'm just working in a bar for now.* There was an unofficial free-wine perk, of which I made judicious use. And in slow moments, I watched the customers. There was a GAA commentator who had a different accent to the one he used on TV. There was a judge who sat at the bar in full judge rig-out, her wig sitting neatly on her head like a vestigial brain.

One regular, Liam, bounded in at the same hour each night, always in a suit, always slightly dishevelled. He was forever getting into arguments about 'funding'.

Tim explained. 'He's the local TD, Grace. Ah, you've heard of him. He used to be Justice Minister. Resigned in disgrace a few years ago?' I shrugged, prompting Tim to sigh, '*God*, you're young.'

I didn't care about politics, but I watched with interest as Liam dealt with his irate constituents. His accent betrayed his origins in the farming heartlands, and he was a good herder of words. When he made a point, it was like a bolt sliding home, neat and precise. He was a constant fidgeter, and handled others with as much ease as he did himself. Women, of course – he was an expert at the hand to the small of the back, of the sincere hand-clasp – but men too he touched warmly in conversation, a hand on the arm, on the shoulder, and they were easy with it, pleased even. He listened patiently to everyone's complaints, but invariably turned back to the bar – to me – with a dark grin and a generous rolling of the eyes.

★

It turned out I was doing better than most of my former classmates. I wasn't on the dole, at least. As Music Composition graduates, we were not the most practical souls. We tended to be on the precious side; my classmates would emerge grinning from three straight hours' piano practice, invoking the 'better than sex' chestnut. My own relationship with the piano was less romantic; I treated it like a horse I was trying to break in. My father had always chastised me for that.

Growing up, Jen had always been the better pianist. She'd made it – a successful stint with the National Symphony Orchestra, a score for a worldwide smash-hit Irish dance show. Then she had Ruán and devoted herself to motherhood full-time. She always insisted it was her choice, but I was sceptical; Ruán's father was on tour in Asia, and there was no suggestion of *him* putting his career on hold.

Our father had taught us both – we'd compete for

space next to him on the piano bench. I'd stare mesmer-
ised at his hands, at the curly gold hairs on his wrists.
And I was a hesitant player from the start. 'Eyes up!' he
would say. 'Don't overthink it. Skip, skip, skip along.'
Dad never hinted at Jen's superiority, and so made her
determined to prove it, over and over.

It shouldn't have surprised me that she would shield
her contacts jealously. 'I'll put in a good word for you,'
she'd say, 'if I get around to it.' Then, when I reminded
her: 'Jesus, I'm already putting you up – would you have
a bit of patience?' Other times, over wine: 'I'm just not
sure you'd *suit* the National Symphony Orchestra! All
that rigid discipline? You're a *different* sort of musician,
Grace.'

At night I lay on my back in the spare bedroom,
sometimes woken by Ruán's thready cries, Jen's awards
shadowy on the shelves above. I resigned myself to
teaching children in their living rooms as pushy parents
hovered in the doorway.

★

A slow night in the bar turned into a sing-song, and I
found myself at the piano. It needed a tune-up, but I was
able to work around that. I played one of Chopin's trip-
pier pieces, showing off, revelling in the looks I drew. It
was so different from playing in draughty practice halls. I
didn't even feel like a pianist. I felt like a seductive starlet
in an old movie, draped over the back of a baby grand in

The Recital

a puddled cocktail dress. *That's right, and you all thought I was just a barmaid.*

Then Liam was prevailed upon to sing a ballad that had been written about his late father, from whom Liam had inherited a name and a Dáil seat. 'I don't think I can follow *that*!' he protested, but eventually he put his hands in his pockets, closed his eyes, and sang. It was more of a recital; his voice was nothing special. Still, it was mournful and deeply felt.

I said as much to Tim, who made a face. 'He isn't half the man his father was. It's a good thing Liam Senior was long dead, God rest him, when Liam Junior resigned from cabinet. The shame would've killed him!'

'Tim, that makes no sense.'

He poured a pint, yanking down the tap handle. 'Ah, don't be smart. He's an amiable enough man, but I wouldn't trust him as far as I could throw him, the arrogant hoor.'

I caught Liam's eye. He was looking at me intently, worrying his glasses in his hands. The weight of an admiring gaze was not unpleasant. He signalled for another whiskey.

'That was something else, Grace.'

I poured him more than was strictly a measure. 'Thanks. You too.'

He swatted at the air. 'I've no voice, but that song still gets to me. We didn't always get on but that man was my idol. Hard to believe it's twelve years since he died . . .'

203

I didn't know what to say. 'I was ten,' I said eventually.

He barked a laugh. 'You'd hardly be expected to re-member him so. Tell me something – what is it you want to do with yourself? Talent like that, you hardly want to stay behind a bar your whole life, working for *that* tyrant.' Liam winked at Tim, who scowled.

'I just finished a postgrad in music.'

He drummed his fingers along the edge of the bar, a parody of 'Chopsticks'. 'And how's that sector doing?'

'Not great. Though I haven't been very proactive, to be honest. My sister's a musician too – well, was – so I'm kind of relying on her for contacts. Her name's Jen – Jennifer Whelan?'

Recognition animated his tired face. '*That's* your sis-ter? I saw her perform a solo at the National Concert Hall once. Christ, she was amazing.' I must have looked crestfallen, because he added, 'You're exceptional, too. I mean that.'

I felt my cheeks darken, tighten. I hated the bitterness I felt about Jen's success, and he'd picked up on it in-stantly. His restless fingers caught the back of my wrist, tapping gently. No ring, I noticed.

'A college friend of mine is a conductor with the Philharmonic Choir. He's always on the lookout for young talent. I'll put in a word for you.'

We ended up leaving at the same time. He stood swaying gently in the car park, looking up at the sky, where the moon was a fierce yellow disc. He threw me a smile, which – I had just begun to notice – seemed weighed down with sadness, always, like that of the recently bereaved.

'The moon's not where I left it,' he said, as though it were his chariot home and now he was stuck. I looked up: the moon did seem to be on the move, clouds streaking across it like shadow puppets.

Before leaving he kissed me goodnight. I closed my eyes, and the dry leaves skittered around our feet like insects. It was brief, and not quite inappropriate, but I could tell from the look he gave me that he was surprised at himself.

★

There was a framed newspaper clipping of Liam in the bar. It was on the way to the women's toilets; I suspected he didn't know it was there. In it, a younger, slimmer Liam sat beaming at his new ministerial desk; behind him were portraits of his predecessors, including his father. The accompanying article was a long, thinly veiled warning: he'd better not let down the family name. It was after reading this that I decided to sleep with him.

I'd only been with young men before, and it was different. There was the paunch to be negotiated. His arms, always in shirtsleeves, were almost translucent. His greying stubble chafed my face. But he still had his hair, thick and springy, and up close his eyes were beautiful; they pinned me down as he moved over me, twin blue follow spots. Afterwards we lay side by side, laughing quietly, and he held my hand at arm's length, examining my fingers, measuring, saying, 'Oh Grace, I must get you a job.'

I believed him. I fizzed with possibilities. I liked the way people looked when Liam would lean across the bar to kiss my cheek, or when he put his hand on my back, his fingers chiselling either side of my spine.

Tim didn't like it. 'Have you got daddy issues or what?' I suspected that he wanted to bar Liam, or fire me, or both.

I was making a spectacle of myself. I was arriving in the real world.

★

One particular night, Liam said an early, lingering good-bye. He was attending a business breakfast – whatever that was – in Naas the next morning, and would be expected to 'work the room', he told me, making deadly serious air quotes. I didn't mind. I had taken to pulsing Bach through my headphones on the walk home and the quiet afterwards seemed like something precious. I wanted to go to bed in that quiet, not be confronted by a frazzled, sleep-deprived Jen. But I could hear Ruán crying from the corridor.

The apartment was dark, except for light under the toilet door. I tiptoed into Ruán's room, picked the furious bundle up. I shushed him, rocked him. I was good

with him now. The first time I'd held him, in the hospital, I'd been a wreck. Instead of enjoying the moment,
I'd thought of the cold tiles flooring the ward, of his
breakability should he slip from my arms. I remembered
touching a hesitant finger to his cheek, feeling the slight
give of his skin, realising how rough my own hide really
was.

'You're home late,' said Jen, from behind me. 'This
fella's been kicking up all night, haven't you?'

Jen took the baby from my arms; something about
this transaction still made me anxious, and I tended to
hold on too long. This night, however, I felt warm and
happy, and I ended up telling her, through Ruán's cries,
about the night of the sing-song; how the charming, if
borderline alcoholic politician had promised to help me
find work.

'Wait,' said Jen, 'wait, this isn't Liam Kelleher we're
talking about? You do *know* his story, right?'

'Yeah, he got chucked out of government. So Tim
says. Whatever.'

'Do you know *why*?'

My buzz was slipping away. 'Does it matter?'

'He shagged his secretary. Got her pregnant, for fuck's
sake. She was really young, like your age? The wife left
him. It was a total circus, it was all over the papers and
Vincent Browne and everything.'

The news hit me like a drenching. 'Well, he . . . he
wouldn't be the first politician, I guess.'

She smirked. 'Ah, he's hardly Clinton. It wasn't glamorous. He was after refusing to bring in a civil-partnership bill, banging on about the Constitution, about *family values*. And then the secretary broke her silence. Yeah, he was a bit undermined after that. He had to go.'

I nodded slowly, my throat thickening.

'God!' said Jen, jiggling Ruán on her shoulder. 'What kind of creeps do you *get* in that place?'

'He's not the worst,' I said, and Jen laughed lightly in my face.

★

Google gave me more on Liam Kelleher than I really cared to have. I loaded up my iPod with podcasts and took long walks with his voice in my ear, by turns manipulative, defensive, reasonable. I used Jen's credit card to get past website paywalls, digging into Liam's archived past. I found his children on Facebook – they were not so much younger than me. I watched videos of him at election count centres, being hoisted and bounced on shoulders, trying to look dignified and somehow managing it. I read the secretary's exclusives to a Sunday redtop, gushing about being whisked away to London and Paris, about champagne in bed. *I* hadn't got champagne in bed.

At work, I tried to pretend everything was normal, but I couldn't do it. We got bad at the kissing. The timing was off; we even started missing each other's mouths. It was only later I realised it was because he was drawing back. 'Oh, that was a one-time thing, Grace,' he told me eventually, as if I'd tried to use expired coupons.

One night he came in with a man who could only have been a conductor, which is to say he looked like a maths professor and used his hands a lot. I tried not to look at them. Liam's voice, to my ear, rose above the rumbling din of wine-bar conversation. I could sense his confusion at my distance, the sidelong way he watched me. I let Tim serve them. When I had no choice but to walk past them to fetch a bottle of Châteauneuf-du-Pape, Liam seized my wrist.

'I want a word with you.'

I couldn't look at him. I focused instead on the triangle of white shirt beneath the lapels of his jacket – the skin underneath, I knew, was almost as white.

'This is Kevin, my old college friend. Kevin, this is the girl I was telling you about.'

'Jennifer Whelan's sister, my my,' said the conductor, smiling in a way that made me wonder how much he had been told. 'You'll have to give us a recital, so.'

I backed off, feeling Tim's stare on me. But I knew, whether he fired me or not – whether I had an audience or not – by the end of the night I would be sliding onto the piano's polished bench like I was taking cover. It was all I was good for; it was my way out. I would flex my fingers, skim them along the surface of the keys. Eyes up, don't overthink it. Skip, skip, skip along.

A Winter Harmonic

Mike McCormack

Blood Horizon

So I got word: there was a man out there and this man had a cure and I could have it at a price. And if I found my way to him and told him what was wrong or needed fixing I could be fairly certain that he would lend an ear. All I had to do was give him the facts, lay them before him as clearly as possible. And while the chances were that he wouldn't have the cure on him straight away I was assured that I would only have to wait a few days, a week, max. He would go away and do whatever he had to do and then get back to me.

One way or another he would sort me out.

He wouldn't see me stuck.

That was the word.

So I waited in a car park outside town; I must have been there a good hour. Cars coming and going in the grey light and the rain pissing down, a filthy day in November.

I had the sheet of paper with the diagnosis and the list

of symptoms I'd logged over the last month. Dizziness, nausea, jelly legs, feet on fire, vertigo . . . There was a knock on the side window.

'Is that the list?'

'Yes.'

'Show it here.'

He shielded the sheet of paper from the rain while he scanned the list up and down. Then he turned it over to make sure that there was nothing on the back.

'And this is your phone number?'

'Yes.'

'Sound,' he said, folding the sheet into his anorak. 'You've set up the payment?'

'It will transfer the moment I get what I need.'

That statement hung in the grey light, the rain spilling off the hood of his anorak. 'Make sure it does, I don't want meeting you again and you don't want meeting me again. That would make neither of us happy.'

He straightened up and struck the roof a heavy wallop with his open hand before turning away.

Halloran

You wouldn't know what sort of shit you'd come across out here: fridges and washing machines and bags of domestic rubbish; abandoned cars once in a while, burntout vans. Wads of silage cover as well, twisted into balls and fucked into drains and culverts; all sorts of shit.

I came across two hundred bottles of piss once. No

labelling or source markings on any of them. I thought it was whiskey when I first came upon them, a stash of whiskey, the same colour and everything. What the hell was a load of whiskey doing out in the open air like this I wondered. But there was no mistaking it when I screwed the cap off one of them – piss, two hundred plastic bottles of stale piss.

But these other things I'm talking about – pages glaring white against the burnt heather, fanned out across twenty or thirty yards. And two heavy rubbish bags torn back from the mouth, ragged strips flapping in the breeze. These old manilla folders lying across each other. A couple of hundred I thought at first. Later I would learn that this particular cache contained over three hundred and seventy files. Some had already been opened by the breeze and the pages were scattered off in a stream across the bog – some snagged in the heather, yellowed and bleached from sun and rain.

Overhead a massive blue sky with a few clouds and a thin breeze blowing through the knee-high heather. And if it was odd to be out here in late November in the middle of the bog looking at a cache of files labelled with names and numbers it was no less odd than the files themselves – these old manilla folders which obviously dated from a time before our digital age. And that's what struck me about them, not the fact that they were scattered here in the bog but that they themselves had been cut adrift from a world which had passed on.

I took out the phone and snapped a few pictures,

tagged them with a time, date and GPS reference and then gathered up as much as I could to carry out to the van on the road. Three trips before I had the whole lot gathered up. Then I drove into the village and called on Nevin because he was the guard on duty that day.

Of course Nevin was glad to see me.

Nevin

I was not glad to see him.

Community wardens – they're a fucking nuisance, don't let anyone tell you otherwise. Bad news and nothing but. They have this arsehole of a job fostering relationships or mediating between the County Council and the community. And this gives them some sort of quasi-judicial powers – slapping fines for parking offences and various environmental infractions and signage violations and so on. Then monitoring the Nitrates Directive, Farm Plastics regulations, various quarrying guidelines and turf-cutting directives . . . all these new regulations which do nothing but criminalise so many rural practices and make the ordinary guard's position awkward in the community.

So you have to be cautious when you see those lads pulling up in their little vans outside the barracks. Halloran and the hi-viz jacket on him.

I was sorting through a pile of summonses when he stood in the door.

'You're flat out,' he said.

'Doing a bit,' I conceded. 'What can I do for you?' I wanted him to get to the point quickly because I knew full well that anything he had to say to me would bring nothing but trouble and hassle.

'There's something in the van you should look at.'

I sat back and shook my head. 'I've told you before, if I go out and find that it's a lump of silage cover you've pulled out of a drain or a culvert I won't be happy.'

'It's not silage cover.'

'Or a few fucking bags of rubbish.'

'It's not rubbish.'

'But it's something stupid no doubt.'

'Come out and have a look, it'll save time guessing.'

So I followed him outside into the grey afternoon. Halloran opened the back door of the van and I saw the pile of folders lying in a heap. I flicked over a couple of pages, then threw them back.

'Let me guess. Out on Shannamaragh bog.'

'Yes.'

'Beyond the handball alley?'

'Yes.'

'That's the third time in as many weeks.'

'The third?'

'That's what I said. You took pictures?'

'I'll send them on.'

'Okay. Grab one end, we'll carry these in.'

Blood Horizon

So I got a call about a week later.

I was changing the sheets on her bed when the phone went off in my pocket; a text message with a name and policy number topping a connected list of dates and place names and other info.

'Did someone call?'

Sarah stood teetering in the doorway wearing a fresh set of pyjamas, her hair damp from the shower. I put the phone in my jacket. 'No, just a text from work, nothing that can't wait.'

'You can't stay with me for ever.'

'Just a few more days, you're on the mend.'

'You know that's not true, there's no sign of me getting better. Still puking and sweating myself into oblivion.'

'Get into bed. I have a good feeling about the next few days.'

'You live in a world of optimism.'

'You have to have faith.'

Later that evening I looked up the insurance company. When I found the number I got into the car and drove twenty miles to the far side of Westport and pulled in on the side of the road. I took out a second phone I'd bought earlier that day, and with the other phone open in my hand I rang the insurance company. With a bit of stumbling and stammering I submitted the name and policy number and RSI number. Then the security questions: the mother's maiden name was Reidy and the godchild's name was Eoghan. And that's it, I was through. Now I had complete access to a new medical insurance policy.

'How can I help you, sir?' the voice asked sweetly.

I had my retreat ready. 'Actually I was just checking up on our insurance policy. We have moved house recently and all our documentation has got messed up in transit.'

'And you want to change the address?'

'No, that's fine, the change of address is only for the next few months. All I wanted to do was to check that I remembered the codes and the passwords to it. But it's fine now.'

'Yes it is, sir.'

'Okay so.'

'Is there anything else, sir?'

'No, that's fine, thank you.'

So I said goodbye, and before I could finish the call properly I threw open the door of the car, leaned out and got sick.

Plasma Chorus I

A couple of nights later. Halloran on the high stool, five or six druids like himself along the bar, well down in their pints. The street lights beyond the window have come up and the village is asleep in its sodium glow; a quiet night in the middle of the week. Behind the bar,

Shamie Thornton is standing with his back to the optics, his arms folded across his chest.

Halloran has the floor.

'A big pile of summonses on the desk when I went into him. Stroking through them with the pen.'

'You didn't spot our name on any of them?'

'I didn't spot yours if that's what you're asking?'

'If you're so worried you can ask him yourself soon enough – he'll be on Morrison's corner with his flashlight in another hour if you want to know.'

'That's his haunt all right.'

'In fairness to him he's not the worst; he has a job to do like anyone else and he gets little enough thanks for doing it in a place like this.'

'He's smart too, the same lad; he didn't make sergeant at twenty-eight for nothing.'

'And he'll square with you – but he'll let you know he's squaring with you. It's not so long ago he served me with a summons – it was six o clock in the evening and I was sprawled out on the couch watching the news when this hand reached in the small window over me and dropped the envelope down on top of me. Only that I saw the gold button on the cuff of the jacket I would never have known who it was. He must have spotted me through the window.'

'So were all these files named?'

'They were all named from what I could see, no one I recognised. I just handed them over to him; he took the lot into the barracks with him.'

'And he wasn't pleased?'

'According to him this is the third one in three weeks, the third load that's been found on the bog.'

'That's hardly a coincidence.'

'Hardly, there's talk of someone attempting to discredit the Health Board, trying to make them look foolish.'

A swell of laughter runs along the bar. 'By Jesus, they have their work cut out for themselves trying to make that crowd look foolish.'

'They'd want to be up early in the morning all right.'

'They need very little help to look bad and that's a fact.'

Halloran is in his element. It is too early for a consensus like this to close out a night. There could be telling on it yet.

Plasma Chorus II

The following Sunday, Halloran standing on Morrison's corner.

It's coming up to half eleven but there's still time for a fag before he goes down to Mass. He'll wander down when he has this last one smoked – give the priest time to put on his vestments. Then he'll stand at the back of the church with the rest of the true believers.

The last cars move down the street, parking along the Westport road, out past the grotto.

A few pints after Mass, he decides. He's stayed away

from it the last few days and he feels good about it. But you can have too much of that as well. It's good to get out and meet people; it doesn't do to get too cooped up in yourself.

A minute later he is joined by a man with whom he exchanges a few words. The opening topics are easily brushed aside; yes, the weather has taken up but not before time either, there's been a solid month of rain but there's a break promised later in the week . . . The man leans towards Halloran and lowers his voice.

'Tell me, what's the word on Emmett Coyne?'

'The last I heard he wasn't good.'

'So I believe.'

'I met Alison coming out of Durkan's two days ago. She had the kids with her and she looked harassed; I hated stopping her but you couldn't not ask either, I couldn't let her pass.'

'You could not.'

'Seemingly he lost a lot of blood while he was lying there. A vein or an artery in his leg was severed and he was very lucky that he didn't bleed out. But when he was transfused at the hospital he reacted very badly. Seemingly he picked up all sorts of infections with it – whatever the cause they don't know. Anyway, they have him jacked up on antibiotics and that's all I know. I didn't want quizzing her too much with the kids and everything.'

'I suppose no one's allowed in to see him?'

'No, he's in Intensive Care. Alison was in a few times

but he was out cold. The two kids haven't been in to see him and she's having an awful time trying to explain it to them.'

'He was a lucky man. I saw the truck on Corcoran's low-loader heading over Kilsallagh that evening. It was some sight – there wasn't a panel that wasn't buckled or twisted and two big holes torn in the tank.'

'It slid down on its side when it left the road.'

'About a hundred feet – Christ he was lucky.'

'I'll leave it so and call to the house when he's home.'

'He'd do it himself if it was one of us.'

'He would and nothing surer.' Halloran dropped the butt and ground it with the sole of his shoe. 'God willing he'll pull through. Time to wander down,' he said.

They set off together; down the quiet street lined with cars. At the church gate they stood for a moment to throw a few coins into the collection box for the Knights of Malta.

Plasma Chorus III

Halloran and the lads in the bar again. A Thursday night, generally one of the quietest in the week but word has spread. In a small community these things have to be talked out. So the lads have turned out and with Halloran's arrival there is now a quorum, they can start the discussion. 'In fairness, he's been driving that truck for how long now – ten, twelve years . . .?'

'It must be that anyway, it's a good ten years since he

took the job over from Joe Needham.'

'Twelve years, I'd say.'

'Driving those narrow roads and never spilling a drop or getting a scratch on her till today.'

'And you could set your watch by him five mornings a week, going along the line at ten minutes past eight.'

'I used to see him from the kitchen window.'

'But it wasn't a mechanical failure?'

'No, it wasn't a mechanical failure. I was talking to Mairtín who came upon him first, and he said you could see where the verge had given way under the wheels just as he came round the bend.'

'This is the bend before Tully bridge?'

'Yes, the bend before you rise up onto it – the whole margin gave way under the wheels.'

'And once she started to tip at all.'

'Straight over.'

'Straight over.'

'And that road as well, it's deadly dangerous.'

'It's high and it's narrow and it's twisty.'

'And it's all potholes – once you leave the main road at Katney's till you arrive above at the crossroads for the Killary there's nothing but potholes, pure gravel underneath it and it was only a matter of time before someone took a spill off it.'

'And with all the rain we've had this past month.'

'It hasn't stopped raining since Halloween.'

'That's what softened the margin, all that run-off down the incline towards the river.'

'Well, they might do something with it now.'

'They'll have to do something with it, there's a big bite gone out of the side of it, it's sectioned off with tape and bollards.'

'And is it still open, the road?'

'It's still open, it was open yesterday evening, it's either keep it open or have cars do a ten-mile detour to take a three-mile spin into town.'

'They were up there yesterday, a County Council crew going around with levelling rods and tapes – Marcus Conway was there.'

'That's Conway's thing all right – bridges and roads and that kind of thing.'

'They might do something with it so, not before time either.'

'They'd want to do something or they better not go coming round here in the spring looking for votes in the Council elections. They'll be told where to go.'

'And the milk tank torn to shreds?'

'Seemingly it slid down the incline and tore a big strip out of the side of it, a thousand gallons of milk then washing down into the river as far as the hatchery.'

'Tore open like a bag of Tayto.'

And so it winds on. This is the news going through its village cycle. Nothing much added to it or clarified but men will bring it home to wives and families and this is how lives in a small village hold together.

Halloran looks at the watch. Twenty past eleven, not too bad. One more pint and he'll head.

So all I needed now was a referral letter.

That's why I was sitting across from a GP who had never seen me before but who was now gazing at the small pile of notes that lay on the desk between us. Twenty in all, totalling €1,000, a good price for the single page that would give Sarah access to the monoclonal treatment that the secondaries in her liver urgently needed.

It was clear to me the moment I had stepped into his office that I had miscalculated. I had come braced for an encounter with someone who carried himself with the same blunt belligerence as the man who had met me in the car park, someone fashioned to the same crude responses. This, in my short experience, was how I imagined criminals carried themselves. What I met instead was a broken man who offered nothing at all in the way of combat or belligerence. Whatever fear or dismay my presence may have caused him, it was well sunk beneath a fatalism that had him already reaching for a headed sheet of paper and filling out the first details before I had properly explained myself.

'This will go out in the post tomorrow morning?'

'That's what you want?'

'That's what I want.'

We had nothing else to say to each other. I was halfway to the door when he called.

'Watch this.'

In his left hand he held the sheaf of notes between

thumb and forefinger; in his right, he held a cheap plastic lighter. He brought the lighter to the notes and ignited the flame. The flame caught, and he turned the notes so that the flame consumed them all the way up to his hand. Then two steps to the window and he dropped what remained of the flaming notes into the rubbish bin. He turned to me.

'You saw that.'

The pleading look in his eyes left me in no doubt as to what he meant.

'If I don't get my letter I saw nothing.'

'You'll get your letter.'

I left him standing there in the smoky air. As I was getting into the car, the fire alarm went off.

Plasma Chorus IV

It's into December now, Christmas only a few weeks away. Nevertheless, there are a few men along the bar. Shamie Thornton is glad that anyone at all is coming out for a pint – he knows well that there is nothing as lonely as an Advent barman.

Halloran is running late – the topic is up and running but he hasn't missed much. He stands inside the door for a moment shrugging himself out of a bulky anorak: it's rainy and blustery out tonight. He is quick to pick up the note of disbelief that drives tonight's topic.

'How the hell is it possible to give a man the wrong blood?'

'In this day and age?'

'You'd think that with everything they know it would be a simple thing to get that right?'

'However it happened, it's happened, and he's on life support as of yesterday evening.'

'I still can't get over it, don't they have records and files? Christ, it's hardly a year since he was in with gall-stones – surely to God they had a record of his blood group and whatever then?'

'Was it a year ago?'

'It was less than a year ago, about eleven months; I'll tell you how I know. I was in Castlebar at the time because the tax was up on the car, and I was just coming out of the County Council offices when I remembered he was in – so I called in to see him, just a walk around the corner. Sitting on the side of the bed he was, reading the paper. His only worry was that he wouldn't get the whole thing done before Christmas and that he'd have to come back again in the New Year.'

'And that was a year ago?'

'That was a year ago.'

'And he went under the knife for that?'

'He did go under the knife. They sent him home for the Christmas and brought him back in the New Year. They don't do procedures like that in December because the hospital is clogged up with people signing themselves in for the Christmas.'

'But that's what I can't understand; if he had surgery they surely had all his records on file?'

'Seemingly there was some error in his file. Either that or his blood group had changed since the surgery.'

'Your blood group can't change, can it?'

'How would I know?'

'You're asking the wrong man.'

'Not in any way I know of.'

'So he got the wrong blood and that was it.'

'That was it – everything came to a halt.'

'A total collapse?'

'Total collapse.'

'Jesus Christ.'

'Just like you'd put diesel into a petrol engine. You'll go a few miles of the road but that's about it, you'll soon pull over to the verge.'

'I'd rather you put diesel into me than the wrong blood.'

'You might get further on it, all right. It could hardly be more dangerous, a total organ collapse and now he is on life support. They are waiting for the rest of the family to come.'

'Jimmy and Oliver and the sister in London?'

'Agnes?'

'Agnes, that's her.'

'That's one phone call you wouldn't want getting.'

'You can say that again.'

The mood is set in gloom now. So much disbelief has exhausted it.

'It's not all bad news, though.'

'How so?'

'I was at the bottle bank the other evening and I met J.J. I asked him how Sarah was doing. Seemingly she's getting on well, improving. Her first treatment didn't go so well so he moved her to that private clinic in Galway. Apparently she is doing much better.'

'I'm glad of that, Sarah was always nice. As for himself – it wouldn't bother me if I never spoke to the cunt.'

'Same as that, there's no nature in him.'

'Never was, the first day ever.'

'But what were you doing at the bottle bank?'

'What does anyone do at a bottle bank?'

'You were throwing in a few jam jars, hardly anything more?'

'Jam jars, my hole.'

'That's the first sign of a problem, you know?'

'What, jam?'

'Not jam, drinking at home like that. That's how it starts.'

Halloran nods to Shamie for another pint. He won't stay out late tonight; home early and a mug of tea and a sandwich, then half an hour of Sky News before he turns into bed. He has an early start in the morning.

Nevin

I spotted him again today, Halloran. Around one o'clock, he had the van parked in front of the chemist. There he was with the cup of tea and the sandwich up on the dash. I didn't stop – I just waved the hand and kept going – if you got stuck talking to that lad you could be there all day.

I watched him once, out on his rounds. It was about a year ago and I was back in Altóir delivering a summons to Ja Frazier. It was early in the afternoon when I got there, about two o'clock, and who did I see through the window but Ja himself stretched out on the couch sleeping, the television on – *Countdown*, something like that on it – and the buck himself snoring his head off in the middle of the day. There was no reason to disturb him – I dropped the summons in the window down on top of him and left him there.

Coming home, I took the high road over Thallabawn bog with the big view out over it. And who was there on the low road, pulling up in the van only Halloran. I pulled over on the side of the road to watch him; I always wondered what it was he got up to out there alone on the bogs.

He got out of the van and took the hi-viz jacket from the seat beside him. Then he went around the back and pulled out a pair of wellingtons and slipped off his shoes and threw them in. There was no rush about him, these things got done in their own time, and, if I were to tell the truth, it was a pleasure watching a man about his work with no hurry on him. Things were allowed to expand to their full weight and measure. He took out his mobile phone and spent a few moments looking at it, then stowed it away in the pocket. Now he was ready. He took off over the bog, a long stride carrying him along swiftly as if his feet hardly touched the ground at all. I watched him walk on, a low winter sun slanting across the day and Halloran walking across the burnt bog. But where the fuck was he going? Nothing ahead of him as far as I could see but red bog all the way out to the slopes of Sheaffrey, miles of it in every direction. And now the rain coming on. Clouds swelling on the horizon, rolling in from the west. If the fucker gets caught out in that . . .

And then he was gone. Disappeared from sight. The sun and a dip of the land and he was nowhere to be seen.

And I was all alone then looking out over the empty land and feeling very foolish in myself as if Halloran and the day had made an eejit out of me, led me here to this spot on a winter's afternoon so that I might spend my time looking out over a tract of bog with nothing in it. And as I stood there I was glad to be alone, glad that no one could see how ridiculous I was or have any part of my foolishness. And I stayed like that for a while with the sky darkening over the bog and the rain closing in and no sign of Halloran anywhere in the distance.

And then I had to laugh. That was Halloran all right, a law unto himself. Let him off I thought. He's no worry, the same buck. Out there on his rounds, making work for both of us.

Halloran and the hi-viz jacket on him.

Joyride to Jupiter

Nuala Ní Chonchúir

The year was set up wrong from the start – wavering sun on New Year's Day and snow on the seventeenth of March that stopped every parade from Malin to Mizen. I didn't know the whole thing would fall asunder but I knew something was going to go wrong, as sure as I knew west was west.

I first took notice at Easter when Teresa disrupted the plans for our usual dinner.

'We won't have any of that yoke,' she said. 'What do you call it? Legs, you know. Woolly. It jumps.' She leapt and laughed; I was startled – it was a move so unlike her. 'Woolly little fellas,' she said, and wiggled her fingers.

'Are you talking about lambs?'

'Lamb!' She seized the word like a biblical wolf. 'Lamb. Yes. None of that.'

So it started that way. Teresa began to change her mind about things that were sacred to her: there were no more fire-and-wine Friday nights. No more wedge heels or skirt suits. And she wanted sweet food to eat above all else: custard, Petits Filous, Jelly Tots.

One Saturday morning I asked if she was going to the hair salon; she had missed two Saturdays by then.

'Is it salon or saloon?' she said. 'I'm beginning to think it's saloon.' She made a gun of her fingers. 'Bang bang!' She cackled and I sat and looked at her, wondering what was happening to us.

At first I thought she must have found another man and she was changing for his pleasure, but she was never missing, never anywhere but at work or at home. Then she left work abruptly and gusted about the house putting things in odd places – loo roll in the drinks cabinet, frozen peas under the stairs. And she hummed high, pointless tunes all the time. She talked less, too, as if words didn't hold weight anymore.

The push-me-pull-you of married life, all the compromises and stand-offs were waning. We became separate and distant but I was not going to give up on Teresa, not at all. I got a girl to come in – Marguerite – and she's gentle with Teresa, a gift.

'How's the form, Mr Halpin?' Marguerite says, bustling in the door in the mornings, all wide-hipped and capable.

'You make me feel old with your "Mr Halpin",' I tell her.

'The thing is, Mr Halpin, you *are* old.'

That's the way Marguerite is. But she cherishes Teresa, keeps her voice low and coaxing with her, and Teresa smiles, accepts her firm, friendly help in a way that is contrary to the woman I married. My Teresa never wants help; she's a one-woman show.

Before her mind sagged she was bad at being sick – a play actor. She took pleasure in her performance as Disgruntled Patient. She luxuriated over tablet-taking – lined them up like gems to be admired. Each headache foretold a brain haemorrhage, every leg creak was bone cancer. She endured but enjoyed hospital visits, complaining non-stop. Now she is truly sick and she neither knows nor cares. My poor, wandering girl.

This morning I found Teresa standing by the chest of drawers in a vest and nothing else. She had taken off the pants and blouse I'd dressed her in an hour before.

'What are you doing, sweetheart?' I said.

'I can't find my tracksuit.'

'You don't have a tracksuit.'

She wrinkled her nose and made slits of her eyes. This we called her angry koala face, and, when I used to say, 'Oh, the angry koala is here,' it melted things, and the koala went back up its tree. But Teresa continued to frown, thinking – if she thinks much at all – that I was thwarting her.

'Tracksuit,' she said.

'I'll tell you what, why don't I go to Penneys and get you a tracksuit? When Marguerite gets here.'

'Marguerite? Who's that?'

And then she laughed because laughter falls from her now as it never did; it falls and pools around us, the one good thing. I knelt and stepped her feet into her knickers and pulled them up. I put her arms into the sleeves of her blouse and fiddled with the tiny buttons. She was doll-like in her pliancy. I kissed her forehead.

'You're my dolly,' I said.

She put her arms around my neck and we held each other for a long time.

. ★

I started my jaunts, on the little train that snakes up and down the shopping centre, shortly after I found Marguerite. She said I should get out of the house. 'Out from under my feet' was what she actually said. Today Marguerite isn't here so I have to bring Teresa with me to the shops. The train driver sees us; he waves and stops the engine.

'All aboard,' he says, tipping his head towards the carriages. He asks where we're headed and I tell him. 'I'll spin you down so.'

Teresa sits with her hands folded in her lap, staring regally at the shoppers sloping through the centre. It is the same expression that shy children wear when they sit on the train – they want to be there, enjoying the trip, but it embarrasses them too because people turn to look. These are the kids I love the most. They are rooted in themselves and they shoulder the world warily, like I did as a child.

We sit in our tiny compartment and I sing a verse to Teresa, from a song we knew as youngsters: 'The Dingle train is whistling now / 'Tis time to make the tay / That's what they said in Tralee town / When evening came the way.' She looks at me like she has never heard this before, so I sing it again, trying to plunge the tune into her mind, willing her to sing along. 'The Dingle train is whistling now / 'Tis time to make the tay . . . '

In Penneys Teresa stands in front of the make-up rack, picking up lipsticks and pots of eyeshadow and blusher; she is contained, at a distance from everything. She never did have that Irish capacity to linger, after dinner or at pub closing time – when she was done with a place she was done, and we were always the first to leave a gathering. But, in her new state, she lingers over everything, examining and waiting, with stores of patience that weren't hers before. I leave her and do my bit of shopping with one eye clamped on her. She stands, studying the make-up containers with care. I come back, and, when Teresa sees me, she hands over the little pots one at a time. I read out their names to her, before pressing them back into their slots.

'Sparkling Miracle. Glamour Queen. Mystic Purple. Yes Eye Can! Nude Candy. Fairytale. Disco Diva. Joyride to Jupiter.' Joyride to Jupiter makes her laugh like a girl – a sweet gurgle from her throat – and I hold it up and ask, 'Would you like this?'

'Can I have it?' She takes the small tub of eyeshadow and clutches it as if it's a jewel from Derrynaflan. 'Joyride to Jupiter,' Teresa says, looking at it in wonder.

I am the worm in the dementia apple; I will tunnel through it, I will not let it get the better of us. Things are different, and will be different, but there are things I can hang on to.

I take Teresa to our bedroom. The room smells of talc and dirty socks; it has always smelt like this. I undress her with care, tumble out of my own clothes, and we tuckle under the duvet. Her skin is buttermilk soft, and I hold her close and caress the neat hollow in her back.

'Chancing your arm, as usual,' she says.

'You love it,' I say.

She presses her breasts to my chest and heat rushes through the length of me. I have long treasured the honesty of our lovemaking; we could always look each other in the eye in the middle of it all and grin, heated up though we were. That hasn't changed, though she gazes at me with bewilderment sometimes now. But she looks happily bewildered, because I know what to do to make her feel good and she responds as she always did, with grunts of pleasure and fierce kisses.

Afterwards we eat. This has been our ritual for fifty years. Today I have a bowl of cherries beside the bed and I de-pip them one at a time with my lips, and, like a bird, I drop the soft flesh into Teresa's mouth. She sucks and chews the scarlet pulp and smiles up at me. It pleases me somehow that she is childlike; she is the girl I courted and won. Gone is the snappy, impatient Teresa she grew into. Back is good-natured, sunny Teresa.

★

The children on the train in the shopping centre are often plump. I love that slight pudginess that most kids have, their hands 'swollen with candy' as the song goes. Sometimes, when they are struggling to board, I lift them into their seats and their cushiony flesh amazes me. How so soft, so wielding? If my hands stay a little too long on their fat waists they shrug me off, impatient to take their seats. A mother gives me a sharp look from time to time. But it's worth it for the sweet feeling imprinted on my hands.

I travel up and down on the train for hours at a time. The driver doesn't mind; he only ever charges me one fare. Once, instead of going to the shopping centre, I went to Heuston Station and took a real train as far as Portarlington. I squinted at the views from the window – a hump in a field was either a very small cow or a very large rabbit; either way I didn't care, it didn't interest me. The muffled tannoy announcements were irritating; it took me ages to figure out what the announcer was saying. I heard 'sex and savages' for 'snacks and beverages'. I drank caramel-tinged tea from a paper cup and paid €2.10 for the experience.

No, all in all I prefer my little shopping-centre train to the real thing. There are better things to see, like the balloon man and the sweetie cart and all the children with their families who trundle about together, lost in a fug of shopping and fast food.

Our daughter comes to visit; she doesn't come much – some long-nursed wariness of me keeps her away. She turns up less and less since Teresa began to flounder, since she began to forget things and wander and dress strangely.

'Seven walnuts a day, that's what she needs,' our daughter says to me. 'Seven walnuts a day, Mam, OK?' she half-shouts at her mother.

'Oh, yes,' Teresa says, as if this makes sense to her. She blinks at our daughter, trying to place her.

'Walnuts?' I ask.

'For her memory,' she says. 'They have polyphenolics or something. Anyway, they help.' She plucks at the hood of Teresa's tracksuit with her fingers. 'What in God's name is she wearing? It's beat onto her; she'd be mortified if she could see herself.'

'Your mother asked me for it. She wanted it.'

Our daughter pokes through the things on the top of the chest of drawers, to distract herself from Teresa, who is perched on the bed in her pink velour tracksuit, looking ridiculous and wrong but content.

'What's this shite?' our daughter says, holding up the pot of Joyride to Jupiter. 'This stuff is total crap. It's for teenagers.'

Teresa barrels across the room and slaps our daughter's cheek, *phwack*. She grabs the eyeshadow and pockets it. The three of us stand, suspended.

'Jesus, Mam.' Our daughter holds her cheek and moves towards Teresa but I wedge myself between them.

'She was a good mother to you,' I say. 'A good mother. She needs your respect.'

'What she *needs* is to be in a home. A hospital. Somewhere.' Our daughter grabs her handbag and heads across the room. She turns. 'But you, you selfish old prick, you have to have it your own way, as usual. She needs help!' She slams the door.

'She has help,' I say, pulling Teresa close to me. 'You're OK, aren't you? My girl, my love.'

*

The pub is not the kind of pub I like; it's manufactured, unorganic. Even the barmen look plastic. I sit, feeling stiff, on a green leather banquette, under a television screen the size of a car. But the pub is here for the convenience of the shopping centre, and, today, it is certainly convenient. I sup a lager then gulp another. I crunch through a bag of bitter nuts and read a discarded *Herald*. More lager and then a Jameson, to pile sour upon sour.

Very little makes me happy anymore, and, conversely, it takes very little to make Teresa madly happy. It is all topsy-turvy. Teresa was a terror, really; the girls she worked with were afraid of her and probably didn't like her much. Not one of them has come to see her since she left work. Not one.

I down the last of the whiskey. By the time I take my place on the little train, my ears are buzzing and my stomach doesn't feel the best. A slender girl with huge grey eyes takes the seat beside me.

'Hello,' I say.

'Hi.'

'And what's your name, little lady?'

'Mary-Kate.'

'You're not serious?' I place my hand on her leg. 'I had a dog called Mary-Kate once. A big fucking ugly wolfhound. A horrible bitch, she was.'

The girl's face contorts, and I put my arm around her. 'Not to worry,' I say. 'She's dead now. Dead as doorknobs, Mary-Kate.'

'Mam,' the girl says, a plaintive squeak as she looks over her shoulder for her mother.

The train lurches forward, and my belly gets left behind until it lands in my throat, and I throw up, all over myself and the train and Mary-Kate.

'There's a crow I want to pick with you, Mr Halpin,' Marguerite says, meeting me in the hallway.

'Oh, yes?' I have a wogeous headache; the hangover is already pounding through my body and it is barely two o'clock. I can still feel the pinch of the security guard's fingers braceleting my arm.

The train driver came to my defence.

'Leave him go,' he said, putting his hand on the security guard's chest. 'Are you all right?'

I swayed and retched, muttered, 'Sorry, sorry,' over and over. I tried to wipe the sick from my jacket.

'You're barred,' the security man said. 'Do you hear me? Don't let me catch you near the place again.' He walked me to the exit.

A single coral rose bloomed from a patch of dirt at the shopping centre's door. I plucked it.

'You can't take that,' the security man said.

'Watch me,' I said. He lunged for the rose and I ran. When I got near the bus stop I slowed to a trot. I walked home, carrying the flower for Teresa in front of me like a chalice.

'Mr Halpin? Are you all right?' Marguerite says, taking my arm.

'I'm grand, grand.'

She puts her hands on her hips. 'You never told me Teresa was going into Emerald Sunsets.'

'She isn't.'

'Well, that's not what your daughter says. She was round here earlier looking for Teresa's pension book. She says Teresa has a place in the home from next month.'

I sit on the bottom of the stairs and weep. I know already that I will acquiesce.

The driveway up to Emerald Sunsets is a blood valley of fuchsia. Teresa and I sit in the back; our daughter drives, glances at me in the rear-view.

'It's just to orientate her. Give her a feel for the place,' she says.

I grunt.

The three of us walk around the home behind the owner. I gag on the faecal smell and hang back when we intrude on the rooms of sleeping residents. There is a horrible calm to the place.

'We'll make sure Mrs Halpin gets the best of rooms, the best of care,' the owner says, a line she spools out for every family no doubt.

'See, it's lovely,' our daughter says, once we're back in her car. 'She'll settle in no time.'

I take Teresa's hand in mine and say nothing.

★

Teresa sits on the bed; I pull her nightdress over her head. She giggles and nods.

'You have a lovely smile,' she says. I want to cry because that was one of the first things she ever said to me when we met at a dance in the Banba Hall.

I make love to her slowly and carefully, enjoying every press of her body. I push my hands into her hair and feel her breath on my neck; it's like nothing has changed. She is my girl, my small thing, my tender, yielding doll. There has always been a softness about Teresa and me. Some couples look like they'd break each other in bed but not us; we always left our spiky selves at the bedroom door.

Afterwards I hand her a paradise square, and she nibbles at it, pulls out the sultanas with her fingers, licks the jam and savours the cake's almond tang. When she has finished her cup of tea I pat her lips with a napkin and she lies back.

'There now, Teresa.'

Soon she drifts and settles, her little silver head quiet

beside me. I lift my pillow. Teresa pushes and fights; I stop, think of letting go, but I grip the sides of the pillow tighter and carry on. I hold it down, push my own face into the top of it and sob. Then, jerk one. Jerk two. And she's gone. I pull the pillow off her face and take her in my arms until I fall asleep myself. The detritus of my mind gets locked down in dreams – Emerald Sunsets, paradise squares, our daughter's nervous glancing in the rear-view, dancing in the Banba Hall, a single coral rose, the spongy hump of the pillow. And though Teresa is safe in my arms, even in sleep, I know she is gone.

City of Glass

Molly McCloskey

The locals used to say of my father-in-law that they remembered him when he came to town on a bicycle. They meant before the Mercedes, before the big hotel and the multiple properties and the house with extensive gardens. They didn't mean it nicely, as in, *Well done, you.* They meant: *You're still nobody, underneath it all.* He is dead now, he grew gnarled and bitter, then expired in his sleep without a sound. His son is no longer my husband.

I came to town riding shotgun in the van of a Donegal farmer. I'd hitched a lift from him somewhere just beyond Ballybofey. It was May, and the gorse was all aflame along the hillsides, and the farmer wanted me to kiss him when he dropped me off. I can't remember if I did. I might've. He was harmless, if grizzled and a bit smelly, and I was twenty-four and saw adventure in each unprecedented moment. It was 1989, and the good old days were about to begin.

They would come to an end six years later, during a freakishly hot summer, in a bedroom not five kilometres from where I might or mightn't have kissed that farmer, where on the floor there were heaps of clothes and broken glass that had been there for months, on a day I wished could go on forever.

★

I had come to Ireland from New York, via Heathrow and Holyhead. It was early evening when I disembarked in Dublin, my stuffed pack like a snail's shell enormous on my back. I'd booked into a hostel on Gardiner Street but instead of dropping my pack I stopped for a pint. I chose at random a pub called Doyle's, where a guy named Declan joined me. Declan's line was that he had recently been released from prison for bombing a house. He wanted me to think: *IRA*. He wanted me to think: *Ho! How hot is that!* He said I should forget about the hostel and spend the night at a B&B with him. I had no desire to go to a B&B with Declan, though we did make a night of it, moving from Doyle's to Bachelor's on Ormond Quay, or maybe it was the Ormond on Bachelor's Walk. Everywhere was too brightly lit and the sofas were all covered in the same prickly maroon upholstery that reminded me of AstroTurf. When the spins set in, Declan walked me to the hostel and left me there.

The next day I hitched out of Dublin. In the grey old days, such things were still possible. The motorways did not yet exist, and I took a local bus to the edge

of the city and stood on a grassy verge as the lorries
rumbled past. It wasn't long before I got a lift. I climbed
high into the cab and the driver offered me a Silk
Cut and we smoked companionably, like old cronies.
From my perch I could see over the hedgerows into the
fields. They looked soggy, like sponges you could wring
out. Low walls crawled this way and that. The sky was
the colour of dirty soap suds. The driver quizzed me
about my itinerary. I told him my plan was to begin
in Donegal and move south along the coast, hitching
the rim of the Republic before boarding the ferry again
and returning to America to begin my life proper. He
answered with a quick in-suck of air and a nod like an
apostrophe. He told me I was a great girl for wandering
aimlessly around Ireland all by myself, and the way he
kept saying, *Aren't you great*, made me feel like I might
just be great.

In Donegal, I hitched from village to village, from
damp to damper hostel, living on chip butties and
Guinness and the thrill of so much sky. One night in
Killybegs, in a pub down by the harbour, I fell in with
a middle-aged couple from Derry named Bill and Lil.
Overweight and florid-faced, their exuberance tainted
with despair, Bill and Lil swept me into their orbit with
a kind of desperate generosity. They drank buckets of
Black *Ta-ar*, and I drank it with them, over a dinner
they treated me to of grilled plaice. By the pavlova
we were promising to keep in touch. We took instant
Polaroids of each other, then sat staring slack-jawed as

they developed, as though something other than our selves might appear.

After a week on the mainland, I escaped to the island of Arranmore. The weather had turned by then. The big black skies had stopped rolling in, and every day dawned fresh and clear. The afternoon I approached the middle-aged skipper in Burtonport to enquire about the next departure for the island, I was wearing a modest pair of shorts. Jimmy had a head of curls that looked like small waves breaking all over his head. He gazed up at me from the boat, gave me the sailing time, and then, with a cock-eyed leer, accused me of not wearing any underwear.

On the island I checked into a seaside hostel and sat on the pebbled shore watching the low waves slide in and out and trying to imagine, behind me, the tumbling of walls in time-lapse. I tried to hear the call of ancient things. I wanted to experience myself as a blink in the eye of time. But I just kept thinking about Jimmy. Eventually, I gave up and went down the road to Early's where I fell into conversation with a handsome dark-haired guy who told me he worked for the UN. I thought he meant a diplomat. I tried to picture this guy, who lacked the gravitas I associated with diplomats, wearing a suit and listening to simultaneous translations on a headset.

At closing time we got a bottle of wine and drank it back at the hostel, kissing a bit until I passed out. When I woke in the morning, the diplomat was gone, but he had left a note – something nice and innocuous and, well, diplomatic. I fell back to sleep, and the next time I opened my eyes, there was the hostel owner, towering over me, *arms akimbo*. When she saw I was conscious, she said, in a tone of great declarative contempt: 'You're some cookie let loose on Arranmore.' She said it as though my few hours revelling had thrown the local population into a tailspin of lust and confusion. As though I were a nightmare of modernity come to screw with their venerable traditions.

I spent the day in a fug of headachy shame, tromping the island's laneways, attempting to appear robust and Teutonic. I did not stay another night but caught the evening boat back to the mainland. As we spluttered out into the channel, Jimmy gave me the nod like an apostrophe and produced a plastic shopping bag. He asked me had I forgotten it the day before. I looked down into the bag. Inside was a tangle of pastel-coloured girls' cotton underwear – cheap-looking but new and clean.

★

Back then, if it wasn't jagged and dramatic cliff faces shearing off into the sea, and greens and blues that glistened silver in a sudden clearing after rain, it was a dreary and a stunted world. The people were ashen-faced, and lots of them were out of work. They stood in dole queues, looking iconic and fated, the way Russians used to, queuing for bread. Birth control was

illegal, a prohibition I mistook for a quaint anachron-
ism, like those laws in places like Alabama outlawing
oral sex. Remnants of middling folk bands wandered
listless and greying about the place. I felt like a time
traveller from some riotous and colourful future.

Because there wasn't much to lose, there was also
a recklessness in the air, a lack of censure that made
the place easy to fall in love with. Everyone smoked,
and no one complained about the fouled air. Driving
drunk was something people did frequently, naturally,
and without serious remorse, as though it were a harmless indulgence, like having a second piece of pie. And
everywhere were those pockets of beautiful dereliction
– the gable walls toppled, creepers laying claim to what
once had been bedrooms, floors now nothing but scutch
grass. The country was like a beautiful failure – verdant,
profound and full of laughter. There was a sense that we
were all in it together, whatever *it* was. In the pub on
Sunday mornings there were men who drove Mercedes
and were big deals at the pharmaceutical plant, and there
were others who were on the dole, and there were
guys home on leave from the Lebanon, and there were
grandmothers and children; there were christenings and
first communions, and there were holes in every family
where once had been the sisters and brothers who were
now abroad, and there were many, many funerals. It was
all this dying – it was a wonder there was anybody left
alive – that kept us mindful of the truth: that our fates
were unknown, that the great leveller awaited us all.

I decided to stay for the summer. A week after the farmer dropped me off in Sligo town I got a job at a pub and restaurant called Carroll's. It catered to the square singletons, the bank tellers, nurses and civil servants. I earned one-pound-forty an hour, taking orders for drinks I'd never heard of from people whose accents I couldn't understand.

Most nights they were three deep at the bar, and by eleven o'clock the place was sweaty and heaving with hormones. At closing time, everyone migrated to one of the two 'discos' in town − less like the shimmering palaces I'd imagined when I'd heard them spoken of and more like high-school dances. During the slow numbers, couples shuffled rigidly in tight circles, the kisses prolonged and adolescent in their monotony. When the fast songs came on, there was a great dash to the dance floor, and over the bobbing heads a field of arms flailed, as groups of women shouted into one another's faces: *I will survive . . . hey-ey-hey!*

One early evening at Carroll's, when the place was quiet, my future husband walked in.

Someone else served him, and we didn't speak. He sat alone at the end of the bar. He was wearing a crisp striped button-down shirt. He had a strong nose and broad shoulders and a way of seeming in charge of himself. I could see in a glance he had substance. He was like no other man I'd met in town. Those who frequented Carroll's struck me as dull, while the druggier guys seemed damaged and unsure, suffused by a vague, self-defeating disdain. Eddie drank his pint and put a tip on the bar and left, and though I forgot all about him, when I saw him again some weeks later, I recognised him immediately.

'I know you from Carroll's,' I said.

'Oh yeah,' he said, cool as could be, but nice.

I'd kept myself busy in the interval. I took to partying with a guy named Animal and the members of the Pretty Felons, a local pop-rock band. I'd met them at one of the edgier bars, where the stuffing erupted through the seats and the air stank of patchouli. Animal had tight curls and a driven intensity that seemed to have no possible outlet, and he was thick-chested and borderline sexy. The Felons were different, slender and listless. They had lank, rained-on-looking hair and an air of aggrieved entitlement, like people done out of an inheritance, but they were gentler than any men I had ever met. In a bedsit above a butcher's shop we smoked sprinklings of hash mixed with tobacco that burned my throat and gave me only a dim, headachy buzz. This way of getting high, so parsimonious and approximate, seemed just another instance of the way people here made do, and I would sit gloomily on the mud-brown sofa, ruminating on how history had diminished them.

One Saturday afternoon, Animal and I were smoking and drinking, and we did what everyone did back then after a few joints and several pints: we went for a drive. Out to Lissadell, where we lay on the white sand beach and watched the blue heavens pull away from us, breaking up into a profusion of dots. When I closed my eyes I felt the sunlight drifting down like snow, and I thought I'd dropped out of nowhere and landed smack in the centre of my life.

The following week, I began an affair with a married journalist.

Aiden worked for the national television station, and he was down from Dublin moving round the country covering that summer's election – all tattered bunting and megaphones on the roofs of cars and tricolour posters that buckled in the rain. He came into Carroll's one day. As I served him his meat and two veg, he looked me in the eye and said in a voice so mellifluous I nearly sank to my knees, 'You're not from here.'

Aiden was a *Gaeilgeoir*, fluent in Irish, and a passionate nationalist. In another age, he might've wandered the byways and earned his meagre crust declaiming epic poems of dispossession. As it was, he sat beside me on various bar stools expounding on key episodes in Irish history; the phrase 'eight hundred years' came up frequently. He gave the impression that he carried in his breast the collective memory of his tribe. He recited poems for me by Eoghan Rua Ó Súilleabháin, talked about the *Táin* and Cromwell and the Fenians, and how all of it related to the general election of 1989. Then he would throw back his head and laugh, with a wicked affection, at the thought of his own people hauling their tragicomic selves through history.

I had moved from town to the nearby beach village

of Rosses Point, where I shared a ramshackle Victorian with two other women. We had no washing machine, and my housemates boiled their underwear on the stovetop, then hung the bras and panties from a clothesline strung across the dank kitchen. The carpets were brown-and-tan swirl and stiff with invisible grime. In the front room where I slept there was a huge bay window that actually overlooked a bay.

I had also quit my job at Carroll's and was working at a posh restaurant in the Rosses frequented by local fat cats, old money and rich American tourists. Instead of chicken and chips, it was all *confit de canard* and *gigot d'agneau*. There were mussels plucked fresh from the rocks and the day's catch being coolly filleted on the butcher block; there were delicate little breads baked each morning and a herb garden from which we tweezed aromatic miracles, and there was always something reducing on the stove. Everything felt exquisite and fussed over, and we – the whole staff, down to the woman who ironed the aprons – carried ourselves with a slight imperiousness, as though we were the keepers of something fine.

One side of the restaurant was glass, and you could see across the inlet to Coney Island, and every night we watched the sky turn with stunning slowness from a pale sunlit blue to a richer cobalt to a navy that looked the texture of velvet. The days stretched to breaking point, and for weeks the sky didn't once turn a proper black. The rain had all but stopped. It was a rare, hot, magical summer, and every day someone would say to me, 'This isn't normal, don't go thinking this is normal,' as though to spare me the pain of a misplaced trust.

A couple of times I joined Aiden on assignments – once to a grim border county where the air was tight and oppressive. As we pulled out of the driveway of a big house where they'd been doing some filming, he asked me, by the way, what I thought of such-and-such a woman, one of the crew. He was already lining up his next lover. I was strangely unoffended by the query. I was that young.

I went to Belfast with him, too. We stayed at the Europa and had dinner at La Belle Époque. After much red wine we had our first proper fight, a drunken doozy up and down Victoria Street. There was something flouncing and erratic about the scene, one of those fights that seems contrived even as it's unfolding, like the urgent melodrama of bad theatre. By the following day all was forgiven, as though it really had been a piece of theatre. He drove me to Dublin and left me at Connolly Station from where I would take the train west, to my careless and impermanent life. As I rode the escalator up, I looked over my shoulder to where his car was waiting at the light, its windows fogged with condensation. The sky was a purply grey, and all the eaves were dripping from a just-finished rain, and I was certain that I had never loved the world in quite the way I did just then. Certainly, I was in love with him. I had told him so – an admission he rather sensationally declared an act of valour on par with the exploits of some great warrior he'd pulled out of a hat.

I smiled and thought: *whatever.*

In July, he took the family to northern Spain for six weeks.

'Six weeks!' I cried.

It wasn't that I thought I couldn't bear his absence. It was that where I came from no one went on six-week holidays. He sat up late at night at tiny kitchen tables in a scattering of rustic villages, composing letters to me, great thick packets that would arrive at my door. He wrote about the poems of Ó Raifteirí and Basque nationalism and how brave I was to love him. Often, halfway through the letter, his smooth loopy script would lapse into a jagged scrawl, the slant of lines across the page growing abruptly steeper.

Aiden was five weeks into his holiday when I met my future husband for the second time.

It was midnight on a Saturday, and I was in town drinking with some friends. Animal was there – his cameo in my life not yet concluded – and it was he who suggested we crash a wedding reception at the local hotel. The ballroom was nearly empty, and Eddie was sitting at the bar.

'I know you from Carroll's,' I said.

'Oh, yeah,' he said. He crossed his arms over his chest, nodded towards the stool beside him and said, 'What can I get you?'

I hoisted myself up and ordered a pint. We chatted

about the restaurant in the Rosses and what I was doing over this side of the world, and he told me about the people who had just got married. At some point it dawned on me that he owned the place. The family did.

I took out my Silk Cuts and said, 'Do you mind if I smoke?' and he said, 'I don't mind if you burst into flames.'

I smiled.

He asked if I'd like to go for a drink sometime.

'Sure,' I said. And then, 'But I'm not looking for anything, you know, *serious.*'

The things we say. Some of them just don't bear thinking about.

'Me neither,' he said, and took a large but seemly swallow of his Guinness.

Next thing I knew it was jaunts to all the beauty spots. There were fresh mussels in Mullaghmore and smoked salmon in country pubs and there were cool milky pints in snugs up and down the coast. I thought I had never known anyone quite so solid, quite so devoid of agendas.

With autumn came Sunday lunches with the family, gleaming crispy roasts and linen napkins, silver that made me think of medieval banquets. There were glasses for each drink course – the aperitif, the gin and tonic, the red and white wines, the liqueur – and as I sat there with a crystal tumbler heavy in my hand, I felt as though something reassuring and true had entered my life at last. It's not that the family was terribly rich; the father had come to town on a bicycle, recall, and had done okay. But there was an old-world aesthetic about their domestic lives – the civilising influence of Eddie's mother. The way they planned menus. The way they arranged flowers from the garden for their table. The way they retired to the sitting room for a smoke and a cognac after dinner, the fire crackling demurely on windswept evenings.

Eddie and I married the following summer in the church where he'd been christened. There were lots of big hats, and outside the church the women periodically clapped their palms atop them to keep them from flying off in the fresh summer gusts. Afterwards we all drank champagne and ate *boeuf en croute* and danced in a marquee to a hokey quartet, and I knew that I need never be alone again.

Within a couple of years of our marriage, the new Ireland had begun to show its face. I had my first glimpses of it on our visits to Eddie's brother. Peter and his wife Siorcha lived in the suburbs of south Dublin, and we stayed with them whenever we were up. Peter worked for one of the banks, and Siorcha had a job at an investment firm. They talked about their home alarm system the way people talk about their kids. They didn't cook anymore but ate *feckin delicious* pre-prepared meals from what Siorcha coolly called Marks and Sparks. She waxed rhapsodic about the latest addition to the line – korma! cannelloni! brie quiche! – tips that were lost on us: there was no Marks and Sparks where we lived.

Sometimes we thought Peter and Siorcha were a bit

full of themselves. We had no idea that they were merely
the vanguard, the earliest glints of materialism and convenience culture, the first trickle of what would soon
be enormous obliterating waves. I imagine that once it
happened, and their own minor indulgences were left in
the shade, they too were appalled. But by then I didn't
know them anymore.

One night, Siorcha and I found ourselves having dinner alone in Dalkey. I was trying to tell her something,
to tell her I was scared, and she was giving me the old
all-marriages-go-through-that advice. She couldn't get
what I was talking about. It wasn't her fault. Whatever
it was that was wrong with Eddie and me was too insi-
dious to explain or describe. The spirited bonhomie of
our early days was morphing into careless disregard. We
lacked direction. We couldn't get our footing. We drank
bottles of fine wine and dined on delectable food, and
it's a cliché to say it but it was the very ease of my life
that made clear it was wrong, because there was nothing
– no want, no trauma, no lack of love – that could account for my unhappiness.

It was not long after that night, in the summer of that
same year, that I found myself travelling west by train
from Dublin. I was with a man named Kevin. We were
drinking bottles of cold beer, standing in the no-man's-
land between carriages, bracing ourselves against the wall
while the floor plates shifted under our feet. It was like
being on a ride at the amusement park. The day was
glorious, and the country slid past in alternating panes of

pastoral, industrial and domestic. The fields were green and empty, or full of sheep who didn't look up when we whooshed by. Then patches of weedy cracked tarmac surrounded by cyclone fences. Then the backyards of houses, all in slots, with their propped bikes and their coal bunkers and the random flotsam of family life. And then all was green again, and there were cows where sheep had been, and a breaker's yard, and a bungalow sitting proud on a knoll. In the distance, a road on which two cars were moving tinily away from another. We leaned out the window, and the wind whipped over our faces in an invigorating wash, and I felt as alive and unencumbered as if we'd hopped a boxcar.

Kevin and I had met when he was down for a weekend from Dublin. We were in a pub, sitting with friends on a row of high stools, and we sat there for so many hours that finally I slipped, with an unusual grace, right off of mine. As though I were a sheet of paper or a feather, making its unhurried way to the floor. It didn't phase him in the least.

He was like no one I had ever met. Intelligent, self-deprecating, shockingly irreverent. All the ideas and people I took seriously, the pretensions I bowed to, the collective obsessions of the nation, everything I thought sacrosanct, Kevin lampooned. He was an autodidact. He'd never been to university but he'd read everything, including *Beowulf*. Kevin was a grafter, too. He had the fierce drive of a young man determined to be someone. He had a deal with a London publisher for his first novel and a hot agent who kept telling him he was on the brink of being big.

About a week after our first meeting I had reason to travel to Dublin. I checked into my hotel and went to meet Kevin. My appointment was in two hours. I never made it, nor did I make it the next day. By the time we boarded the train to go west, with the floor moving under us and the country sliding past in frames, the world had cracked wide open.

When we got off the train that evening, back in the town where I lived, we went to a poetry reading. There were too many people we knew there, and it was a self-destructive act that can only be explained by the compulsion illicit lovers feel to exhibit themselves. The only empty seats were in the front row, and we crept up the aisle and sat stiffly through the next hour, resisting the urge to giggle or touch each other or rise from our seats, raise our arms to the heavens and shout *Hallelujah!* The reading was being given by a fleshy guy from California with a goatee and a Latino surname who remained poignantly unaware of the scandal that was unfolding in front of him.

Afterwards, a friend named Johnny offered Kevin and me a bed for the night. He said it out of the side of his mouth, like we were on the run. Which in a way we were. But Johnny said most things out of the side of his mouth. He spoke in long circuitous sentences that ended back where they'd begun.

'Yeah, well it's a kind of ah . . . yeah, ya know a sort

of a . . . right, you know what I mean, yeah?'

Johnny's house was out in the Rosses, not far from where I'd once lived in the Victorian with the swirly carpets and the big bay window. It was on a quiet lane-way overlooking a white powder beach, a piece of real estate that would very soon be worth a fortune. The house had charm, but Johnny, who had inherited it from his parents, was too disorganised to keep it up, and the place, frankly, was a disaster area. For Kevin and me, it had the combined charms of a honeymoon cottage and a safe house. We slept in the spare bedroom, which, even in the context of the general disorder, existed on another plane of chaos. It was not simply messy, it was hazardous. On the floor, mixed in with the piles of dirty clothes and the faded paperbacks and a few split-open cigarettes, were several large isosceles triangles of broken glass, as though from a window or a picture frame. It was a sign of our own disorder that we regarded a floor full of jagged glass as amusing. Kevin christened it the City of Glass. He was a master of literary allusion. We spent hours in there, lying in bed discussing books and people, our fathers and mothers and their broken marriages, our plans, our hopes, the funny and the sad things that had happened in our lives. It felt less like we had met than like we had rediscovered one another, and in that find-ing was a happiness that bordered on delirium.

On the third day, we decided to walk across the big open fields out the back of the house to a pub in the village. It was hot – freakishly hot – and our progress was slow. Our initial brisk gait degenerated to a trudge. It was becoming hallucinatory. I was a few steps behind Johnny and Kevin, and with the sweat rolling off them and their pale skin so unsuited to the sun they made me think of malarial explorers on the verge of expiry. It is one of my most enduring images of Kevin, plodding across the field in safari gear and a straw boater, though of course he was wearing nothing of the sort.

Upon arriving, we collapsed dramatically at a picnic table in the gravel yard. The bay was an icy blue. I could hear Kevin talking to Johnny but I may as well have been listening to my own thoughts. My boundaries had dissolved, and he was as much me as I was. To leave him, or to lose him, would have been as impossible just then as taking leave of myself.

That evening, back at Johnny's place, when the air had cooled and we were lying in the front yard, our dinner plates scattered like frisbees on the grass, I felt utterly, deludedly complete. At that moment, I would happily have committed the rest of my life to laughing at Kevin's clever witticisms, following the train of his allusions, catering to his inexhaustible desires, and getting drunk. I didn't ever want to work again, to earn money, or even to be required to think straight. I never wanted to leave that house or the City of Glass or the Rosses. I saw no reason – no compelling philosophical or moral or existential reason – why, once we had found our little Edens, we should ever have to leave them.

But I was in hiding, and the clock was ticking. I made

calls from the phone in Johnny's front hall, and people tried to coax me home, like I was like a spy coming in from the cold. Finally, on the fourth day, I went.

★

There is nothing, in theory, that a marriage cannot accommodate. It expands infinitely in order to contain itself. Somewhere, in a parallel dimension, I stood humbled by my own appalling selfishness, which shattered the mould we had and allowed us to begin again as different people. Somewhere, we were reconciled. What I had done was blistering and flagrant and ineradicable. But it was not the case that we were incapable of surviving it; it was only the case that I was.

Once, a few years after the divorce, when I was back in the town where Eddie and I had lived, I saw him walking towards me over the bridge. We had bumped into one another a few times since the split, and the split itself had been amicable enough. But there was always something uncanny, unsettling, about seeing him. It was like seeing a ghost, yes, but at the same time like becoming a ghost myself. When we reached each other, he shook his head ruefully and said, 'Jesus, I was saying to myself *there's a nice looking bird coming over the bridge*, and then . . . it was you.'

I could hardly speak. We were just across the road from where he'd said to me that first night 'I don't mind if you burst into flames.' It was a throwaway comment,

262

but it was an indication of everything he was to offer me: generosity, indulgence, forgiveness. A lifetime of
occasionally heedless celebration.

There was a day, some months after Eddie and I had
separated and I was still scratching around in the rubble
of my life, that Aiden came to see me in the west. He
parked his red Camaro in front of the cottage where I
was living. It was like an alarm throbbing in the tiny
drive. He was all sparkle and sobriety. He drank Cidona
in a way I found self-congratulatory and described his
letters to me from Spain that summer as the diary of
an illness. Whatever magic had once existed between
us had curdled – I looked at him and saw a philander-
ing smoothie, and I detested myself for having allowed
him to visit. As I watched him pull away the following morning, the wheels turning on the gravel, the car
a slash of red against the chill blue dawn, I felt a dozen
different kinds of sad.

I went back to Johnny's house only once, eight summers after the fact. I was living in Dublin by then.
Johnny was on the dry and I had long since straightened
myself out. I brought a bottle of Perrier, and we sat in
the bright clean kitchen like two suburban housewives.
The floors were clear of debris. Johnny's sentences had
an end point. He told me he'd been near wet brain, and
I couldn't argue with him.

Out the back he'd planted a small garden, and he
picked herbs and different kinds of lettuce and made us a
salad. He had edible flowers, too – one a sunburst yellow

and the other burnt orange – and he added the petals to the salad, and I nearly wept at the small remarkable beauties life throws our way. The house felt still and reconciled around me, and one minute it was as simple as that and the next I'd feel it swarming with the ghosts of us all.

We talked about the people we knew or used to know. We talked about Kevin. His life had run wild for a time. I'd heard stories. It was easy to imagine. He was reckless, and unable to protect himself from his own sharp edges. But by the time we'd bumped into each other again – in a Tesco, of all places – Kevin was in the process of reconstructing himself. He was doing some radio work in Dublin. We went for coffee on Clarendon Street, and, as such encounters go, it was not the worst. I felt acutely self-conscious, but there was also something tender, like a kind of compassion for whoever it was we had once believed ourselves to be.

I wonder sometimes if anything was ever really as we recall it. Standing on the escalator at Connolly Station and realising that the grey sodden world was perfect in itself. The crystal tumbler and the hearth, a solid house around us. Watching the earth flash past from the window of a train, as free as if we'd hopped a boxcar. Now, it was like we all existed in some nebulous afterlife, a vantage point from which we gazed down on everything we had destroyed and all the parallel dimensions in which we were reconciled. Where we had learned, finally, how to put to better use all those Edens we'd stumbled on.

While You Were Working

Neasa McHale

She stares up at the ceiling where wispy cobwebs flutter in the draught. Her eyes follow the cracks a fresh coat of paint would cover. They are superficial. It's a Tuesday morning, the worst day for traffic but she isn't going to work today.

He turns over in the bed and faces her back. The radio plays some song she doesn't know – recently, the radio has been left on throughout the night. She has another twenty minutes of lying there before it's time to get up. She closes her eyes.

When the alarm clock goes off, he stretches his hand out and ruffles her bed hair.

'I went first yesterday, it's your turn today,' she says as she reaches out to the alarm. 'I'm on a go-slow today. I'm not going into the office.'

'Think I'll be having a go-slow myself,' he says. 'I'm knackered.'

'The quicker ya do it, the easier it is.' She wipes sleep from her eyes.

He stretches his whole body, scratches his head, gives

a loud sigh and gets up. He walks towards the bathroom, turns on the shower and closes the bathroom door. A few moments later the toilet flushes.

She reaches out and flicks a stray hair from his pillow. The pillow is still warm. Picking up his upended book from his bedside locker, she scans the page. Yet another book about Ancient Greece. She never understood what that was all about. All those myths and made-up stories. She had watched one of the films before, guts and gore, all in 3D. He had tried explaining, and she had tried understanding but still it confused her. She leaves the book back the way it was. At least it's not one of those books that makes him laugh out loud.

'What ya laughing at?' she'd said one time.

He turned his head and looked at her.

'Ah just the fella in the story? He's after fucking up again and his boss is giving him a bollocking. The excuses he's giving are priceless.'

'There must be some really funny excuses.'

'Ah ya'd have to read it to really get it.'

'Suppose so.'

Putting her feet to the floor, she bends down to pick up a sock, aims it at the laundry basket and misses. She goes and takes her light-blue dressing gown from the back of the door. The collar is stained from when she went blonde to brunette. Not owning a pair of slippers, she puts on socks.

Turning the tap in the kitchen, she fills the kettle. The shower stops, and she hears him pad across the landing into the bedroom. Opening the fridge, she takes out an almost-full carton of milk. Leaning on the worktop, she waits for the kettle to boil. The steam gradually rises a little and then hits the underside of the presses and travels away towards the window. Looking out, she sees a sunny day with a clear blue sky. The kettle comes to the boil; she pours the hot water into the cup over the tea bag. He doesn't drink tea so there is no need for a teapot – when people call to the house, she is more likely to go looking for the corkscrew. Taking a bowl from the press and bringing it to the table, she pours cereal in first and then milk. She doesn't sit down but stands there and eats a few spoonfuls of her cereal. She picks up her cup from the worktop and warms her hands.

Last night she had tried to talk.

'Say if we couldn't afford the mortgage this month?'

'Wha'?'

'Just say.'

'Savings.'

'None.'

'Loan.'

'Couldn't get one.'

'I dunno.'

'That's it.'

'Wha'?'

'Those kinda things.'

'I don't get ya.'

'We're just flying along.'

'And that's bad because?'

'I dunno.'

'Ya want us to be strugglin' along?'

'Ah no but . . .'

'We work,' he said.

'Wha'?'

'Us two, together.'

'Yeah.'

'So it's easy.'

'What if it's the other way around?'

'Cos it's easy we're working?'

'Yeah.'

'I dunno, are you not happy?'

'No, it's not that.'

'Then what?'

'I'm happy, yeah.'

'But?'

'I don't know.'

'I'm gonna head up after this, it's nearly twelve.' He opened a packet of cigarettes.

'Ah wait till we finish this.' She pointed to the bottle of wine.

'Right, go on, top me up, and we've the mortgage so we're grand?'

'Yeah.'

She rinses her cereal bowl and then takes the back-door key from the cutlery drawer and takes the tin from the window sill above the sink, retching a little as the smell of cat food catches her off guard. She opens the door and then taps the side of the tin with the spoon.

She waits. Nothing happens. She does it again. Still nothing. She walks out into the back garden and calls out. Then the cat walks slowly out of the garden shed and lazily up the garden path. She spoons the food into the bowl as the cat nudges her hand out of the way. Scratch greedily devours the food as she stands there watching.

'No darling, you're not getting any more. You're turning into such a fatty catty.' The cat rubs against her ankle as she makes her way to the back door. She goes inside and turns the key in the door. She'll leave Scratch out until later. Someone told her before about smothering cats' paws in butter when they move to a new place, how it stops them getting lost.

He comes into the kitchen.

'Has your da given ya that invoice for me yet? Just hate having it hanging over me, ya know, just want to get it paid,' he says.

'No but he said he's gonna. He wasn't sure of a price, one of the parts I think, like a casket or something.'

'Do you mean a gasket?' he says.

'Ah yeah, that's probably what it was.'

'Sure I'll wait so, and if I don't hear from him we might drop over on Saturday. You all right with that?'

'Yeah, yeah,' she says. 'That's grand.'

'Right so, I'm off now. Is there anything in for dinner?'

'Could ya pick up something on your way home in case I don't get a chance.'

'Ah yeah, no bother. Chinese?'

'On a Tuesday! Ah yeah, go on, I'm only messin'.'

As he walks towards the door, she calls him back. Reaching out she takes hold of his tie.

'Ya look great,' she says, and kisses him.

'Ah thanks, babes, I did what ya told me. Ya know, light-blue shirt with dark-blue tie? See ya later.'

He leaves and she watches him go. She had called him back and kissed him. There was no need for that.

She used to love his eyes.

Her da said he'd collect her at eleven; 'It'll be easier if I bring the van, get it done in one go.' When she takes her suitcase from the top of the wardrobe it's dusty. It looks older and more worn than she remembers, she's had it for years. It isn't even one you can wheel along – well, it was, but a delay and the chance of missing a connecting flight has left it a wheel short. They had laughed all the way though.

'If we miss it we miss it, but if we get it all the better.' He gave her a wink. He kept turning around with a big smirk on his face, a couple of hundred yards ahead. Her laughing had made her struggle even more with the case, and every time he had turned around she laughed again. 'I'm trying, I'm trying.' They had made it, more's the pity, what they both would have given for another week, she thinks to herself.

She'll have to carry the suitcase out to the van later. She had a picture of just sauntering out the door with her stuff, all in the one go, but now it looks like she'll have to make a few trips to get everything in the van. She told her da not to get out of the van. She doesn't like when he comes into the house. He usually barges in and comments on the size of the place and sure what was the point of having such a big house? The kitchen was now all stainless steel enclosed by vast white walls. When they had put the extension on the kitchen, he had asked them was it a restaurant they were opening.

As she puts her clothes into the case, she begins to shake. Opening drawer after drawer and putting clothes into her case, she packs all her stuff, and when that's full, she starts filling black sacks. She hears the news begin on the radio and realises she hasn't rung work. She throws around all the stuff lying on the bed as she looks for her phone.

'Hey Cathy? It'll just be yourself and Siobhan today, I'm not going to be in.'

'No probs, everything okay?'

'Yeah, just have a few things to do.'

'Ah yeah no probs.'

'I'll check my emails later, and if there's nothing urgent I mightn't be in tomorrow. I'll ring ya later and let you know.'

'Grand, talk to you then and have another think about Galway. It'll be fun.'

'Okay, I'll have a think about it, bye.'

She has an hour. She gets a pen and some paper from a drawer in the hallway. She sits on the third step from the bottom of the stairs remembering the last note she had written him. It was the week she had gone to Spain with her ma. The note was about the cat. He had called her the minute he had read it.

'Are you serious that the cat has worms,' he had asked, 'cos I'm not going near it, so does it?'

'Yeah, Scratch has got worms, that's why I'm gone away. If ya read it properly it says *so the cat doesn't get them*. Now give it to the cat on Friday, cos that's when I usually give it, otherwise it will be the worms.'

'Ah ya know what I'm like with things like that, I'll forget. Ya know I'll forget.'

'Well just try and remember but sure the cat'll probably remind ya itself.'

'Would ya stop. Anyway how ya gettin' on?'

'Yeah grand. Ya know, not doing much but like sure it's nice, bit overcast today but sure it's better than being at home.'

'Don't hold back whatever ya do.'

'Ah no, I didn't mean that. Ya know, just good being away for a while.'

'Right, go on and I'll talk to you later. And tell your ma I seen your da down the pub with some young wan the other night.'

'If ya said auld wan she'd probably believe ya. Right go on, talk t'ya.'

She chews the cap of the pen. Changing her mind, she stands up and places the pen and paper on the hall table and walks into the sitting room. She scans the room for the remote. She spots it sticking out from under the oversized cushion on the cream three-seater. Her sister, Elaine, calls this room an adult's oasis.

'Ya couldn't let my lot in here,' she said. 'They'd have the place destroyed in seconds. Jumping on the couches with their mucky runners and spilling their drinks?'

Forty minutes now before she leaves. She presses a couple of buttons on the remote, he's been mad about that mini-series, he mightn't get to watch it tonight but at least she'll record it for him now.

Now there is only thirty minutes until she leaves. She goes into the bathroom and gives the sink a wipe and pours bleach down the toilet – no doubt his mother will be over this evening, no point in giving her another thing to complain about. The hoover is out on the landing but she isn't bothered so she just puts the hoover into the junk room. Then she decides to move the hoover into the office; it'll probably be his mother who uses it next, she could fall over something in the junk room.

In the kitchen, she decides she doesn't want to use any more of the milk so she drinks juice instead. The kitchen becomes brighter as the sun beams down from the skylight. She finishes her juice and goes back up-stairs. She brings the bags and suitcase downstairs. Her phone beeps—

'Got last min job on. Will be there before twelve. Da.'

She thinks for a moment – no, he needs to be here sooner than that, just in case. She clenches her right hand and puts it against her mouth and thinks again. But she's not completely ready herself, there's a few things she needs to do. She goes up and gets dressed quickly. Then she scrapes her hair back from her face and ties it up. She is ready in minutes. Her nails – she can do her nails now to pass the time. She first needs to take off the varnish. Finding remover in her bag, she does this with a wipe in the bathroom. She takes a bottle of nail varnish from her bag and sits on the edge of the bath and begins to paint her nails bright red. When the first hand is done she starts on the other but her hands are shaking now and she is smudging her nails, and the more she tries the more her hands shake. She eventually finishes the last nail but needs a wipe to wipe away the smudges. He'll probably be longer than an hour. She looks in the mirror at her eyebrows and sees a few stray hairs and goes downstairs and gets her tweezers from her handbag and uses the mirror in the hall. She starts plucking but the doorbell rings. Through the frosted glass door she can see the outline of someone, a man. The bell rings again, and the ding-dong travels through the house. Ding-dong again. She thinks about opening the door, but then she hears the letter box being pushed open and watches a leaflet fall to the floor.

She goes into the sitting room and turns on the TV again and sits in the armchair beside the window. She looks out the window and then back at the TV. A quick look out the window again. Red car, green car, black car. Next, a silver van, not the one she is looking for, she watches it go past. She remembers she left a wash in the machine and goes into the utility room. She opens the machine, drags across the empty basket from the dryer and puts the wash into the basket. Clothesline, clothes horse, tumble dryer, she's not sure where to put them. The bathroom mat, towels, tea towels – it would take her five minutes to hang them out, but when would they be brought in, and they could go unnoticed in the tumble dryer for days. She decides to put them on the clothes horse. She opens the dishwasher; there aren't enough dishes to run it.

The doorbell rings.

'Well?' He says, stepping into the hallway.

'Think I'm nearly ready.'

'Ah yeah, grand. Sorry, love, for getting held up.'

'Ah no you're grand, sure. I wouldn't have been ready anyway.'

'So how are ya? Now you're sure about this?'

'Well it'd be a lot easier if we were fighting or like not getting on. But it would only be a matter of time.'

'It's only yourself who knows what's best, love, ya know. But ya have your poor mammy in bits with worry so we better get home as soon as we can.'

'Well she shouldn't be worrying.'

'Yeah but ya know what mammies are like, like.'

'Remember egg dinners years ago?'

'Wha'?'

'Us all getting different egg dinners.'

'There was nothin' else.'

'Elaine fried, me poached, Denise always crying cos her boiled egg wasn't runny enough.'

'Yer ma had to feed yiz.'

'Yiz were great.'

'Only having eggs for yiz.'

'It's not a dig, Da, just the way yiz managed.'

'Barely. Right, I'll start bringing the bags out.'

She watches him pick up the bags and struggle down the garden path. She walks back into the kitchen and sees the cat box. Oh shit, she still has to pack Scratch. Her da has all the bags in the van now. He is sitting in the van waiting for her. She walks to the front door and signals to him that she'll be another minute. With an anxious look he taps his watch and mouths, 'Your mammy.'

She runs through the house and opens the back door and calls 'Scratch!' She walks out into the back garden and looks around, 'Scratch, puss! Puss! Scratch pss, pss, pss! Scratch come on, where are you?' She goes to the shed and finds the cat, curled in a box, helplessly looking up at her, and with two tiny black and white kittens.

'Oh Scratchie . . . ya poor little thing and me slaggin' ya cos ya had a big belly! What are we going to do with ya?'

She strokes the cat but Scratch lets out a low hissing noise.

'Don't worry, I'm not going to . . . '

Closing the shed door quietly, she heads towards the house.

'The cat,' she says. 'It's . . . it's having kittens.'

'You're jokin' me, love?'

'What'll I do, Da?'

'Ah ya can't leave the poor creature.'

'I know, Da . . . Will ya help me bring me stuff in?'

'Ah pet, are ya sure this is what ya want to do? Stay?'

'Da, I've no choice.'

'Ah love, do you really want to stay for the sake of the cat?'

'No Da, I want to stay.'

'Sure ya've got more to worry about than the cat.'

'Come on and we bring the stuff back in.'

Her da brings her things back inside and tells her to ring her ma to let her know she's okay. He gives her a hug and heads off. She goes back into the kitchen and opens the fridge. She takes out the carton of milk. Then she turns and opens the press and takes out a small plate and heads out to the garden shed.

'Here ya go, Scratch, and I'll bring ya food when you're done.' For the next few hours, she stays with the cat and two more kittens arrive.

Drained from the day, she makes her way back to the sitting room and flops onto the couch and flicks through the channels.

The front door opens and she wakes from her doze.

'I'm in here,' she calls.

'Grub's up. Got you the house special fried rice, beef and black bean for meself and some spare ribs for the both of us.'

She gets up from the couch and walks into the kitchen. He has his back to her. He is taking plates from the press. She spots two cans of cola on the worktop.

'Ah ya didn't get me diet,' she says.

'I didn't get ya diet fried rice either, will ya not be able to eat it?'

'What's the point in wasting calories on a bleedin' drink?'

'Well then just don't drink it. Problem solved yeah?'

'Here,' she says. 'When Adam and Elaine gave us that cat, why did we call the cat Scratch?'

'Wha'?'

'Why did we call Scratch Scratch?'

'Cos he was scratching things . . . I don't know.'

'You said everything I thought was too girly.'

'Oh yeah, and you said Tom the tomcat was bloody stupid . . . Do we have serviettes?'

'Yeah in the bottom drawer . . . Well, Scratch the tomcat did something miraculous today.'

'He's not bringing the dead birds again?'

'No, better.'

'Wha'?'

'He had kittens.'

'No way.'

'Way.'

'Whose cat's it? If it's yer one from down the road with that manky-lookin' excuse for a cat, she'll be after us for maintenance.' He smiles.

'No, ya fool. Scratch had the kittens, they're his . . . I mean hers.'

'No way? Ha! That's gas. Did you not have a look when we got . . . it?'

'I think we just thought she was a he, you and your Tom the tomcat.'

'Where are they?'

'The shed.'

'Right, well, I'll have this,' he says, looking at the plate of food, 'and then have a look at them.'

Walking through the hallway towards the sitting room, he shouts, 'What's the craic with the bags out here?'

'Shit,' she says to herself.

'The black bags?'

'Making room for the kittens, we've got four new mouths to feed.'

'I'll put a light in the shed,' he calls. 'We'll manage something.'

Brimstone Butterfly

Desmond Hogan

Zapamtite. Remember.

Arriving in Zagreb on a freezing November evening. Like Prague – subdued city lights, the coloured ones at intervals from one another, like lighthouses, a peculiar kind of pharos.

Posters all along the airport route for Lenny Kravitz who sang once for the California Boys' Choir.

I give a girl in a pinafore patterned with steam irons 50 *kuna* for 29 *kuna* of groceries in a shop on Palmotićeva. Makes to return 20 *kuna* change but swiftly puts it back in the till.

When I manage to argue it back I feel like the woman who found the lost silver coin and rejoiced.

Dimitris – musclé like Cristiano Ronaldo, mermaid's-tail green eyes, in a T-shirt with a sad Cherokee chief on it, under a three-dimensional photograph of elephants, one moment a solitary elephant, the next at a slightly different angle an elephant with a baby elephant – in a flat by the Royal Canal in Dublin had told me the joke. The Demon arrives in Stockholm and causes havoc. He arrives in Berlin, and there is chaos in Germany. On arrival at Zagreb airport he immediately screams, 'The Croatians have robbed my suitcase!'

At Zagreb airport, Petar, born year of the Vukovar massacre in Daruvar, a Titan with a bottlenose-dolphin face who plays basketball and soccer in St Louis now, had stood in front of the candle. Small lights in red glass along the edges of boulevards, arrangements of these lights in green spaces.

Zapamtite. Remember.

A sixteen-year-old boy had been among the two hundred and sixty people taken from Vukovar Hospital who were massacred near the village of Ovčara, bodies dumped in a wooded ravine.

'I first learned to ride a motorcycle,' Dimitris told me. 'Then I stole my aunt's car when I was thirteen and learned to drive. Two years later drove my aunt's car in the war.'

'To a cruel war I sent him, from whence he return'd his brows bound with oak.'

Dimitris came back from war with a tattoo on his leg of Japanese samurai Miyamoto Musashi, in Japanese pantaloons and hose with a top-of-Mount-Fuji pattern, killing an opponent with a *bokken* – a staff.

Leontis had done the tattoo.

Hair like mashed bananas and eyes the colour of a crown of thorns which had verdigris.

'Keep it quiet.'

Dogs of War. Christopher Walken mercenaries.

Bear goulash and hog goulash between sneak attacks.

At seventeen they entered an eighty-year-old Serbian woman's house near Vukovar. Her scarf patterned with butterflies hovering over garden flowers. Dimitris and another youth went upstairs.

Leontis entered her sitting room, which had a Mr and Mrs Duck in it, he in blue dungarees, chocolate polka-dot scarf, she in blue bib dress not unlike her husband's outfit.

Old hogs going blind run at everything.

She threw a grenade which killed Leontis beyond re-cognition.

'We put her on the stick,' said Dimitris, sipping li-quorice liqueur – *licor à la sambuca* – as his budgie Hannibal and his canary Lecter, called after Dr Hannibal 'the Cannibal' Lecter in *The Silence of the Lambs*, chir-ruped in their cage.

Impaled her.

This was a partisan method of revenge immediately after the war.

Pointed wooden pole greased with oil, forced into the anus, pushed through until it emerged around col-larbone, wide end of the stick placed in a hole in the ground, and the victim hoisted for all to see.

'Toblerone, Turkish Delight, weed helps me with post-traumatic stress syndrome. And she does.'

Zyna, Dimitris' girlfriend, went to her job in a Dub-lin bakery with her honey-blonde hair like a cluster-bomb explosion, black boa, shoulder bag like a lamin-

ated magpie's or wren's nest, face the colour of a Steve
Reeves movie – *Romolo e Remo* maybe – jackboots that
Kaiser Wilhelm's favourite Count Philipp zu Eulenburg,
banished for his proclivities, might have worn.

★

Beech, lime, birch, maple leaves, the ground outside
Alojzije Stepinac's Cathedral of the Assumption of the
Blessed Virgin Mary, the verdure by the cathedral,
covered with the leaves of a Japanese pagoda tree, like
gold coins, riches you have saved up.

Smell of chrysanthemums, candytuft, mistletoe, dried
figs from Dolac market.

A nun in black and white veil comes down Skalinska
– a wynd near the cathedral.

The fragile Alojzije Stepinac welcomed and had close
links with Ante Pavelić's Nazi satellite Independent State
of Croatia, many against him, many for him, his
strongest supporters the Jews who know of the assistance
he gave to Croatia's Jews. It is widely believed that the
body which lies in the cathedral was poisoned by Communist agents.

'My grandparents were Ustaše. The People who
Rise,' Dimitris had told me. 'They said times were good
then. The old people said times were good then.'

From childhood Croatians hear how Saint Nikola
Tavelić was cut to pieces by the Muslims in Palestine in
1391.

As we drank Turkish mocca coffee from Croatia I had it recounted: Poles thrown over cliffs; knives, saws, hammers, wheatsheaf cutters, machetes, piano wire, wooden mallets, clubs, rifle butts, bayonets as a method of death; the crane gallows by the river Sava at Jasenovac Concentration Camp the winter before final defeat, bodies slashed and throats slit before being flung in the current; throat-slitting competitions; heads sawn off; children's heads severed and thrown on mothers' laps; children's heads dashed against schools' walls; arms and legs cut off, eyes, tongues, hearts cut out, breasts severed; not to mention death by gas, by fire as happened to those locked inside Glina Orthodox Church (this the reason for a letter from Stepinac to Pavelić); eyes and human organs gloatingly displayed in the cafés of Tkalčićeva in Zagreb.

'Pavelić escaped to Argentina, was shot in Buenos Aires, died in Madrid, and there's a gold tomb for him there.'

Dimitris' mother's grandfather had been a lieutenant in Treblinka, executed after the war.

His grandfather received toxic barrels of waste from the Soviet Union. Most people had car licences for certain days. He had a car licence for all days. He opened one of the barrels and his organs became disarrayed. He died in one week. Dimitris' father, who was imprisoned for going to Mass, was near one of the barrels and got an ulcer.

Zyna's grandmother, her mother's mother, a Russian, was put in Dachau.

★

'You'll be sent to the cells,' I was warned.

Packing your belongings into boxes, sacks, possible imprisonment. Who will collect the boxes and sacks? Who will collect the life, the existence?

A Jewish woman has recently managed to reclaim her family heirloom of Gustav Klimt paintings stolen by the Nazis and you remember in gold Jewish women taken to concentration camps in fur coats, wearing excess jewellery, wearing their jewellery so it could be saved. Jewish people rounded up at a theatre in Amsterdam, Hollandse Schouwburg, a stop for a day before the train to Westerbork, then further east.

★

After a front-page Sunday tabloid article my mountain bicycle is grabbed outside my basement bedsit. I find it wrecked on the other side of the eighteenth-century building, white splashes from the carrion crows nesting above all over the place, as if they were engaging in amateur painting.

Frame kicked in. Two wheels mercilessly buckled. Brake wires pulled out. More damage done by stomping on it, by a man whose face looks like a plate of rashers. I am thrown on the ground and kicked like a Kerry football. A Stella Artois bottle is thrown at me.

'The newspapers never lie,' declares his girlfriend in a

diamanté halter top, matching hot pants, her body like a pudding stuffed into this attire and supported by stars-and-stripes block-high heels.

A Japanese Spitz dog is watching this from afar. 'Get back on your lead at once,' a lady in a summer dress with lotus flowers and South Sea sunsets on it says to him and walks off with him.

★

A crowd comes and bangs on my door some nights later. 'Where's the paedophile?' Like a lynch mob in Alabama. Do they intend to hang me from a lime tree in the Belfry?

A mug with vintage cars and car horns is thrown through my window. I keep very silent and they leave.

Romanians greet me cordially. Offering sweet anadems – a watch with enamelled dial, crystal surround, gold-plated, for sale outside Lidl.

★

A man who used drink with Pecker Dunne, author of 'Sullivan's John', in Jet Carroll's in Listowel, drives me across the Curragh – a heroic landscape – playing Margo, 'West of the Old River Shannon', and Mike Denver, 'I Want to Be in Ireland for the Summer'.

Pecker Dunne, whose grandfather Bernie used to busk at the Country Shop Café in Dublin, claimed he wrote 'Sullivan's John' when he was eleven.

A farmer's son, Johnny Sullivan, fell in love with a Traveller girl at Pecker Dunne's site in Kilrush, County Clare, and ran away with her. Off to England where he started a tarmac and trucking business. The song has him carrying a Traveller's box of tools.

★

In a glory hole by the Royal Canal with a view of Mountjoy jail I find a traumatised brimstone butterfly – yellow with orange spots – who has stowed away among images wrapped in cotton teacloths my mother sent me when I lived in Limerick – images numerously scrutinised, even my Madonnas, as possible pornography, Antoine-Denis Chaudet's *Cupid and the Butterfly* from the Louvre, posthumously finished by Pierre Cartellier, naked crouching teenage boy with pigeon wings feeding a butterfly on a plinth, eliciting even leers because of his committed buttocks.

In 1702 there'd been the Brimstone Butterfly Fraud when brimstone butterflies had been painted with eye-spots and declared a new species.

I release the butterfly in the direction of Mountjoy jail.

★

'It's a terrible thing, Mountjoy,' a youth by the Grand Canal, with a turf cut that looks as if it's been done by a lawnmower, face the red of someone who's just been up and down the Sugarloaf, eyes like Badlands fires, yellow and emerald Manchester United protest scarf around his neck, tells me.

'Grown men using a bucket for urinating as a toilet. Mountjoy is terrible. You light a cigarette on a bunk in the middle of the night and you see cockroaches. The cockroaches have been there since it was built. When I was first put in Mountjoy in the middle of the night it was the caravan cell. Four bunk beds. Eight people, four sleep on the floor. Travellers thrown in there a lot. Young Travellers go on suicide watch. Twenty-three hour lockdown, padded cells.'

★

'I was in jail. Zagreb. Ljubljana. Italy.' Dimitris wears a chocolate-coloured T-shirt with a deranged Mr T from *The A-Team* on it.

When they first moved into this flat they were robbed – socks, toilet paper, even things in the fridge were stolen.

Their fridge magnet shows four completely covered Muslim women and a small boy with the word 'Mom' in a dialogue bubble.

Dimitris was shot in left foot in Milan, stabbed on right side on Via Roma, Rijeka, which Gabriele D'Annunzio and three hundred supporters occupied in 1919 and which he ruled as dictator until December 1920.

Their fathers killed in the war, children start sniffing glue by the canal there.

One of them, a boxer, beat people up and threw them in the canal.

Ships travelling to Rijeka from the south throw food into the sea, and sharks follow – *modruy*, Zyna calls them – when they come into the archipelago. Then they get trapped because of shallow water.

*

Helicopters – choppers for Dimitris – shoot when they see a shark's tail in summer.

Post-traumatic stress syndrome.

After the war – the clean-ups in Muslim Bosnia – life is a collage. Berlin, Munich, Stockholm, Amsterdam, Rome, Palermo, Dublin.

Armed robbery – jail.

He stole Marshal Tito's watch from a museum in Zagreb and sold it to a Jewish man in Piazza Goldoni, Trieste.

Hid on Cres island for a while before being sent to jail.

Then armed robbery again. International journeys ending in Palermo.

Return. Jail.

Organised crime. He and Zyna manage to get to Dublin the year a design of a woman with plentiful hair playing a harp, which Ivan Meštrović submitted for the coins of the Irish Free State in 1927 but too late for consideration, is finally used on a commemorative coin.

Before he left he started kicking a Jewish youth with whom he'd had an argument on the ground, and the youth clung to Zyna's boots.

He didn't know why he did it.

Ustaše?

Black Legion? The Nazis got the uniforms for them.

Didn't I know of Ivica Čuljak? Panonski after the Roman Pannonia Inferior. Painter. Poet. Actor. Punk singer. From Vinkovci near Vukovar – Chicago of Yugoslavia.

Mental Casualty. How the Punk Defended Croatia.

Five seconds after the concert begins in Maksimir Stadium in Zagreb, riot squad called in. Used cut himself during performances so he looked like a mutilated ant. Twelve years for killing a man in self-defence. Spent time in a mental institution near Zagreb. Wore the uniform of the Croatian National Guard when war started. Joined the army to defend his mother. Turned up in a Belgrade nightclub during the war. Dimitris says that because of his enthusiasm with hatchet and chainsaw in combat he was shot in his bunker by the Croatian army.

And even just now Marko Perković and his group Thompson who sing songs in praise of Ustaše Croatia get 60,000 people in Zagreb, many wearing Ustaše insignia.

What does she think of Alojzije Stepinac, I ask Zyna?

She's wearing a T-shirt with a mannequin cat's face on it.

'He was a good man.'

★

The world's borders changed. Old acquaintances faded into the night like the ghosts of yesteryear. Your only friends a Croatian couple. He involved in clean-up operations in Bosnian villages at fifteen. From Bosnian villages to Plunkett Tower in Ballymun.

Wars have brought us together.

★

Arriving in Dublin Dimitris and Zyna initially lived in the only occupied tower in Ballymun, Plunkett Tower.

Towers at Silloge and Shangan were waiting to be destroyed. They burnt rubbish under them.

At the reception youths, scamgany, skaggy boys, some on drugs, would ask for money, would ask for sweets.

'Arriving in a new place you must always get to know the social bottom first.'

Daso, aged eighteen, Sonic the Hedgehog hairstyle, injected himself. Water bubble in syringe went through his body as blood clot to his heart and killed him.

Rozzer, aged fifteen, hoodlum in hoodie look, took too much methadone, went home, got sick in his sleep, choked on his own vomit.

While they were there some boys stole six rabbits, set

a deaf pit bull terrier on them in Coultry Park, mutilated the rabbits with their own hands.

Dimitris and Zyna threw their passports into a fire
under a tower at Silloge.

As a fugitive the only job Dimitris could get was as
gravedigger in nearby Glasnevin Cemetery.

There he worked with Robo, a gravedigger from
County Antrim.

Inebriated pike expression, long face, flinted features.

Robo's grandmother – his father's mother – had
ninety-three grandchildren. Mother Shiggins.

Robo's uncle used drive Robo around Antrim on a
Bill Wright pot cart. Mending pots and pans on the way.
They'd go to small fairs. Sleep under the cart.

Robo's uncle's house was a shed. Donkey in shed too.

He raised chunky chickens for Christmas. Stole wood
from building sites. Gathered fallen trees with Robo's
help. Sold them as logs for Christmas. He used a bow saw.

Some of the Shiggins beat the Lambeg drum at two
Orange gatherings each year in Tennessee.

Robo came south to see the site of the battle of the
Boyne and became a gravedigger, often exposing the
Eve with very nude breasts on his back from Sailor Bill
in Portrush.

'He was a sailor. Did tattoos in Portrush and Colraine.
His son Bruce carried on the business.'

Nuns had babies, threw the babies into lime he informed Dimitris.

Digging seven feet deep one day Dimitris broke a

coffin and stepped in yellow jelly.

A mother asked him to put a cross on a three-month-old baby's neck. He opened the coffin and the head fell off and he had to pick up the head.

Memories of Second World War Ustaše massacres of Serb children.

The mother started spitting at him. The priest was alien to him, Dimitris said.

'On my twenty-eighth birthday I buried five babies.'

*

'Arriving in a new place you must get to know the social bottom first.'

Arriving at the house by the Royal Canal Dimitris and Zyna immediately got to know Mosher and Peggy's Leg who drank Brasserie beer by Tesco.

Eyes swallowed in Mosher's face the way insects are swallowed in the pitcher plant that grows in Roscommon and Westmeath, leaving an echo of deep sea blue, youngish face that has Patriarch's scrolls.

Peggy's Leg wears a rainbow-striped woollen hat and her hair is the colour of Marie Antoinette's wig.

'You meet the nicest people in the Joy,' Mosher tells me. 'The ones outside should be inside and the ones inside should be outside.

'Some get out and are in again on a running charge after a week. They're used to it. It's a way of life. The way it is, you get fed. It's cheaper to be inside.

'I've lived on the streets for years and I know every-one. If you're with me you're all right.'

★

'I've been a landlord for twenty-five years and every nutcase in Ireland has passed through my hands,' the landlord, a man from Carlow with a face the colour of marmalade, says.

The house we live in is peaceful now but Dimitris and Zyna tell me about some of its recent occupants.

A man from Kazakhstan who thought Muslims were after him and going to bomb him and who set the cur-tains and mattress on fire and threw the mattress on fire outside on the landing.

A man who thought Dimitris and Zyna were spies and that Tesco was a spy ring.

A Bosnian Muslim who was always banging drawers, shelves, doors.

A woman from Moldova with three children, includ-ing an ice-blonde, almost narcissus-haired boy. 'I am divorce-ed.'

Kookie arrived with a bottle of Scottish sparkling water and nothing else.

Three times she'd run away from a mental hospital.

She used wrap her body in tinfoil, put clothes over tinfoil, then don a tinfoil headdress, sleep in the hall in this apparel. Thought there were a million people in her room.

Once went naked to Tesco except for bits of tinfoil wrapped around her, many of which fell off.

'She was a 'phrenic,' Dimitris whispers.

*

'I have a friend. Painter.'

Age of consent is fourteen in Croatia but Slavko was accused of spiking a seventeen-year-old boy with drugs and drink and then having sex with him.

Due at prison hospital with his solicitor – his 'brief' (Dimitris uses a word he learnt from Mosher), Dimitris picked him up.

The escape route was florid. Naum in Bosnia. Montenegro. Serbia. Kosovo.

Going south to Albania, to keep the map, the atlas of desire alive.

Dimitris got Slavko to safety in Tirana, Albania.

Dimitris picks up a photograph from over the fireplace of Slavko swimming with a fifteen-year-old Albanian boy in Lake Ohrid, Macedonia, Slavko in briefs with a jabberwocky pattern, blue, yellow, red; the boy, who has a pencil-line moustache, in sailor-stripe jersey briefs with a red rim.

'There are twenty Croatian mercenaries in Dublin,' Dimitris tells me. If ever I need help.

Croatian mercenaries in Burma communicate video footage to Dimitris' computer of people being executed in Burma.

A Pakistani couple with a child move into one of the unoccupied flats, and soon there are broken Chivas Regal bottles all over the back. The council won't take the rubbish because of bottles in it, and rubbish bags accumulate, and one evening I come home and find that they're on fire near the central heating exhaust.

It takes four buckets to quench the fire.

Two Chinese youths move into another flat. They grow hash with hydroponics. Bio-fed hash. A ventilator goes off regularly at three in the morning – at first Dimitris and Zyna think it's a sausage maker – for the benefit of the hash.

The Pakistani couple move out because of the noise but the young Pakistani man still has a key and visits the house once a week, opening the accumulation of letters in the hall – casualties, traumas, mental-hospital cases, junkies, psychopaths – reading them and leaving a litter of unopened letters on the hallstand.

One of the Chinese youths tries to sublet his smelly, claustrophobic room. Advertises for a room-mate.

A black youth in a beanie comes, his bumster jeans show boxers with a pattern of leprechauns. China youth rejects him, and the black youth screams outside that he's been rejected because he's black.

The Chinese youth does have a Polish youth, whose black hair is so shaven his head looks like ash, staying with him for a while, and who's hit on the head at three in the morning on the North Circular Road, with a baseball bat.

There is an almost daily noonday concert of someone kicking the hall door and beating it with a chain. We take this in our stride. With Dimitris at work on a building site, Zyna wanders around in a pongee though Hannibal and Lecter are twittering louder than usual. It never occurs to us we should inquire into it. One January evening Dimitris had turned away a shaven-headed man with a prison tattoo on his neck, 'Down for Life', who had come looking for me.

A junkie who looks like a mackerel head still attached to a bone body, a body of bones – an alleycat's delight – who's fleeing a drug gang in Coolock, and his girl-friend whose hair is a despairing flamingo, arrive, and he immediately starts stealing bicycles, advertising them in *Buy and Sell*, amputating some of them, bits of bicycles all over the place.

Dimitris and Zyna play host to a youth just out of Mountjoy who showed up in Bermudas patterned with cheetahs and rajs' palaces and rajs' leopard-spot um-brellas, his legs golf-ball white, his entire belongings in a green Carroll's Irish Gifts paper bag, and their flat sounds like a fanatical rookery. They leave their door open at night and noise penetrates your room. They suddenly decide to play Panonski top volume, so you wake in fright as if being strafed by a helicopter attack. Feels as if a Balkan war is going on.

A woman is attacked on the street and her terriers –

ankle–biters – hanged.

I leave this savage Golgotha of microwaves that sparkle like a rocket about to take off when turned on, or toasters that kamikaze after two slices of rye bread, of Dickensian hot plates – one of the pair having given up the ghost – for another part of the city.

*

Shortly after I leave an old man who looks as if he's going to disintegrate or blow away like Traveller's Joy in autumn, comes to live in the house.

'I have come here to die.'

A black youth, drug trafficker, moves briefly into my room. He was born and bred in Galway but his parents are from the West Indies. Guards come looking for him and he disappears. The junkie comes down and robs money and a PlayStation from the next occupant of my room, a youth who looks like a frazzled snowdrop.

The postman had placed a book of Jean-León Gérôme reproductions for me in the junkie's arms one morning, and I was lucky to have got it, that he didn't advertise it in *Buy and Sell*. I was lucky to be able to put the colour copy I'd made from it in my new room, Christ entering Jerusalem on a donkey followed by its milk-white foal, greeted by Mary Magdalene dressed as a dancing girl – an *almeh* – as a woman of Cairo.

The junkie frequently comes down and asks Dimitris if he has his bucket.

The junkies multiply like garbage rodents. The new junkie couple immediately sell the house hoover. He wears a hat all the time. The junkie who was already there hammers a hole in his door so he can shout abuse at the new junkie opposite who does the same thing with his door.

'I'll fucking break your jaw. I'll fucking break your throat.'

'Fucking handicaps. Fucking spastics.'

The junkie girl who was already there, nine months pregnant, has a knife fight with the new junkie's girl-friend, who in leggings has a plucked-chicken look, cheeks inflamed – like a rare steak, and the old man downstairs drops dead.

Hannibal bites Lecter on the neck and Lecter drops dead. Then Hannibal dies.

Dimitris decides to put on his silver suit, white shirt, turn himself in at the Croatian Embassy with Zyna in her turquoise dress with *matreshka* dolls and Russian spring flowers on it, and ask for papers to return to Croatia.

Mosher and Peggy's Leg give them a good-luck card which shows three children going up in a balloon bas-ket.

> Sorry you're leaving.
> You'll be missed.
> It was nice knowing you.
> I hope you return someday.
> Have a nice flight.

★

One of the main access points to the Royal Canal as it journeys from the Shannon to the Irish Sea is in my mother's village in County Westmeath.

She wrote to me once about how she returned and visited the Church of the Nativity and knelt and prayed that if she had done anything wrong, that if she had made mistakes she should be forgiven.

★

The only people who offer you a meal in Dublin are a Croatian couple. This is before they leave Ireland. They wanted to make scampi *buzara* but there were only mussels available so it is mussels *buzara*.

Collecting date shells from the sea is forbidden in Croatia – they're not as old as the sixteen-hundred-year-old olive tree on Veli Brijun in the Brijuni Islands – but some are hundreds of years old, and as soon as he gets home he hopes to get a tweezers, a hammer and sub-aqua outfit and dive for them.

When they go the city is lesser, lonelier without them, their stories of concentration camps and massacres and sudden, epic flights.

★

When they leave a golden thread is lost in the city –

they've taken an Aladdin's lamp with them – something that on being massaged gives back images, stories, legends.

You follow the story as the raven flies into the teeth of the wind. Croatia Bus and Dublin City buses have the same jazzy pattern, navy and tango orange. They get their upholstery from the same company.

There are deer, goats, ducks in the fox-coloured hills, and there's an exodus of foxes from the mountains to the lowlands – sign of a bad winter to come.

★

'We miss rashers, Leo Burdock's quarter-pounder, fireplaces,' Zyna announces outside Isadora Duncan's villa, an annexe of a lambswool-yellow Austrian Empire hotel with marine-blue lettering, a tall palm tree Isadora Duncan loved beside the villa.

'We come from the Beverly Hills of Croatia,' Dimitris had told me in Dublin. 'Untouched during the war.'

'Isadora Duncan was killed here,' Dimitris proudly claims, who was handcuffed immediately on his arrival in Croatia and put in Rijeka jail for three months, later in the year getting a further two weeks for having magic mushrooms sent to him from Amsterdam.

'If you know everyone in prison it's not so bad.'

'Isadora Duncan wasn't killed here,' I contradict him. 'She was killed in Nice.'

No use contradicting a Croatian fact. Isadora's scarf

became entangled in the wheels of an automobile here, in this town with its *lungomare*; its belle-époque hotels all shades of yellow – Easter primrose, buttercup yellow, old gold, rose-yellow, lemon-yellow, Naples yellow; its Mediterranean-Gothic villas of Frankenstein hue; its youths like mahogany lizards, one of whom said to me: 'There was a were, and refugees came here during the were'; its outbreaks of urban wood – chestnut, laurel, gingko trees, sequoias, holm oak, Japanese camellia, bougainvillea, baby banana trees, Japanese banana trees in which the soundtrack of Elvira Madigan is piped – Vivaldi's Violin Concerto, Mozart's Piano Concerto No. 21; its German and Austrian tourists in Tyrolese hats, Alpine hot pants, white loin-stockings, with quarterstaffs; its historical list of visitors – Isadora, Chekhov, Puccini, Mahler, Coco Chanel (who was interrogated by the Free French Purge Committee for her Nazi connections but who, unlike Arletty, who was forbidden to act, was acquitted for lack of evidence).

'Before the war,' says Zyna who's carrying a shoulder bag with a lion, a rhinoceros and an elephant on it, 'there were orchestras everywhere. Evergreen music. A river of people at four in the morning. Dancing all over town to orchestras. After the war the streets are empty at eleven.

'Before the war I was in the Young Communist Pioneers. Love your country. Tito was a Croatian but he hated Croatians.'

'All the celebrities came to his funeral in Llubjana,'

Dimitris breaks in. He's wearing a striped T-shirt – blue, white, orange, white, green, white, aquamarine, white.

'He loved being photographed with celebrities,' Zyna adds, 'Elizabeth Taylor, Gina Lollobrigida, Sophia Loren, Queen Elizabeth.'

'The partisans stole my grandfather's bicycle during the war,' Dimitris complains.

'They threw the gold Virgin which was by the sea, into the sea. She was put there by an aristocratic woman whose son was lost in a ship at sea. The partisans re-placed her with a maiden holding a gull. Bikers threw bottles at the gull during the war. The Virgin was found and was put beside the church.'

There are button chrysanthemums under the Virgin now, and a passing woman in a scarlet cardigan with a swallow at each shoulder flutters her fingers at the Vir-gin.

'The last witch in Europe was burned here,' Dimitris proudly announces, pointing to the beginning of a copse.

Never contradict a Croatian fact.

I knew there were executions of women accused of being witches in Switzerland and Prussia at the end of the eighteenth century and the beginning of the nine-teenth.

Darkey Kelly, who ran the Maiden Tower brothel in Copper Alley, Dublin, which had a clientele of Hellfire Club young bloods, was partially hanged and publicly burned alive in Baggot Street, Dublin, January 1761.

Believed to have been a witch for two and a half centuries, recently revealed as a serial killer who hid men's bodies in the vaults of her brothel, possibly the real reason for her terrible end.

'Never trust a cop or a hooker,' Dimitris would say.

Witch hunt . . .

The template of prosecutions builds up, clerics who taught the classics. But I suspect, I know there's a lie. A misinterpretation of history.

'Tender grapes have a good smell . . . '

A priest who taught the classics investigated the lonely Aughrim, the battlefield of a thirteen-year-old boy's body.

★

Flavio – gaunt eaten face like Saint Oliver Plunkett's, Russian camp pale-rye haircut, ascetic glasses sitting on his face – plays his guitar on the *lungomare* in front of Isadora's villa. He was lost in the war for eight years. They declared him dead. His parents died. They took his house, cancelled his social-security number. He doesn't exist. They looked at records going back to the 1930s. He can't get a new number.

What is a person who doesn't exist supposed to do? He knew ten numbers on the accordion, including 'Lili Marleen' – 'The German version,' Dimitris is quick to say, 'Lale Andersen's version was played in Croatia all during the war.'

Then Flavio got a guitar, and he sits in front of Isadora's villa and plays all day, looking towards the shimmering round-the-year azure beloved of Habsburg empresses and Russian tsars, sipping alcoholic beverages made from crushed walnuts or from honey and herbs.

Isadora Duncan had many homes. There is a statue of her behind Flavio. She dances nude among the shrubs grown from seeds brought back by sailors from their journeys. She dances to Flavio's tunes, but she knows that the last four tenants were recently evicted from another of her homes, the Carnegie Hall Artist Studios, including a woman poet in remission with cancer and a ninety-eight-year-old woman photographer, she knows that this is the world we live in.

Sky and sea are a torrid thrush's egg blue at evening, a penumbra of orange on the sea and the mountains. You might expect the historical visitors to this place, Chekhov, Puccini, Mahler, Isadora Duncan, and even Coco Chanel, if she wore the black she looked best in, to come down from the mountains, a much-needed confederation.

*

When I first went to live in County Limerick after returning from England, in a dream, I came out of a pothole in the Warsaw Ghetto after the rising. There were no survivors in my life. But there was a great menorah in the sky.

Zagreb is a hall of mirrors for me; it mirrors exactly past friends.

I walk through Zagreb from early morning to late evening, with its Popeye the Sailor blue trams, by the nineteenth-century paternalistic building, the Balkan stucco, the Stalin functional, the Stalin Gothic, the Stalin Titan, high rises with the words *The Exploited* written at the bottom of them.

City of curd cheese and circuses. Tea towels with patterns of tiny owls or tiny houses with cloudlets above them and trees beside them cover shopping baskets. A man in a Stetson performs Gospel karaoke. I frequently hear Freddie Mercury 'I Want to Break Free'.

Federiko Benković, like Dimitris, exiled himself from Croatia but returned, and his *Sacrifice of Isaac* is tenebrist like the roasting chestnuts which are sold throughout the city – Isaac's head bent towards his adolescent genitals which are covered by a trail of gauze but we are reassured by edges in the painting that his pubes are growing. While his father points a dagger to kill him, Isaac is curious about his sexuality. His left nipple is bright as a girl's.

'Tender grapes have a good smell . . . '

'Zagreb was a bunker then,' Dimitris had told me. The Croatian Army bombed Zagreb themselves. There were 10,000 skinheads in Zagreb during the war. Books by the white supremacist Matthew Broderick were popular.'

He was talking about another place when he told me,

'There was a man. He was the best neighbour. When the war came he lined thirty of his neighbours up in the corridor and shot them.'

As winter dark intensifies I am outside a barber shop with bay rum in the window in glass containers shaped like cannon guns or culverins – phallic – or in glass containers shaped like Prussian helmets.

On the wall inside a photograph of a 1930s barber in white coat standing beside a line of customers like people waiting to be executed.

In the shop window is a photograph of a modern counterpart, a youth in tank top, with Teddy-boy roach, lip gloss, who doesn't look unlike Slavko's fifteen-year-old Albanian friend.

Zapamtite. Remember.

'I was in war. It's not a game of chess.'

They fought with hunting guns, bows and arrows, homemade grenades, potato mines, pineapple mines. They have grenades at home as souvenirs of the war.

Dimitris and I have been through the wars, and once you've been through the wars you're marked; Toblerone and Turkish Delight may palliate, but you'll never forget.

Paper and Ashes

William Wall

I got the death certs for the crows. I call them the crows.
When someone dies they all come pecking. I got five. I
came out of the office, and it was still daylight like when
you come out of the pictures. I'm there blinking and
looking around me and everyone is wearing T-shirts.
I'm thinking there was a reason why people used to
wear black, like you're obviously a widow and people
show respect. I probably look like just a thirty-five-year-
old woman with a handbag full of death certs. Except
they don't know about the death certs, that's the whole
point.

So I went down to the river. The sun was shining.
My late husband liked water.

So then I thought about his ashes, standing there. I
thought, *Wouldn't it be nice?*

Would anybody notice? There was just this old tramp
asleep on a bench with a bottle in a brown paper bag.
Even if he saw. I looked down over the wall, and the
tide was out, and I could just see a shopping trolley in
the mud. That gave me a laugh. Then I started to think

wouldn't it be even better if I left the urn in a supermarket trolley. Someone would find it and report it. Would the person who lost the human ashes please come to the information desk. Better again if I put him on a shelf. In the pickles section. Or in the fridge with the soups. If I could get one of those stickers. 'Reduced to Clear'. I remember my late mother saying once, That man of yours knows the price of everything and the value of nothing. Everybody says that about accountants.

So that's what I was thinking when someone hit me right between the shoulder blades. I don't remember falling out onto the road, but I remember the sound of a car passing right near me. I remember thinking, *That one missed me.* Then someone was helping me up. It was the tramp.

My death certs, I said.

No fear of that missus, the tramp said.

No, I said, they were in my handbag.

The tramp pointed up the street, and I saw the boy who hit me. He was running and throwing things. The things were from my handbag. Bits of paper. Keys. My mobile went over the wall into the river. Some of the death certs were going up on the wind. I could see one drifting over the wall. I started to run but my back and shoulders hurt. I had to stop. All of a sudden I had a bad headache. The tramp started to run too, and he got about three feet ahead of me. Now he was leaning on his knees wheezing.

We walked. We did not say anything to each other.

I was thinking, *Why is this tramp walking with me? We're like an old couple.* When we reached the place where my bits started I found my car keys.

I saw the certs going upriver. The tide was coming in. They were just floating. Now how am I going to prove he's dead?

The tramp looked at me.

It's just paper isn't it? he said.

My late husband, I said.

I liked saying *late*.

I'm sorry for your trouble missus, the tramp said. I found myself shaking his hand. I never touched a tramp before. I let go as soon as he let me.

My credit cards, I said.

My late husband would have thought about the cards first, then the phone. He wouldn't have bothered about the certs. All I had to do was go back into the registry and queue again and they'd give me out a hundred if I wanted them. It was stupid.

Suddenly I thought, *I have only this old man.* Even at the funeral they were all laughing behind my back. Those that aren't owed money.

I had the ashes in the boot of the car. It was in the car park. I could be back in five minutes. If we tipped him into the river he'd go upstream with the certs and end up in a bog somewhere. He'd have his papers anyway. Or stuck in the bank. He might even drift up some disused sewer and spend the rest of his days hoping nobody would flush. From what the solicitor told me, that's the way he's lived for the past two years anyway.

At that moment I felt up. It was the end of a stressed-out week. Waking up in the morning and finding your husband dead in the en suite is no joke. He had his pyjamas down around his ankles.

What's your name?

Saddam Hussein.

I stared at him.

My mum called me after my old dad, didn't she? he said. That was before he was famous.

Is that true?

No. I don't give out names. I got issues, see.

Can I call you Saddam?

He grinned. His upper false teeth fell down, and he closed his mouth quickly. After a bit of chewing, he said, Lost them before that way.

He moved away from the river wall.

I'm going to be gone for a bit. If I come back will you still be here?

That's my bench, he said, pointing. Unless it's raining I'll be over there under that stairs.

I went to the police station first. I told the duty officer about my bag. He wrote it all down. He let me use the station phone to cancel the credit cards. He asked me if I had a witness. I told him about the tramp. He sighed. That's not a witness, he said. Name? Saddam Hussein. It did not go well.

I went to the car park. The ashes were under the passenger seat not in the boot. I remember putting them on the floor. They must have rolled.

So what do we say?

The tramp looked at me. Then he composed his face in sorrow and joined his hands in prayer.

For what we are about to receive we thank thee Lord, he said. No that's not right, he said. Hang on.

I could see he was thinking because he was chewing. I suspected he was moving his upper false teeth around. After a bit he coughed and then coughed again and said, Man that is born of a woman hath but a short time to live, an is full of misery. He cometh up and is cut down like a flower; he flieth as it were a shadow, and never continueth in one stay. In the midst of life we be in death.

I stared at him. I was crying. Where did that come from?

C. of E., he said, my old dad was a vicar wasn't he?

Your old dad was a vicar?

Why I don't go in houses see, I got issues.

Because your dad was a vicar?

Oh yes.

My husband left me penniless, I said.

The tramp nodded at me. I like a nice chat, he said. Get things off my chest. It's good that.

But he looked worried. He took a step backwards. He held his hand out low and flat like he was patting a child's head.

Idle hands, he said, get on with it.

I was still holding the urn. It was surprisingly light.

Is that all we come down to? I was thinking this was better than he deserved. My late husband, accountant, investor extraordinaire, hopeless case. Maybe it was better than I deserved myself. I remembered a time when we were courting. Down here at the river. We had a cardboard box of Colonel Sanders' Kentucky Fried Chicken. I could identify the actual spot a few hundred yards along the quay. A crow and a seagull were arguing over something. We ate the chicken facing each other, sitting on the wall like people sitting on horses. I met him at a disco. He was a smooth talker. The tide was in that time. And it was the night. I confess I was happy to have hooked a fast talker, a man with ambition. I remember he explained the stock market to me. Greasy kisses too.

Chuck it in missus, the tramp said. Get on with it.

He pointed at the urn. He was agitated, I could see that. He didn't like me changing my mind.

I don't want to.

Now he was shifting from foot to foot as if he was running in place but he wasn't lifting his feet. He was looking around him. There was a thread of spit on his chin. Then he said, Discipline discipline discipline, that's what makes a man, self-discipline yes. We had a nice house. We had a disused tennis court.

Your dad?

We had a flush WC didn't we? He used to come in my room very late very late and examine the sheets. 'Forgive, O Lord, for Thy dear Son, The ill that I this

day have done.' What if I fell asleep? Where was my
mum you ask?

He walked away. I watched him going along the
street. He was still talking. He was waving his hands. I
could see he was arguing. He didn't sit on his bench. He
turned a corner. I felt I had let him down.

The sun was sinking behind buildings.

I opened the urn. It was a screw-cap. I tipped the
ashes out, and the wind took them up. The ashes were
a pale yellow colour. There was a man on the other
bank watching me. He blessed himself. The ashes blew
out along the river, and the tide carried them upstream.
They were headed for the country. Ashes and paper.
Like someone had thrown a fire away.

How I Beat the Devil
Paul Murray

I was ten years old when I first met the Devil, in a small village in the south-west of Ireland. My family was on holidays there; he was renting the cottage down the road from ours.

My parents were geologists, and our summer destinations were always chosen for their geological interest. If you think you can imagine a more potent recipe for boredom, then you don't know geologists: you don't know the endless hours of pleasure they can derive from looking at rocks, or the lengths they'll go to find them. The so-called holiday was a daily field trip into the hills, and I, of course, was press-ganged into coming along.

In previous years I hadn't minded; I'd traipsed along happily beside them, with my bucket and my magnifying glass. But ten is a funny age. Adolescence is still just over the horizon; nevertheless, something has changed. The glister of magic has gone from the world; it has become resistant, obdurate, like a friend that, without explanation, suddenly stops talking to you. Home seems to offer nothing but limitations, and extended periods of time spent with one's parents no longer have the same unqualified allure – particularly if they revolve around what my mother called 'some of the most interesting pre-Cambrian lithologies in Europe'. That week, standing around in the rain while my parents chipped at the ground with small metallic instruments, I had for the first time an overpowering wish to be somewhere else.

I knew that to tell my father I was bored would only provoke him. My father didn't believe in boredom; he said boredom was an illusion that existed only in the minds of lazy people. Instead, when we came back to the cottage for lunch, I told them I had a sore tummy and was going to lie down. They were concerned, of course, and wanted to stay with me. But I persuaded them to go back to their work. The sun had come out at last, and the pre-Cambrian lithologies were just up the road; they could see our cottage from the hill. All right, they said, just for an hour. Through the window I watched them walk back up the lane, already lost in conversation. Then I threw off my bedcovers. I went to the back door and stood on the step, breathing in the rain. I was free.

Unless you wanted to dig up rocks, however, in this particular village freedom was of limited value. There were a couple of pubs, a shop that didn't sell comics, a few fields of cows. There were various scenic vistas, but nothing that did anything. For an hour I wandered back and forth with a gathering sense of frustration. The trees dripped emptily, the placid chomping of the cows seemed to mock my impatience. I could hear my father's voice in my head, telling me *Everything is interesting if you look at it long enough*; but I could find no purchase on this damp Arcadia, no matter how long I looked, so I gave up and went back to the cottage.

Things weren't much better here: the TV only had one channel, and wouldn't work with my video console. The meagreness of my own company was really beginning to distress me, and I was thinking seriously about rejoining my parents on the hill, when in a drawer in the living room, I found a box of marbles. Although in entertainment terms these were only a marginal improvement on rocks, I seized on them without hesitation. I went out onto the lane and began to play, me against me; that's what I was doing when the Devil came sauntering along. He stopped and watched me play for a while, and then said, 'Wotcher.'

I knew right away who he was – knew in a strange precognitive way, the way you might arriving at some place of your ancestors, which although you've never been there before at once starts up an inner machinery, a series of calls and responses that fly back and forth through the silence. I wasn't scared, but if I'd had hackles, they would have stood up. This was the old Enemy, there was no doubt about it. Still, I could see in his eyes the same rural boredom I was suffering myself: so when he asked if he could join the game for a moment, I said yes.

He cheated from the very first throw, but with such

dazzling artistry that I didn't say a word. As well as standard magicianly stuff, sleight of hand and marbles up the sleeve, he made full use of his supernatural powers. For instance, if he was on the brink of certain defeat, he'd pretend to cough and turn his threatened steelie into a worthless threesie – or a frog, or a butterfly, that would hop or flutter away; he'd alter the gradient of the road so my marble rolled off harmlessly into a tuft of grass; sometimes, when he missed a shot, he'd momentarily accelerate the revolution of the earth, creating a G-force that would cause his marble to U-turn back into mine. He made no attempt to disguise his chicanery; I wondered if he even knew he was doing it, if he realised there were rules he was flagrantly ignoring. I didn't care: it was definitely the most interesting thing I'd seen on this holiday, and anyway at the end of the game he gave me back all the marbles he'd won from me.

After that we went into the village and bought Cokes, then went wandering down the laneways while he told me about famous figures from the past who'd sold him their souls. 'I mean many of the names you'd expect,' he said. 'No one's going to be shocked to hear Genghis Khan got rid of his soul pretty early on. But there are others in there who would really surprise you. Great leaders, thinkers, pillars of the community. People you'd feel ought to have much more of an insight into the whole thing.'

'Why would someone sell their soul?'

'Various reasons. Power, fame, a place in history.

Frankly it's a bitch to get into history *without* selling your soul.'

'Why would they want a place in history?'

He shrugged. 'I suppose it's the biggest thing they can get in exchange for their souls.'

There seemed an unsatisfying circularity to this, but before I could question him further, or ask who Genghis Khan was, he'd stopped in his tracks and was pointing at the cows in the field. 'Will you look at these f—ing things?'

I looked at them. I couldn't see anything extraordinary about the cows. 'That's my point. They just stand around all day long, chewing f—ing grass.'

'What's wrong with that?'

'Their lives are f—d, that's what's wrong. Their lives are f—d, and they don't even care!' He picked up a stick and threw it at the small brindled group nearest us. 'The f—ing farmer is going to turn you into burgers, you c—ts!' The cows lumbered away from the stick with the minimum possible effort, resumed their rumination with their filthy tails turned to us.

'C—ts,' the Devil said again.

Something happened when he swore – which was often, particularly when around cows, whose peaceful-ness and satisfaction with their lot he seemed to take as a personal affront; the words came out muffled or smudged, like rap songs when they're played on the ra-dio, as if he was being censored or redacted as he spoke. I wanted to ask him about it, but I also felt it might be a sensitive subject, like a handicap.

Initially my parents were uneasy about this new association with the man from the neighbouring cottage. Then one evening the Devil called over on the pretext of borrowing a torch. He told them his name was Dave, and he worked for an oil exploration company; he feigned astonishment when he heard they were geologists, and asked if they were interested in pre-Cambrian lithologies at all. It was like watching an expert criminal pick a lock: with a handful of well-chosen questions, he had completely disarmed them. For the rest of the night, I watched as my parents jabbered away to him not only about fissures, tectonic movements, developments in the industry but also their own hopes and dreams – awards, grant applications, university contracts, things they had never spoken of to me. Desire made their eyes shine: suddenly they looked much younger, almost like children.

They must have wondered how 'Dave' knew so much about what it was like here six hundred thousand years ago; they must have had some inkling of who he really was, the same way I had. But perhaps adults are less attentive to the voices that murmur within – or maybe the way he lied, like the way he cheated at marbles, was so entrancing, so intoxicating, that they simply stopped caring it wasn't true. His lies were better than truth; truth, by comparison, became something dowdy and tired and limited, like an ancient TV set with only one channel. He had the same effect on everybody. Even the taciturn locals lit up when he came into a room. It was as if he could jump at will into their heads, see through their eyes; he could intuit exactly what it was they wanted, the specific lacks and yearnings that gave them traction on the world, he could *understand*. That was the men; their wives, like my mother, and every other woman I saw cross his path, just simpered and giggled and twirled their hair.

One day I called to his cottage. There was no answer when I knocked, so I just went in. The Devil was watching one of those afternoon quiz shows. He seemed to know the answer to every question. 'AQUARIUM! It's staring you right in the face, you stupid b—d!'

'You should enter one of those things,' I said. 'You'd be good. You might win, even.'

'I'm banned,' the Devil said darkly.

His cottage was disappointing. I had imagined a cockatrice, a three-headed dog, at the very least a few chalk pentacles scrawled on the floor, but other than some pictures of his friends from Hell, all shiny-faced and smiling, stuck to the fridge, and a slightly less antiquated television, it was exactly the same as the one rented by my family. The dullness of it nagged at me, and, after sitting on the couch for a minute or two, I asked him a question that had been on my mind for some time. What was he doing in West Cork?

'I'm on holiday,' the Devil said.

'On holiday?'

'My doctor prescribed a two-week holiday. For my ulcer.'

'Ulcer?'

'It's something you get when people keep repeating everything you say,' he said, rather shortly.

'Oh,' I said. 'But why did you come here? Why didn't you go somewhere nice, like the Algarve? Or Disney World?' For these were the places my friends, whose parents were not geologists, had gone to this summer.

'It's contractual,' he said, then, seeing my blank look, expanded: 'On business, I can go wherever I want. The Algarve, Disney World, under the sea, wherever. But leisure, that's a different story. When it comes to my own time, "purgatorial" is as much as I'm allowed. Unimaginative, middle-of-the-road restaurants. A two-drink limit in bars. Holidays in places like this. That's the contract.'

'I didn't think *you'd* have a contract,' I said. I meant it in a flattering way, but it seemed to annoy him even more. 'Of course I have a contract. You think I do this for the good of my health? You think I want an ulcer?'

'No, but it's sort of funny when you think about it. Isn't it?'

'I don't find it particularly funny.'

'Well, you know,' even as I said them I knew the words weren't coming out right, but I kept going anyway, 'you having an ulcer and getting stressed and stuff, when you're the one responsible for everything being like this in the first place.'

'Ha!' he exclaimed. 'Oh sure, I'm responsible! I invented war, and smog, and telemarketing! And ulcers too, why not?'

322

'What I mean is,' I tried to make it sound as non-judgemental as I could, 'you're the one who got us banished from the Garden of Eden, which you just did because you got kicked out of Heaven, for the sin of Pride—'

'F—!' he yelled, springing off the couch. For the next few minutes he stormed around the room, swearing and gesticulating. Finally he returned to me. 'The "sin of Pride",' he repeated contemptuously. 'Let me tell you a few things about that little episode. God . . . God is not what you'd call reasonable. God is not a pleasant person to have to deal with. It's very sad to meet an omnipotent being who is such a petty man.' He frowned. 'You've probably heard the saying, "there's no such thing as a free lunch"?'

This was new to me – my mother always made my lunch, and to this point hadn't charged – but I didn't want to interrupt, so I nodded.

'Well, that's God all over. Every little thing he'd do for you, he'd want something in return. Worship me. Sing my praises. Unless everyone's constantly telling him how great he is he throws a tantrum. Dare to suggest you might occasionally like some time on your own and the next thing you know you're out on your ear.' I must have looked doubtful, because he said next, 'Look at the Flood, for instance. He gets out on the wrong side of bed one morning and out of pure pique he practically destroys his entire Creation. Is that the kind of mentality you want in the guy running the show?'

'He did invent a rainbow afterwards,' I remembered.

'Yeah, I'm sure all the annihilated rabbits and anteaters and whatever other completely blameless animals really appreciated that. A big multicoloured metaphor, thanks a million. That totally makes our needless deaths worthwhile.'

'So . . .' this time I put the question together in my head first, 'all the bad things that happen are God's fault? Not yours?'

The Devil began to reply, then stopped. 'Look,' he said. 'I'm not claiming to be a saint. But all I do is give people what they want. They ask, and I give it to them. When's the last time God gave you something you asked for?'

'Then you take their souls.'

'I told you, they don't *want* their souls,' he returned. 'It's a free and fair exchange.'

'What do you do with all those souls anyway?'

'Put them to work in my dry cleaners,' he answered, switching the sound on the TV back on.

'What's it like not having a soul?' I persisted.

He sighed, brought his hand in a slow melancholy circle about the room. 'It's like this, kid. It's exactly like this.'

When I got home, I couldn't stop thinking about this contract that prevented him from enjoying anything. It explained a lot, such as why every time he bought an ice cream, half of it always immediately melted off onto the street. But I couldn't help wondering if 'purgatorial' applied to his relationships too, and if that was the only reason he was friends with a ten-year-old boy.

I saw him most days, to play marbles or watch TV, but I didn't know how the Devil spent his evenings, until one night I was woken from my sleep by a sudden peal of light. I opened the curtains to see the sky pulsating with unearthly colours; when I lifted the sash it seemed I could hear laughter too, amid minor explosions and other, vaguely animalistic sounds. I put on my shoes and lowered myself out the window.

There was some kind of party going on inside the Devil's cottage. In the brief bursts of scarlet, cinnamon, silver light, I could make out horned heads, baroque silhouettes with enormous, arching wings. I wanted to get closer, but something held me back: so I stayed at the edge of the trees, watching, until I got cold and returned to my bed.

The Devil was alone again the next morning when I called over, throwing beer cans and emptying ashtrays into a black plastic sack, singing along with the stereo: 'Sinatra,' he told me. 'We did some business at one point. Soul the size of a raisin.'

'So you had a little party last night,' I said.

He looked at me and harrumphed. 'I thought I heard someone nosing around outside. Shouldn't you have been in bed, with your dollies?'

'I was in bed, until the noise woke me up,' I said pointedly. 'Can't have been too good for your ulcer, all that beer and smoking.'

'What are you, my mother?' he retorted.

I knew he didn't have a mother and was about to remind him, when the sadness of it struck me: that he'd never had anyone to make him free lunch, or give him his ulcer medicine, or wrap presents for his birthday, although I didn't know if he had one of those either. Instead I said, 'Who were all those people?'

'Oh, just friends of mine. Come here, I'll show you.' He brought me over to the fridge and named the people in the photos. 'That's Astragal . . . Azazel . . . Baal, he's a riot . . . Choronzon . . . and that is Baphomet.' His finger dallied on a winged figure slouched at the edge of the picture. 'Beautiful, isn't she?'

I shrugged. 'If you go for green skin and yellow eyes, I suppose.'

'She and I have been hitting it off quite well lately,' he said airily; then, registering my indifference, he nudged me. 'Come on, let's go and have some fun.'

He was in high spirits. After a particularly impressive bout of cheating at marbles, during which he repeatedly sent himself back in time so he could jump out from behind himself, he turned his attention to the cows. 'Look at these poor chumps,' he said. 'Standing in their stupid field day after day. They have no idea how wonderful life can be.'

'They look happy enough,' I said.

'We need to teach these cows how to enjoy themselves,' he said thoughtfully.

I was about to ask him what he meant when, at the

far end of the field, I noticed one of the cows was hovering ten feet off the ground.

'What are you doing?' I said warily.

'I'm not doing anything,' the Devil insisted, as the first cow's comrades slowly joined it in mid-air. They were uncertain at first, but then they really took to it, swooping about, buzzing the hedgerows, filling the sky with their joyful mooing. One more ambitious cow attempted to loop the loop; until you've seen a cow loop the loop, in my opinion, you haven't really lived. After that he turned us both invisible, and brought us up the hill where my parents were studying the rock formations. 'Watch this,' he whispered. Suddenly my dad stood bolt upright; then he hunched down again; then he jumped up, as if he'd been stung, and called my mother's name. 'Gold!' he cried. 'Gold!'

'Where? Where?' my mother gasped, hurrying over.

My father hunkered down, frowning at the ground. 'That's weird,' he said. Then my mother clutched his arm. 'What's that glinting over there?'

We bit our lips to stop ourselves from exploding with laughter.

I was still laughing about it the next morning when I called to his cottage. The Devil answered the door in his dressing gown, though it wasn't early; he agreed to come and play marbles, but his cheating was curiously lacklustre and he seemed more interested in his phone.

'What's wrong with you?' I demanded when his apathetic play and constant sighing got annoying.

'Nothing,' he said, checking his phone.

'Are you expecting a call?'

'No,' he said, but then added: 'What kind of signal are you getting here? I don't think my phone's getting a signal.'

'Do you want me to try calling you?'

I dialled his number, and he gazed with mounting joy at the phone as it lay inert in his hand – then his face fell, as it began to buzz.

'Who's supposed to be calling?' I asked. 'Is it that girl with the green skin?'

'Baphomet,' he said morosely.

'Maybe she's busy,' I said.

'Oh, she's busy all right,' he said. 'She's a succubus.' Noting my blank expression, he gave me a comprehensive explanation of what this entailed.

'Oh,' I said faintly, lowering myself onto a tree-stump.

'So you see,' he concluded gloomily, 'at any given time I'm sharing her with like ten other guys.'

After that day, not a marble was thrown, not a single cow levitated. Whatever this Baphomet had done to him, all the Devil wanted to do now was moon about his cottage – either staring hopelessly out the window, or throwing the sofa cushions around in a rage, shouting lines of *Paradise Lost*, which he knew by heart.

As for me, I was totally out of my depth. With no experience in matters of the heart, I could do little more than make him cups of hot chocolate and listen to his lengthy enumerations of Baphomet's virtues, which in most people would have been considered pretty serious vices.

'Why don't you call her?' I ventured at one point.

'Me? Call her?'

'Well, why not?'

'What is wrong with you?'

'It's just a suggestion.'

'Me call her,' he repeated, disgustedly.

'There must be something you can do.'

'There isn't! There just isn't!' He got up and went to the stereo and put on *Tracks of My Tears* for the millionth time.

His heartache was exhausting to be around, and my inability to help made it even worse. When the time came for my family to pack up and return home, I found myself experiencing a strange mixture of guilt and relief.

'So you're just going to abandon me, is that it? Like everybody else.'

'I have to go back to school.'

'What if I kill myself?'

'You can't kill yourself,' I said. 'You're the Devil.'

This observation didn't seem to cheer him up at all. On the contrary, I left him with his head in his arms, beating his fists on the table. The next year we took our holidays in France, and it was a long time before I heard from him again.

Ten years passed. I grew up and went to college; my parents retired and moved to an island in the South

Pacific to study the volcanoes. Although I'd vowed to myself, that last day in West Cork, to avoid it at all costs, by now I'd had a few more personal run-ins with love. My last girlfriend, Jennifer, was beautiful but intensely religious and wanted us to 'wait'. Sometimes I'd try and change her mind with one of the Devil's speeches about living for the moment; she would listen patiently and then peck me on the cheek and tell me she'd be late for her seminar. If I wanted to live for the moment, she implied, I would have to do so by myself.

One rainy April evening, just after seven, the buzzer of my apartment sounded. I went out to the step and there he was. He hadn't aged a day; if anything, he looked younger than ever, except for his eyes, which described a decade spent toiling through continents, paying court to the greedy and desperate, hustling the same base fantasies that were the best a never-learning humanity could come up with – that jaded look that comes from trading in dreams.

'What the f—k is this s—t?' he said, looking around my dingy apartment.

'I'm a student,' I told him.

'Rocks?'

'Literature.'

'That's useful,' he said.

Now that we had caught up to his satisfaction, he came promptly to his point. Did I remember Baphomet? 'Of course,' I said. He told me that after years of silent yearning he had at last confessed his feelings to her. It had not been a success. First she laughed. Now she was avoiding him. She wouldn't even return his calls. 'She kept telling me she wasn't ready for a long-term relationship,' he said, honking his nose into a handkerchief. 'I mean she's ten billion years old. How long do I have to wait?'

I was surprised to hear he was still obsessed with her after all this time, but I supposed time for him was not at a premium; he had all eternity to indulge his fascinations. In some ways I could see her point. 'You're both career people. You travel a lot. It's hard to maintain a serious relationship if you're spending all that time apart. Not to mention the nature of your work. Love doesn't always sit well with, you know, the all-consuming pursuit of Evil.'

He folded his hands on the crown of his head and exhaled slowly. 'Well that's just it,' he said. He explained that since the fall of the Berlin Wall and the corresponding ascent of free-market capitalism, increasing numbers of people had been selling their souls to each other, bypassing him altogether. 'Effectively, the whole thing's been privatised,' he said. Given that the greater part of his work was being done for him, he wondered whether the time hadn't come for him to get out of the game.

'Out of the game? And do what?'

'This is what I'm saying. I could settle down. Live a normal life.'

'I thought you hated normal life,' I said, remembering his harsh words to the cows.

'Not your kind of normal life,' he said irritably, waving at the grungy apartment. 'I'd be with Baphomet.'

Warning bells went off in my head, but all I said was, 'Baphomet doesn't feel the same way?'

'Oh, she's obsessed with her work. But her situation's exactly the same! Look out your window! You think to tempt men from the path of rightness and drain them of their sexual energy you need a designated full-time staff anymore? Modern life does all that for you! The Western world is basically one big succubus. She could quit tomorrow and no one would even notice. But she just won't accept that times have changed.'

'So what does that have to do with me?' I said at last.

Immediately he was all business. 'She won't listen to me, but what about a disinterested third party?' he said. 'She's so concerned about work – what if it's her actual work that turns around and says, thanks but no thanks? Believe me, that would really make a succubus stop and think.'

He told me that Baphomet was currently 'working the area'. She tended to concentrate on clerics, saints, people whose minds should be on other things, but if I agreed, he would slip me onto her client roster. ('We share a secretary,' he explained.) When she visited me, I would astonish her by rejecting her advances. Then I would subtly lead her around to thinking about alternatives to her current way of life. 'Tell her she's too good for that damn business! Tell her there are people out there who're ready to make a serious commitment to her! Who could make her happy. That sort of thing.'

It didn't sound like much of a plan. Nobody – man, woman or demon – likes to be told they are obsolete. Even if she accepted that she'd been supplanted by technology, from what he'd told me about her, Baphomet didn't sound, to put it as politely as possible, like the 'settling down' type. And what about him? Could he really spend the rest of eternity with her – in a corner of the field, so to speak, chewing the cud? The whole enterprise seemed a vainglorious folly that would collapse the moment you set foot in it. Yet surely he knew this. He was the Devil! Vainglorious follies were his stock-in-trade. He must have some angle, I thought; he must be counting the cards, he must have spotted some flaw in the system, by which he could make this work.

A few nights later, I stayed up late studying the Romantics, those troubled souls who had struggled so heroically, so hopelessly against their own narcissism. When I went to bed, I quickly found myself lost in a dream, in which I was pinned to my bed by a demon. She had green skin and yellow eyes and was sublimely beautiful: at the same time, her talons, her wings, the capacity of her body for terrible cruelty, gave this beauty an extra intoxicating dimension. She went about her work, stripping back the sheets first and then my clothing, whispering to me wordlessly that if none of this was real, it didn't matter, there was no need to resist . . .

It was with some difficulty that I fended her off me, and sat up in the bed.

'What?' she said, blinking. 'This never happens.'

Anyone who's woken up with a demon straddling them will know that it's not the easiest thing in the world just to strike up a conversation. But I tried, nevertheless. 'So you must be a succubus,' I said, adjusting my pyjamas.

'Obviously,' she snapped, clearly vexed at having her work interrupted.

'I've always wanted to meet a succubus,' I said.

'Well, this is your lucky night.'

'Can I get you a drink, or——?'

'Silence,' she commanded. She pushed me down onto the bed, stroked my eyelids shut and whispered to me, 'Abandon yourself to pleasure.'

I cleared my throat, wriggled out from under her, clambered off the bed. 'It's just that I'm actually a little bit thirsty,' I said.

'I will sate your thirst and your every other desire.'

'Mmm,' I said apathetically.

'I will bring you release so extraordinary you will forget who you are.'

'Well, why don't we have a drink first,' I said, 'and then we can decide what we're doing.'

I went to the cupboard, while she glowered back at me from the roiled sheets. Her yellow eyes were quite intimidating, and her long tail bobbed incessantly behind her, more like a familiar than a part of her body. 'So!' I said, presenting her with a tumbler of wine and then retreating to a safe distance. 'You're a succubus! That must be an interesting job?'

334

She threw back her wine, and then crunched the glass for good measure, staring at me with her yellow eyes. 'I take the filthiest fantasies from the darkest corner of the heart and paint them in sweat on your bedsheets,' she said.

'Right,' I said. 'And you've been doing that for long?'

'A hundred million nights,' she replied, 'of almost unbearable pleasure.' She drew herself up on her knees, and her magnificent torso jutted out like the gates of Paradise. I hurried down another slug of wine and averted my eyes. I was finding it difficult to concentrate on my task. She really was a very attractive woman. Her forceful tone, her faint redolence of brimstone, that magnificent pistachio-ice-cream-coloured skin, when you took it all together it really cast a spell on you—

'A hundred million nights,' I squeaked, catching hold of myself. 'That's a long time.'

She made no reply to this. I noticed a long rent in the bedsheet where she was clasping it and unclasping it between her talons.

'And you don't get bored?'

'No,' she said. 'No, I'd have to say I never get bored.'

'Because from one perspective,' I said, 'I mean, you know, here's you, this beautiful, intelligent, immortal creature, just . . . bouncing around with all these different men . . .'

'What are you getting at?' She drew back, eyeing me suspiciously.

'Some people might find it a little . . . empty,' I said, as delicately as I could.

'Empty?' she repeated. 'Empty?' Tendrils of her hair rose snake-like to hiss around her head. 'After the raptures I purvey, worldly pleasures are as scraps from the table! To enter my body is to stare into beauty's own sun!'

'I'm just wondering if you ever feel like it's time to settle down,' I said.

The hissing tresses and whipping tail froze: she stared at me for a long moment, her eyes turning from yellow to black. Then she half-jumped, half-flew off the bed. I covered my face, but she went right past me, over to a handbag I hadn't noticed before. From this she took a printout, read it, then turned back on me. 'You're not the Archbishop of Fontenoy!'

I babbled out excuses, but she'd already worked it out. 'Satan put you up to this, didn't he?' she exclaimed, with a kind of mock triumph. 'I should have known! Nobody wants a drink first!'

I hung my head, while Baphomet swore and stormed around the room, her great wings beating furiously, sending gusts of charred air to pummel the curtains and rustle behind the posters on the wall. Finally she hoved up at my desk, plunking herself in the chair and lighting a cigarette.

'He gave you this too, I suppose,' she said, picking up a book on the Romantics. 'His little gang.'

I told her I was studying their poetry; I had my finals in a couple of weeks, I said.

'Poetry,' she repeated derisively. But, sucking hard

on the cigarette, she began to flick through the book. 'Byron. I could tell you some things about him. And his flaky sister. Always trying to get me into her room. Those two just did not stop.' Pages turned; the coal of her cigarette glowed in the murky dreamlight. 'Keats, though. He was like you, he only ever wanted to talk. Used to call me his Muse. Asked me to wear togas, and talk Greek to him.' She sighed, closed the book, held it away from her in order to gaze melancholically at the cover, like a mother with a picture of a child who has since gone astray. 'In retrospect, this is when it all went wrong,' she said. 'When he went native.'

I guessed she was talking about the Devil, but I didn't say anything.

'You'd never think someone who'd seen as many souls up close would be interested in acquiring his own. It's like a pest exterminator deciding he wants to live in an anthill.' After a moment she added glumly, 'And bring me with him.'

'He says he wants to get out of the game,' I said.

'The game is all he has.'

'He's in love with you.'

She laughed exotically, twists of smoke interbraiding with the writhing of her tail. 'Love! You know he practically invented that? With the help of your friends there.' She nodded at the book on the desk.

'I know it sounds crazy,' I persisted. 'But he seems serious about it. He says he's ready to make a real commitment.'

'*Commitment*,' she repeated. 'Settling down. Holidays in Ireland, dinners in unimaginative, middle-of-the-road restaurants – do you think he'd actually enjoy any of that?'

'Well, if he got out of his contract he might,' I said. 'Because there wouldn't be that clause, stopping him from enjoying things.'

'The clause?' she repeated, smiling at me.

I gazed back at her stupidly.

'Have you ever heard the famous paradox,' she said conversationally, '*Everything I say to you is a lie?* Imagine if you *were* that person. Imagine how hard it would be to work out what you wanted. But I know what he wants. He's like any other man. They think they want love. But really they're all banging on Daddy's door, begging to be let back in.'

She extinguished her cigarette in the palm of her hand. 'A girl picks things up after ten billion years,' she said.

'Couldn't you try it, at least? Just to see? How could it hurt?'

'How could it hurt?' she repeated to herself. She rose to her feet. She towered over me. She caressed my cheek with a talon. 'Little boys,' she said. Then, soundlessly, she turned to smoke, and hurtled up the chimney.

It was some months later that a parcel arrived from Switzerland with a brief, unusually effusive letter from the Devil inside, thanking me for making him 'a very happy man'. He said that he and Baphomet were renting an apartment together in Lausanne; she was working freelance for the Paris fashion monthlies, while he pursued a trade in carpentry, a long-time hobby of his. There was a photo of the two of them by the lakeside, the Devil smiling goofily with his arm around his girlfriend, she staring coolly into the camera. Also enclosed was a spice rack he had built, a reward for my small part in bringing them together.

By that time I'd graduated from college and started interning at a publishing house; this is where I met Christine, who is now my wife. Voltaire – another sometime resident of Lausanne – called marriage 'the only adventure open to the cowardly'. It's certainly provided all the excitement I could need, and more. We have two children, Lucy and Tom: watching them grow up fascinates me, the transformation from helpless pink blobs into mysterious and complex personalities they've made up all by themselves.

Baphomet was right: this wasn't the kind of adventure the Devil was looking for. The two of them split up after less than a year and threw themselves with redoubled vigour into their former careers. Having got what he wanted, he no longer wanted it: it was an old story, one he'd traded on for thousands of years. The mystery was that he'd expected anything different. Maybe he simply wanted to be on the other side of the bargain for once – to be the dope signing away his soul for a grand illusion, instead of the guy who knew the ugly truth. Maybe he just wanted to want, like people do.

It must be hard not to procrastinate when you're immortal; it must be hard not to put off the lessons life's trying to teach you for some other time when you're more in the mood. After Baphomet, he embarked on a string of tempestuous affairs – with a well-known Hollywood actress, a Slavic princess-contortionist, and latterly a sweet-hearted girl composed entirely of mercury from the spiral nebula of Andromeda.

Sometimes, in between girlfriends, he'll come and stay with us. He likes it here: he gets on well with Christine, as he does with all women, and he loves playing with the kids, who share his anarchic spirit and boundless capacity for destruction. He makes no secret of his loneliness: he is always quoting self-aggrandising bits of *Paradise Lost* to me—

> In solitude
> What happiness, who can enjoy alone,
> Or all enjoying, what contentment find?

But when I try to talk him round – suggest, for example, that he could have this life, if he were willing to accept the compromises – he will merely grimace, or make a smart remark: 'When you're a cow, I'm sure that grass tastes pretty good.'

I can see his point. Why keep to one corner of the field when you can be the whole sky over it? Why be content with a single life when you can dictate the dreams of a multitude? Why tie yourself to a person or place that will finally fail you when you can live for the moment, endlessly changing, endlessly interesting, forever taking on irresistible new shapes? But the moment tends only to have room for one.

He's in the house right now, for Lucy's sixth birthday party. In the living room they're playing musical chairs. If I listen closely, I can hear his hoof beats mixed up with the feet of the children as they dance in a circle, round and round. The song is Smokey Robinson's *Tracks of My Tears*, the same one he played repeatedly in the rainy cottage all those years ago. I wonder if he remembers, if the memory will catch him off guard as he's planning how best to cheat. The music freezes, a moment out of time; I picture the kids charging for the chairs, and the Devil lost in the scramble, out of the game again.

About the Authors

COLIN BARRETT is from Mayo. In 2009 he completed his MA in Creative Writing in University College Dublin (UCD) and was awarded the Penguin Ireland Prize. He has received Arts Council bursaries, and his fiction has appeared in *The Stinging Fly*, the anthology *Sharp Sticks, Driven Nails* and in the Harper Perennial 52 Stories online series. The story 'The Clancy Kid' was shortlisted for the 2011 Bridport Prize. A collection of his stories is forthcoming from Stinging Fly Press.

KEVIN BARRY (editor) has written two story collections and a novel. He has won the Rooney Prize for Irish Literature, the European Union Prize for Literature, the Sunday Times EFG Private Bank Short Story Award and the Authors' Club First Novel Award. His stories have appeared in the *New Yorker*, *Best European Fiction*, *The Stinging Fly* and elsewhere. He lives in County Sligo.

GREG BAXTER is the author of *A Preparation for Death* and *The Apartment*. He was born in Texas in 1974. From

2003 to 2011, he lived in Dublin. He now lives in Berlin, where he writes and translates.

MARY COSTELLO, originally from Galway, lives in Dublin. Her first book, a collection of short stories entitled *The China Factory*, was published in 2012 by Stinging Fly Press and nominated for the Guardian First Book Award.

JULIAN GOUGH sang on four albums by Toasted Heretic. He is the author of three novels, *Juno & Juliet*, *Jude in Ireland* and *Jude in London*, and a poetry collection, *Free Sex Chocolate*. He has won the BBC National Short Story Award and has been shortlisted, twice, for the Everyman Bollinger Wodehouse Prize. In 2011, he wrote the ending to Minecraft, *Time Magazine*'s computer game of the year.

MICHAEL HARDING is an author and playwright. His creative chronicle of ordinary life in the Irish midlands is published as a weekly column in the *Irish Times*. He has published three novels, *Priest*, *The Trouble with Sarah Gullion* and *Bird in the Snow*. His memoir of love, melancholy and magical thinking, *Staring at Lakes*, is published this year.

DERMOT HEALY was born in Finea, County Westmeath, in 1947. He has written poems, plays, screenplays, novels, short stories and a memoir. His works include the novels *Long Time No See*, *Sudden Times* and *A Goat's Song*, the memoir *The Bend for Home* and the story collection *Banished Misfortune*. He is a member of Aosdána, the Irish Academy of Arts and Letters. He lives in Ballyconnell West in County Sligo.

DESMOND HOGAN was born in east Galway in 1950 and lives in Dublin. He has won many prizes, including the John Llewellyn Rhys Memorial Prize and the Rooney Prize for Irish Literature. *The Ikon Maker* (1976), his first novel of many, has lately been reissued by the Lilliput Press. His work has recently appeared in *Princeton University Chronicle*, *The White Review*, *The Stinging Fly*, *American Short Fiction*, *Cyphers* and *Best European Fiction 2012*.

PAT McCABE was born in Monaghan in 1955. His novels include *The Dead School*, *The Butcher Boy* and *Winter Wood*. He has written for screen and stage and is currently working on a novel and a book of short stories. His latest book, *Goodbye Mr Fish/Hello Mr Rat* is due from Quercus in September this year.

MOLLY McCLOSKEY was born in Philadelphia and has lived in Ireland since 1989. She is the author of three works of fiction and, most recently, a memoir, *Circles Around the Sun*, which concerns her brother's descent into schizophrenia. She is the writer-in-residence at UCD for 2013.

MIKE MCCORMACK is the author of two collections of short stories, *Getting It in the Head* and *Forensic Songs*, and two novels, *Crowe's Requiem* and *Notes from a Coma*. Awarded the Rooney Prize for Irish Literature in 1996, *Getting It in the Head* was also chosen as a New York Times Notable Book of the Year. In 2006, *Notes from a Coma* was shortlisted for the Irish Book of the Year Award. He was awarded a Civitella Ranieri Fellowship in 2007. He lives in Galway.

NEASA MCHALE was born in Dublin in 1984. She studied History and English in St Patrick's College, Drumcondra, and is now studying for a Masters in Library and Information Studies in UCD. 'While You Were Working' is her first published story.

LISA MCINERNEY is the author of award-winning blog Arse End of Ireland, a columnist for TheJournal.ie and editor of online magazine Ramp.ie. She's spoken at literary events both at home and in the USA about new media, its effect on traditional publishing and its possibilities for writers. She lives in Galway.

ANDREW MEEHAN was, until recently, the Head of Development at the Irish Film Board. During this time he was the winner of the Cúirt International Literary Festival's New Writing Award, and his short fiction appeared in *The Stinging Fly* as well as other journals. Now, he mainly writes screenplays.

About the Authors

PAUL MURRAY is the author of the novels *An Evening of Long Goodbyes* and *Skippy Dies*. He lives in Dublin.

NUALA NÍ CHONCHÚIR was born in Dublin in 1970. Her fourth short-story collection, *Mother America*, was published by New Island in 2012; the *Irish Times* said of it: 'Ní Chonchúir's precisely made but deliciously sensual stories mark her as a carrier of Edna O'Brien's flame.' Her debut novel, *You* (New Island, 2010) was called 'a gem' by the *Irish Examiner*.

ÉILÍS NÍ DHUIBHNE was born in Dublin. She has written eight novels, six collections of short stories, several books for children, plays and non-fiction work. Her most recent collection of short stories is *The Shelter of Neighbours* (Blackstaff, 2012). She has won many literary awards, and her stories are widely anthologised and translated. Éilís is Writer Fellow in UCD where she teaches on the MA and MFA in Creative Writing. She is a member of Aosdána.

SHEILA PURDY was born in Dublin and studied at UCD, King's Inns and the University of Ulster. Working in industry she travelled worldwide. On her return to study at UCD, she was conferred with a Masters of Arts in Creative Writing in 2011. She is writing a debut collection of short stories.

KEITH RIDGWAY is from Dublin. He is the author of *The Long Falling* (Faber, 1998), *The Parts* (Faber, 2003), *Animals* (Fourth Estate, 2007) and *Hawthorn & Child* (Granta Books, 2012). His short fiction has been published in the *New Yorker*, *Granta*, *Zoetrope*, *The Stinging Fly* and others.

EIMEAR RYAN was born in 1986 and grew up in Tipperary. Her stories have appeared in *New Irish Writing*, *The Stinging Fly* and the *Irish Times*. She is a recipient of the Hennessy Award for First Fiction and an Arts Council bursary. She holds an M.Phil. in Creative Writing from Trinity College and is writing her first novel.

WILLIAM WALL was born in Cork in 1955 and is the author of four novels, one collection of short fiction and three collections of poetry. *This Is the Country* was nominated for the 2005 Man Booker Prize. He has won many prizes for fiction and poetry. His most recent book is *Ghost Estate*, a collection of poetry. Explore his website www.williamwall.net